Sean Black grew up in Scotland, studied film in New York and has written the screenplays for many of Britain's best-known TV dramas.

While writing his first novel, *Lockdown*, he undertook a gruelling 24-day close-protection course encompassing two weeks in an army camp in Wales, followed by a week of firearms training in the Czech Republic. To research *Deadlock*, he 'did time' in Pelican Bay Supermax Prison, home to some of America's most violent inmates.

DEADLOCK

Elite bodyguard Ryan Lock and his trusted friend, Ty Johnson, become convicted felons — sentenced to twenty years in Pelican Bay, California's notorious supermax prison . . . at least that's what the FBI and the United States Justice Department want everyone to believe. In reality, their mission, to keep one man alive for one week, is not straight-forward. The inmate Frank 'Reaper' Hays, founding member of the white supremacist Aryan Brotherhood prison gang, is about to give evidence against members of his own gang for the brutal slaying of an undercover ATF agent and his family. And Hays refuses protective custody. In a world dominated by violent gangs, mistrust and constantly shifting alliances, Lock knows that he faces the toughest assignment of his career — just to stay alive . . .

Books by Sean Black
Published by The House of Ulverscroft:

LOCKDOWN

SEAN BLACK

DEADLOCK

Complete and Unabridged

CHARNWOOD
Leicester

First published in Great Britain in 2010 by
Bantam Press
an imprint of
Transworld Publishers, London

First Charnwood Edition
published 2011
by arrangement with
Transworld Publishers
The Random House Group Ltd., London

British Library CIP Data

Black, Sean.
  Deadlock.
  1. Bodyguards- -Fiction. 2. Undercover operations- -
  Fiction. 3. Prisons- -California- -Fiction. 4. Gangs- -
  Fiction. 5. Suspense fiction. 6. Large type books.
  I. Title
  823.9'2–dc22

  ISBN 978–1–4448–0651–9

Published by
F. A. Thorpe (Publishing)
Anstey, Leicestershire

Set by Words & Graphics Ltd.
Anstey, Leicestershire
Printed and bound in Great Britain by
T. J. International Ltd., Padstow, Cornwall

This book is printed on acid-free paper

For Marta and Caitlin,
my heart and soul

Prologue

The California/Oregon Border

Ken Prager woke to blood at the back of his throat and the barrel of a shotgun pressing hard into his right eye. He opened his left: a burning wooden cross was embedded in the centre of a muddy clearing ringed by giant redwood trees.

Then, as firefly embers from the blazing cross were sucked heavenwards by a swirling wind, came the question he'd been dreading for the past six months. A question that, depending on his answer, might be the last words he ever heard. Worse still, the question came from the blonde-haired woman on the other end of the shotgun.

'Who the hell are you?' she asked him.

Prager cleared his throat to speak and she withdrew the gun just enough to allow him a glimpse of a lone figure flanking the burning cross. Arms folded, face obscured by a ski mask, the figure stood in silence, waiting for an answer,

'You know who I am,' Prager said. His voice sounded cracked and tentative to him — the voice of a liar.

He put a hand down on the muddy ground and tried to lever himself up and on to his feet.

'What's all this about?'

'You tell us,' the woman said, ratcheting a round into the chamber of the shotgun and re-sighting it in the middle of his forehead. 'Now, why don't you try again? And this time we'd appreciate the truth.'

Prager choked back a laugh. 'The truth?'

The truth was, Ken Prager wasn't sure who he was any more. Six months ago he'd been Special Agent Kenneth Prager, devoted family man, and a six-year veteran of the Bureau of Alcohol, Tobacco, Firearms and Explosives. Then he'd been asked by his bosses at the Bureau to go undercover, to become Kenny Edwards, a marine fallen on hard times who'd found a new purpose in life: ridding the United States of America of anyone who wasn't in possession of white skin.

But he'd quickly found there was a snag. In order to convince the others of his new identity, he'd first had to convince himself. Then, to complicate matters further, and despite the fact that Ken Prager had a wife at home, he'd fallen in love. Those six months had blurred the edges of his identity to a point where he was no longer sure he could answer the question of who he was with any certainty. Not even to himself.

He felt the woman leaning her shoulder into the stock of the shotgun, the tip of the barrel pressing painfully into his skull.

'We need an answer, Kenny,' she said.

Prager blinked the rain from his eyes.

Stick to your story. Wasn't that the mantra? They wouldn't ask you if they already knew. If they knew, you'd already be dead.

'You know who I am,' Prager repeated, taking his time over each syllable, trying to inject a tone of certainty into his words.

'OK then,' the woman said, with the slightest of nods to someone standing behind him. 'Maybe this'll refresh your memory.'

There was the low rumble of a diesel engine and a black van squelched its way to the centre of the clearing and stopped. A masked driver clambered out of the front cab and walked round to the side.

Prager caught the flash of a tiny shamrock tattooed on the knuckle of the man's right hand as he clasped the handle and threw open the van's side panel with a game-show flourish.

A dome light illuminated the van's cargo space. Two people crouched on the floor. One a woman in her early forties, the other a boy in his mid-teens. Bar the ropes securing their hands and feet and a single strip of silver gaffer tape covering their mouths, they were both naked.

Turning his head, Prager vomited on to the muddy ground beneath him.

'Jesus, no,' he muttered, staring into the terrified eyes of his wife and son.

Part One

1

One Month Later

450 Golden Gate Avenue, San Francisco, California
The package was sitting on Jalicia Jones's desk when she arrived at her office in the Federal Building a little after seven in the morning. It was a large, padded manila envelope with her name written on it in big black capital letters. Beneath her name was her title. No return address. No stamps. Just her name and title.

> JALICIA JONES
> Assistant U.S. Attorney
> Organized Crime Strike Force

She took a final sip of the skinny latte she bought every workday morning across the street at Peats coffee shop and tossed the cup across the room. It went in off the rim of her wastepaper basket. She high-fived fresh air in celebration of the three-point coffee-cup shot, then sat down and stared at the new arrival.

It wasn't internal mail, that was for sure: they used perforated envelopes for hard copies sent between departments. By rights she should speak to her legal assistant and try to work out who had delivered it. Maybe even have one of the US

Marshals Service guys, who provided security for the building and its staff, check it out for her. But, almost immediately, she dismissed both those notions. Jalicia was a young woman who had conditioned herself over the years to suppress unease and confront fear. You didn't get from the bullet-ridden streets of South Central Los Angeles to an Ivy League law school without that ability.

So, instead of following procedure, she picked the package up and shook it gently. Feeling faintly ridiculous, she held it up to her ear. What was she expecting to hear, she wondered, a ticking clock?

To hell with it.

She ripped open the top of the envelope, turned it upside down with a shake, and stifled a laugh of relief as a single DVD disc clattered out on to the wood. All that angst, and for what? It was probably surveillance footage, dumped on her desk by an over-eager intern who'd started work before she had.

She picked up the shiny silver disc — and that was when she noticed what looked like a strip of meat stuck to the inside of the bubble wrap. Pulling a letter opener from her desk drawer, she lifted the top of the envelope to get a better look.

What she'd taken to be a strip of meat extended all the way down into the envelope. Carefully, she prodded at it with the letter opener. Her stomach gave an involuntary lurch.

Grabbing for a tissue from her handbag, she extracted the paper-thin rectangle of what she could now see was human skin and laid it out on the desk. The edges of the ragged rectangle were charred black. At the centre of the slab of skin, rendered in dark ink, was a swastika.

The sound of the phone on her desk ringing made her jump.

'Jalicia Jones,' she said, her gaze still transfixed by the near-translucent scroll of skin with the charred swastika at its centre.

Silence at the other end of the line.

'Hello?'

There was a click, and then a woman's voice, human, but unmistakably automated. 'You have a collect call from . . . ' There was a pause before the voice added, 'Pelican Bay State Prison. Press one to accept this call.'

Jalicia pressed the number one key on the pad. There was another pause, then a man's voice, deep and masculine: 'Ms Jones?' There was an emphasis on the Ms.

'Yes?'

'This is Frank Hays.'

She opened her mouth, took a deep breath, trying to compose herself.

'You know who I am, right?'

She knew who he was all right. In fact, when she glanced over to the cork board on the opposite wall of her office, his face stared back at her. An old mugshot of a white male in his mid-twenties, with a square head, his hair down to his shoulders, a ratty moustache and a look of utter contempt for the rest of the world.

But the name underneath the photograph wasn't Frank Hays. It referred to him by the nickname he'd earned in prison: Reaper.

Next to Reaper's picture were six other mugshots. Together, these men on the wall of Jalicia's office constituted the leadership of America's most feared prison gang, the Aryan Brotherhood. Violent white supremacists, they'd banded together in California's notorious San Quentin Prison in the late 1970s; what they'd lacked in numbers they'd more than made up for in their ability to terrorise everyone who crossed their path, other violent criminals included. And within their ranks, within their leadership even, Reaper had earned a fearsome reputation based on his complete disregard for human life. It was rumoured that during his first week in prison, having been threatened with rape by the leader of a long-established black prison gang, Reaper had responded by beating the gangster unconscious and nailing him to the wall of his cell with a hammer and four nails purloined from a prison workshop.

Jalicia took another deep breath. 'I know who you are.'

'Good,' said Reaper. 'You get a special delivery over the last couple of days?'

'This morning,' Jalicia said, her eyes drawn back to the parchment of skin. 'Pretty neat trick. Hand-delivering something when you're in prison.'

There was a low, throaty chuckle from Reaper. 'I heard it was on its way, is all. You know who it belongs to?'

Jalicia knew all right. The swastika tattoo had almost certainly been carved from the mutilated body of Ken Prager, an undercover ATF agent

10

who'd infiltrated a white supremacist group the authorities believed was carrying out an assortment of criminal activities on behalf of the incarcerated Aryan Brotherhood leadership. 'Yeah, I know.'

'So, you and me,' Reaper continued. 'I think it's about time we had a talk.'

'About?'

'Just make the arrangements. And make sure it stays on the down low. I ain't gonna be any use to you dead.'

2

Twenty-four Hours Later

**Pelican Bay Supermax Prison,
Crescent City, California**
The seven-hour drive from San Francisco to California's highest-security prison had given Jalicia plenty of time to chew over Reaper's request for a meeting, and what it might mean for her case against the Aryan Brotherhood.

In the administration building she was greeted by Warden Louis Marquez, a dapper Hispanic with a prosthetic left eye, his eyeball having been gouged out of its socket by a disgruntled female inmate early in his career as a correctional officer. Marquez got Jalicia to sign the prison's standard release form, certifying that she understood that the prison operated a strict 'No Hostages' policy, then passed her on to a barrel-chested lieutenant by the name of Williams, who explained that he was in charge of monitoring gang activity among the prison's three and a half thousand inmates. Williams had facilitated Reaper's phone call to Jalicia, but beyond that he was equally in the dark as to what Reaper was so eager to discuss with her.

Williams led her into a white-walled meeting room tucked away from the prying eyes of other inmates. Jalicia took a seat, while Williams keyed his radio.

'OK, you can bring him in now,' he said.

A minute later the door opened, and Reaper was led into the room by two guards. A double set of handcuffs and leg restraints were linked by a heavy belly chain which looped around his midriff. A white spit shield covered his nose and mouth.

Reaper shuffled forward and was dumped into a chair opposite Jalicia by the two guards, who took up positions either side of him, hands poised, gun-slinger style, on their tasers. He sat there in silence for a moment.

Jalicia turned to Williams, who was standing behind her, arms folded, 'Could we lose the mask?' she asked, hoping that the request would go some way towards establishing trust between her and Reaper.

'Hope you got all your vaccinations,' Williams said to her, before nodding to one of the guards flanking Reaper to remove the spit shield.

Reaper smirked at Williams's jibe.

When the shield was off he leaned back in his chair and scratched lazily at a set of SS lightning bolts tattooed across a bicep that was thicker than most men's thighs. 'You know, me just being here, talking to you, could get me killed.'

'Then I guess you must have a pretty good reason for contacting me,' Jalicia said.

Reaper's mouth, partially obscured by the kind of walrus moustache usually reserved for the bad guy in an old Western, broke into a smile, but his eyes remained unblinking. In fact,

13

ever since Reaper had walked into the visiting room with his two-guard escort, she'd felt him studying her, taking in every detail, scrutinising her every reaction. It wasn't so much the feeling of a man mentally undressing her, which she might have expected under the circumstances. No, this went deeper. Reaper's gaze suggested a man staring into her soul.

'This case you're building against the Aryan Brotherhood,' he said. 'And these conspiracy charges you're going to be bringing against them for that ATF agent and his family being snuffed.'

Jalicia took a breath, her mind flitting back to the contents of the envelope. 'What about them?'

'You're gonna be seeking the death penalty for the suspects, aren't you?' he asked.

Jalicia settled for a nod of the head and a 'That's correct.'

Reaper stretched his arms up as far as his restraints would allow, and yawned. 'But, hypothetically speaking, if someone who was, shall we say, associated with the Brotherhood were to cooperate with your office, this person wouldn't be looking at Death Row. In fact, he might even be offered some kind of a deal.'

The truth was that, so far, Jalicia had enough evidence to bring the leadership of the gang to trial for ordering the murder of Ken Prager and his family. An intercepted, and subsequently decoded, note found in a prison cell right here in Pelican Bay proved beyond any reasonable doubt that the Aryan Brotherhood had voted on and directly commissioned Prager's death after he'd infiltrated a group which helped run the gang's

14

operations on the outside. But, whether she could persuade a judge and jury to sentence to death men who were already serving life without possibility of parole was another matter entirely. The one thing that would do that would be a star witness, someone on the inside of the organisation. Reaper more than fitted the bill.

'If such a person were to come forward, we could certainly look at making some kind of an arrangement,' Jalicia said. 'You know, you might want to think about seeking an attorney to represent you.'

At this Reaper stiffened. His fingers interlocked, then steepled under his chin. 'No. This stays between me and you.'

'So you would testify against the other men being indicted?'

'If you keep me off The Row, then yes, I would.'

'What else would you want?' Jalicia asked.

Reaper's eyes swept the floor. Here it comes, thought Jalicia. She knew that cheating death wouldn't be motivation enough for a man like Reaper.

'Time off for good behaviour?' Reaper suggested with a wry smile.

Jalicia matched his smile. Reaper was already serving three sentences of life without possibility of parole for a triple homicide, which included two young black girls, so any kind of early release wasn't an option. 'What is it that you want that I can actually deliver?' she prompted.

Reaper leaned forward. 'I've been in solitary confinement for the past five years. In my cell twenty-three hours out of twenty-four. Out only to shower on my own, or exercise in a tiny concrete box not much bigger than this room.'

'We could arrange for you to be transferred to the THU,' Jalicia suggested.

Lieutenant Williams nodded in agreement. 'We could definitely do that.'

The Transitional Housing Unit was where former gang members lived together inside the prison. It lay, like purgatory, somewhere between the hell of solitary confinement (also known as the Secure Housing Unit, or SHU) and the relative freedom of the general housing units, where the majority of prisoners could move much more freely.

Reaper shook his head. 'I want to be back on the mainline.'

Jalicia laughed. The mainline was the other name for the general housing units. 'A federal witness on the mainline? You wouldn't last two seconds.'

'That all depends,' Reaper said with another wry smile.

'On what?'

'Let's just say I have some new friends now, friends who think the leadership of the Aryan Brotherhood might have had its day.'

So that was what this was all about, thought Jalicia: a power play, with Reaper testifying against his old comrades and being rewarded by the new regime.

'Which 'friends' are we talking about here?' she asked. 'The Nazi Low Riders? The Texas Circle?'

The Nazi Low Riders and the Texas Circle were both up-and-coming white supremacist prison groups who had long envied the Aryan Brotherhood's stranglehold on the prison system's drug and protection trade. If Jalicia and the Federal Prosecutor's office took the Aryan Brotherhood down, it would create enough space for one of the other prison gangs to step in and take over a trade inside and outside the country's prisons worth tens of millions of dollars.

Reaper looked up at the ceiling. 'I can't name names, but you know as well as I do that nature abhors a vacuum.'

'So, you take the stand, testify against the Aryan Brotherhood, and in return I convince the prison authorities to let you back into general population.'

'That's right,' said Reaper.

'But the Aryan Brotherhood would come after you.'

'I'm prepared to take that risk. Plus, like I said, I have new friends looking out for me.'

Jalicia knew that, in the normal course of things, a snitch was an automatic target on the mainline, fair game for everyone. But Reaper was different. Most prisoners would see his treachery as existing on a plane high enough that it wouldn't be their job to intervene. In some ways it was akin to the kind of deals governments cut all the time with other nations when it served their purposes. It was realpolitik at its most base.

'OK,' she said finally. 'We might be able to return you to general population, but only after you testify.'

Reaper's smile disappeared. 'No. I go back before then or you can forget me as a witness.'

Jalicia folded her arms. 'Why the rush? You wait a couple of weeks, you give your testimony, we move you to the mainline — everyone's happy.'

Reaper leaned forward, and once again Jalicia found herself mesmerised by the blackness of his eyes. 'You still don't get it, do you? I'll be safer before I testify out on the mainline. In solitary, all it takes is someone to bribe a guard, a cell door being opened at the wrong time. At least out on the yard I can see them coming.'

Jalicia nodded slowly. Reaper was probably right. To an outsider, he might seem to be safer in solitary, but nowhere would be entirely free of risk.

Reaper rose slowly, indicating that he was done talking. 'So, that's my offer. I get my move, and I'll give you the leadership of the Aryan Brotherhood on a plate. Take it or leave it.'

And then he was gone, shuffling with his two-guard escort through a heavy metal door, leaving Jalicia still seated.

The deal Reaper was offering went like this: if he kept his end of the bargain, the death penalty for the six men who'd ordered Prager's murder would be a slam-dunk, and her name would be right up there with Eliot Ness as the woman who had smashed a seemingly untouchable crime syndicate that operated from inside prison. After the trial, if the Aryan Brotherhood took their revenge on Reaper, that would be his problem.

Those few weeks before the trial, though

18

— that was the problem. Especially the final five days, because five days before Reaper testified Jalicia would be obligated to reveal his identity to the defence lawyers representing the gang.

Five days. That was what it boiled down to. Keep Reaper alive for those five days after naming him and Jalicia would secure justice for Ken Prager and his family, and send a clear signal that if you ordered the execution of a federal agent, you paid with your life.

Jalicia unclenched her hands and tried to let go of some of the tension. There had to be a way to make this work. Some way of keeping Reaper alive during the critical period while he was on the mainline and before he took the witness stand. She just had to find it.

3

Six Weeks Later

Ryan Lock stared out across San Francisco Bay towards Alcatraz Island. The city's trademark fog had briefly given way to a cloudless deep-blue sky, and he could make out not only the sharp outline of the infamous island but also the main prison buildings themselves, etched in chalk-white. Clusters of tourists filed past on their way to the boat that would take them out to the former residence of America's most wanted criminals, but Lock wasn't going on the tour with them. He was here on business. Although exactly what kind of business wasn't yet clear.

The previous evening he had received a call at the New York apartment he shared with his girlfriend, Carrie Delaney, a TV news reporter. Unlike most calls he received of a business nature, this one came direct to his home, and the woman on the other end of the line was insistent but calm. Usually potential clients were insistent and panicked, often with very good reason.

After a career in the military, Lock now worked in high-end private security, often taking on jobs that no one else would touch. At least that was his reputation. In short, he made sure that no harm came to people whose lives were being threatened, or who faced other menaces such as blackmail, kidnap of a family member, or extortion. Outsiders might describe him as a bodyguard, or a bullet catcher, but Lock hated the macho connotations of both terms and saw himself simply as a troubleshooter.

The woman on the other end of the line had identified herself as Jalicia Jones, a Federal Prosecutor at the US Attorney's Office in San Francisco. She'd said there was a matter of a very sensitive nature she wished to discuss with him — in person.

'You're going to have to do better than that,' he'd said, using his free hand to stir the pasta sauce he was cooking for dinner.

Jalicia had given him one more detail: the job involved protection of a witness for a major federal trial.

'Don't you have the US Marshals Service for that sort of thing?' he'd asked her, scooping up some of the sauce and tasting it.

'This is a rather unique set of circumstances, Mr Lock.'

'You can't find someone on the west coast who provides close protection?'

'Not of this type. It's high-end. Super high-end.'

Lock knew that 'high-end' was not-so-secret code for 'might get you killed'. He could only surmise that 'super high-end' was a job *likely* to get you killed.

'Mr Lock, you'll understand when we meet,' she'd continued. 'Your flight leaves Kennedy at six o'clock tomorrow morning. A first-class ticket will be waiting for you at the Virgin

America reservations desk.'

'And why do you think I'm going to fly the whole way across the country for a meeting about this exactly?'

There'd been silence on the other end of the line, then Jalicia said, 'Because I've done my research on you.'

Lock had put the spoon down on the kitchen counter as a trickle of unease worked its way down his back. 'What does that mean?'

But Jalicia had ignored the question, given him the flight number and hung up.

Behind him, Carrie was sitting on the sofa, working through some background material for a story she was covering. Their yellow Labrador, Angel, a rescue dog from an animal-testing unit, was lying next to her, its head resting on her lap.

'Business?' she'd asked, looking up.

'Some prosecutor from the US Attorney's Office in San Francisco. Wants me to fly out there first thing to meet with her about a witness protection gig.'

'And are you?'

Lock had grimaced. 'Hell, no.'

★　★　★

Around four in the morning, having had two hours' sleep, Lock had rolled out of bed.

Carrie stole some more comforter from his side of the bed and said, eyes still closed, 'You're going, aren't you?'

Lock sighed. 'I guess I am.'

'What changed your mind?'

22

'If I don't find out what's so important that they want to hire private security from the other side of the country, it'll drive me nuts.'

Carrie gave a sleepy laugh. 'She wasn't lying about doing her research on you.'

As Lock got dressed, Angel skittered around his feet, disturbed by the change in routine.

Carrie propped herself up on one elbow. 'You taking your partner?'

'No, Angel's staying here.'

'You know who I mean.'

Lock walked back to the bed and sat down. He pushed away a strand of blonde hair which had fallen over Carrie's face, then leaned in and kissed her gently on the lips. Before the lure of climbing back into bed with Carrie properly took hold, he stood back up.

'I'm meeting him there. He's out visiting family in California anyway. He said he'd drive up to San Francisco from LA.'

★   ★   ★

Lock was waiting for him now — his partner, Tyrone Johnson. They'd originally hooked up out in Iraq, where Ty was serving in the United States Marine Corps and Lock, despite the fact he'd been raised in the States, was working with the British Royal Military Police specialist close protection unit. The rapport had been immediate, and when Lock eventually left the military, Ty, who was already working in high-end private security, had secured Lock his first gig with a large pharmaceutical company which had been targeted by animal rights activists.

While he waited for Ty, Lock kept his gaze steady on Alcatraz. Little wonder that no one had escaped from the place. If the freezing temperature of the water surrounding the prison didn't get you, and if the strong bay currents didn't sweep you out into the Pacific, then the sharks would finish you off.

Lock saw Ty before Ty saw Lock, the young African-American's long, basketball player's strides making short work of the ground between sidewalk and pier, Lock caught his friend's grimace as they bumped fists.

'That was a long goddamn drive,' Ty said, massaging the back of his neck.

'Well, let's hope it's worth it.'

'Come on,' said Ty, tapping Lock's elbow. 'My ride's over there.'

Lock picked it out immediately — a 1966 Lincoln Continental that had been resprayed in a migraine-inducing purple.

Ty's chin jutted out. 'Go on, get it out of the way.'

'Get what out of the way?' Lock asked.

'Whatever you're going to say about my ride.'

Their respective tastes in both cars and music were a long-running source of friction between them. Ty thought Lock's choice of both automobiles and music boring, while Lock maintained that in their job the key was to appear as inconspicuous as possible. Something they clearly weren't about to do in a pimped-out purple Continental.

'It's . . . ' Lock searched for the right word. 'It's very striking.'

Lock ducked in the front passenger side as Ty walked round to the driver's door. The interior was black and purple leopard-spot suede. The sound system was a six-speaker Bose model guaranteed to make your ears bleed even at low volume. The two additional JL woofers mounted in the back looked capable of rearranging your internal organs.

Ty popped on a pair of mirrored Aviator sunglasses, gunned the engine and pulled away from the kerb.

'Have to say, Tyrone, we're really blending in this vehicle. All you're missing is a fedora with a feather, Superfly.'

Ty scowled. 'Where's your sense of style, brother?'

'Must have left it back in New York,' Lock took another look around the Lincoln's cabin. 'You know what? I think this is a first.'

'What d'you mean?'

'Well, I don't think I've ever been in a vehicle before and actually prayed that I'd be car-jacked.'

On the way to the Federal Building where they were scheduled to meet with Jalicia, Lock brought Ty a little more up to speed with his conversation the previous evening. After a pause, Ty said, 'Makes no sense. They have the Marshals for this kind of stuff. You sure they want us for witness protection?'

'That's what it sounded like.'

Ty seemed to lighten a little. 'So, we fly 'em

down to Cancun, chill out for a few weeks, then fly 'em back home and pick up a big fat cheque from Uncle Sam. I mean, how hard can it be, right?'

Lock stared out of the window as they drove along Bay Street, past a bar called the Red Jack Saloon. A knot of four or five bikers sporting Hell's Angel patches were chatting outside, as much a part of the local scenery as cable cars and the Golden Gate Bridge, He was guessing that Ty's optimism was misplaced. Someone with Lock's reputation wasn't flown across the country first-class if the job was straightforward.

4

The conference room where Lock and Ty were meeting Jalicia faced out on to Golden Gate Avenue, a busy thoroughfare in the centre of downtown San Francisco. Barely a few blocks east lay the Tenderloin, one of the city's sleaziest areas, where junkies sprawled on the sidewalk and transvestite prostitutes openly plied their trade. Lock wondered to himself whether the proximity of the courthouse to so many dope fiends and vagrants was altogether coincidental.

Ten storeys below, Lock watched a homeless man wrestle with a wonky-wheeled shopping cart. The cart lurched sharply to the left, almost careening off the edge of the kerb. The homeless man pulled it back from the edge, his bedding roll spilling on to the sidewalk. As he let go of the cart to retrieve his bedding, the cart started to move again. Some people's lives were like that, Lock reflected. Soon as you got one thing straightened out, you set another problem in motion. Lock wondered if he was about to get a taste of the same thing.

Behind Lock, the conference room door opened and a surprisingly young African-American woman with sharp, pretty features bustled in, hand out in greeting. Lock watched with amusement as Ty, who was already seated, immediately straightened in his seat. Ty saw himself as a ladies' man, but Lock had a feeling that Jalicia Jones wasn't someone who would share that opinion.

'Mr Lock, I'm glad you made it,' she said with a rehearsed smile.

Ty loudly cleared his throat.

'Ms Jones, this is my partner, Tyrone Johnson,' Lock said.

'Call me Ty,' said Ty, with a wide grin.

A grizzled white guy in his late fifties had followed Jalicia into the room. He identified himself to Lock as Special Agent Tommy Coburn of the Bureau of Alcohol, Tobacco, Firearms and Explosives. Muscular, with hair greying at the temples, and a hangdog expression, Lock would have put him down as an ageing biker or an ex-con.

Coburn eyed Ty with suspicion but stuck out a hand in greeting. 'Coburn.'

'Hey,' Ty said, propping his sneakers up on the conference room table and giving Coburn a wave.

Lock noticed Jalicia shoot Ty a look that suggested his charm offensive was falling flat.

'OK, Mr Lock, Mr Johnson, here's the 411. For the past couple of years, the Organized Crime Strike Force here in San Francisco, along with a number of other federal agencies, has been building a case against a prison gang called the Aryan Brotherhood and their associates.' Jalicia paused for a moment. 'I take it you've heard of them?'

'Bad-ass white supremacist prison gang?' Lock ventured. Living with a career-driven news reporter like Carrie, Lock found himself carrying

28

a trove of usually useless information about all aspects of American life.

'Nowadays, they don't just operate inside prison,' Jalicia continued. 'As well as being linked to a number of far-right racist groups, they also control drugs, prostitution and a number of extortion rackets on the outside. You name it, they're involved.'

'As part of our investigation we had an agent infiltrate a group on the outside who we believed were dealing in firearms and explosives on behalf of the Aryan Brotherhood,' Coburn said. 'When the group discovered who this agent was, and the Aryan Brotherhood got wind of it, they ordered the group to execute him and his family.'

'We're about to open the trial of the leadership of the Aryan Brotherhood on charges of conspiracy to commit murder in the first degree, a crime for which I'll be seeking the death penalty,' Jalicia added, coolly.

Lock raised his hand. 'I'm no lawyer, but isn't conspiracy a pretty hard charge to prove?'

Jalicia sat forward, her eyes on Lock. 'Not when you have one of their own testifying against them.'

'First rat off the sinking ship?' Ty asked.

Coburn bristled noticeably. 'We prefer the term 'confidential informant'.'

'The truth is, we had a decent case before,' Jalicia stated. 'This witness makes the verdict a virtual certainty.'

'Your informant tell you who actually pulled the trigger?' Lock asked.

'He's sketchy. He's thrown us a few names,

but no one we've been able to locate. But if his testimony drives the jury towards a guilty verdict then you can bet the leadership of the Aryan Brotherhood will cough up the killers if they think it'll keep them from Death Row.'

Lock nodded. This made sense. An inside informant was a chink in any criminal gang's armour. When the informant sang, the united front would collapse and the gang's leadership would turn over their killers. It was how a lot of major cases worked. Deals. Leverage. Bartering. And, ultimately, betrayal. Honour among thieves was a nice romantic construct, but it rarely stood up under the shadow of Death Row.

'So who is this guy?' Lock asked,

'His name is Frank Hays, but he goes by the nickname Reaper.'

'And where do you have this star witness of yours stowed away at the moment?'

'The Secure Housing Unit at Pelican Bay Supermax.'

Lock spread his hands, puzzled. 'So why do you need us? Leave him in solitary. He should be safe there, shouldn't he?'

Jalicia glanced down at some papers. 'He's already spent ten years in prison, the last five of those in solitary, and now he's saying that he'll only testify if he's released back into the general prison population.'

'Tell him no,' said Lock.

Lock caught Coburn studying him. 'We tried that, but he's holding firm. Won't give us anything in court unless he's put back on the yard. It's a catch-22.'

'And he knows the risks?' Lock asked.

'He's an old-school con,' said Coburn. 'Been round the block. He seems to have convinced himself that he's got enough juice with another white supremacist gang inside Pelican Bay that he'll be safe.'

'So move him out. Put him in another prison. Or a safe house,' Ty offered.

'Too much of a flight risk,' Jalicia said, with the resigned air of someone who'd already been over all these options a million times. 'And, in any case, if the Aryan Brotherhood send an assassin after him, it'll be easier for them to get to him at a lower-level security facility. At least at Pelican Bay we can keep an eye on him.'

Lock drummed his fingers on the table as he worked through the situation. 'If you don't agree to put him on the yard, you lose your star witness. If you put him back with the general population, there's a greater chance of someone taking him out before he can give his testimony. That's your problem, isn't it?'

Jalicia straightened in her chair. She stared directly at Lock. 'We need some extra insurance in place to make sure nothing happens to him. Plus, like I said, he's a flight risk. It would be good if we could have someone keeping an eye on him before he testifies for a number of reasons.'

'You think he's looking to escape?' puzzled Lock.

'We can't rule it out,' said Coburn.

Jalicia clasped her hands together, her eyes on Lock once more. 'At midnight tonight, we're obliged to reveal Reaper as our star witness to the defence. Five days after that, he takes the stand at the Federal Courthouse in San Francisco. All we have to do is keep him breathing for those five days,' she said.

'You're nuts,' Lock said, getting up. 'Move him to a safe house on the outside, like Ty said.'

Jalicia sighed. 'There's no way a judge will sanction that for a man with his record. Believe me, I've already petitioned for it twice and been laughed out of chambers both times. Another prison? We just shipped the six men he's testifying against to the federal Supermax in Colorado, so we can't send him there. We need him somewhere secure, and right now the most secure facility in California is Pelican Bay.'

'So, you want me to do what? Babysit him *inside* the prison?' Lock asked. 'You're out of your mind.' He turned to Ty. 'Can you give me a ride back to the airport?'

'Sure thing.'

Jalicia started to object, but Lock cut her off. 'You know, my old man has a saying: I may be stupid, but I ain't crazy. I might have a reputation as the patron saint of lost causes, but not even I'm insane enough to take this gig.'

Jalicia caught up with Lock at the door, putting her hand on his arm as he went to open it. 'Before you leave, there's something I'd like you to see. Then you can make your decision.'

5

A video projector hooked up to a laptop threw the blurry DVD footage on to the wall of the darkened conference room. It took a second for the person holding the camera to find the main subject: a man being held at gunpoint in the centre of what appeared to be a clearing surrounded by giant redwood trees.

Shot over the shoulder of the person holding the shotgun, it was clear that the victim was male, but that was about all Lock could make out from the grainy-green images.

'Hang on,' Jalicia said, leaning over to fiddle with the laptop. A volume bar on screen rolled to maximum.

On screen, a heavily distorted voice came from close to the male hostage: *We need an answer, Kenny.*

'This is your undercover guy?' Lock asked.

Jalicia nodded.

The ATF agent stared up at the gun, his face still obscured by the person holding the shotgun. *You know who I am.*

The voice came again, deep and metallic. *OK then, maybe this'll refresh your memory.*

'We had the FBI do a voice analysis,' Jalicia said. 'The person speaking is, in actual fact, a woman, but the footage was doctored to conceal that fact.'

Next came the sound of a vehicle engine, and

then the ATF agent said something that Lock didn't quite catch. 'Jesus, no,' Jalicia murmured, filling in the missing audio for them. From her lack of reaction it was clear to Lock that she'd watched the footage enough times to rob the images of their shock value.

The frame adjusted suddenly, swooping over the ATF agent's head before settling on a black van. The side panel was open, revealing a middle-aged woman and a teenage boy, both naked, gagged and restrained.

Lock froze. He could feel his teeth grinding against each other and his stomach lurching. He recognised the woman, and immediately knew who the agent was. He swivelled round and stared at Jalicia. She had the decency not to meet his gaze.

'Ken Prager, right?' Lock said, his voice breaking with emotion.

'You know him?' Ty asked, unable to conceal his surprise at Lock's reaction,

'I grew up with him. We were good friends. Played football together. I was there when he got married.' Pinheads of sweat were forming on the back of Lock's neck. 'But then you already knew that, didn't you?' he said to Jalicia.

'Ken did mention you more than once,' Coburn said.

Jalicia ran the tip of her right index finger over the touch pad of the laptop computer. Lock tracked the cursor's progress on screen towards the pause button.

'No,' Lock said. 'I want to see it.'

'Don't do this to yourself, man,' said Ty.

Lock turned to him. 'Stay out of this, Tyrone.'

The next few minutes disintegrated into a series of bloody snapshots on screen as Ken Prager's wife and son were dragged from the van. Prager's son, Aaron, whom Lock had last seen as a sweet-natured, boisterous seven-year-old, was forced at gunpoint to cut the swastika from his father's back as Prager's wife, Janet, choked back sobs.

Lock fought the urge to vomit as bile burned the back of his throat. He dug his nails into the palms of his hands so hard that they broke the skin.

Lock had witnessed many terrible things in his life: roadside bombs that sprayed flesh into the air like so much confetti; innocent women and children needlessly mutilated; an endless parade of depravity. Sometimes he'd been able to intervene, sometimes orders from above had meant all he could do was bear witness. His training as a military close protection operator was specifically designed to force him to react but also to analyse situations as they developed. The rules of engagement were simple: if you saw something which didn't impact on the immediate security of the person you were guarding, you noted it but did not get involved. This was different though. Very different. Although they hadn't seen each other in years, Ken Prager had been like a brother to Lock, as Ty was to him now. Lock didn't forge many close friendships, but when he did they were unassailable.

The images stacked up. The cold disposal of Janet and Aaron by means of a single gunshot to the back of their heads. By the time Ken Prager was dispatched, Lock could sense his old friend's relief. After all, who would want to live after witnessing the murder of his wife and child?

When the footage came to an abrupt cut-off, no one spoke. Lock's shock had given way to a cold rage.

Jalicia snapped the laptop shut, and Coburn got up and opened the blinds. Watery San Francisco sunlight seeped across the conference table and splashed against the far wall, which only seconds ago had been bloodier than a butcher's block.

Lock glanced at Jalicia and Coburn. 'Would you give us a moment alone?'

Without a word, they got up and left the room, closing the door behind them.

Ty spoke first. 'You have to do this job now, don't you?'

Lock nodded.

'Then I'm coming with you.'

'It's too dangerous,' said Lock.

'Exactly,' said Ty. 'That's why you need someone watching your back. Listen, Ryan, half the kids in my neighbourhood graduated to one prison or another. I know the turf.'

Lock hesitated. There was nothing he could do now to help Ken Prager. He hadn't even known he was undercover with the ATF. But if something happened to Ty, that would be different.

'I'm not letting you walk into that place on your own, brother,' Ty persisted.

'I really don't want you to feel you have to do

this,' Lock said, studying Ty's look of concern.

'But you feel you have to because he was your friend, right?' Ty asked him.

'Of course.'

Ty reached out and put a hand on Lock's shoulder. 'Then you'll understand why I can't let you walk in there on your own.'

6

Clad in the standard blue uniform of a California Department of Corrections prisoner, Lock peered out of the porthole window as the twin-engine Cessna light aircraft dropped rapidly on its final approach, breaking through a low bank of coastal cloud to give him his first clear view of where he was about to spend the next five days. At first all he could see were vast tracts of redwood forest, which encircled the facility on almost three sides. To the east, the ancient trees climbed to a barren range of mountains, and to the west lay the Pacific Ocean. Then it was there below him, modern America's answer to Alcatraz: Pelican Bay Supermax.

Nothing had prepared him for the sheer scale of the place. Two hundred and seventy-five acres in the middle of nowhere, about as far north as you could venture in California before you slipped into the state of Oregon. Even if a prisoner made it out past the plethora of electric fences, razor wire and gun towers, where would he go? Sure, there was nearby Crescent City, but that was where the guards lived with their families — hardly an ideal place to hide out.

Lock sank back in his seat and ran through the cover story Jalicia had furnished them with. A high-net-worth client in Los Angeles whom they'd been guarding had fired them on some dubious pretext and then refused to pay them.

When they'd gone to collect the money, there had been an altercation with several members of his new security team, during which one of them had been killed. They had both received fifteen-year sentences for manslaughter. In the cauldron of sex, violence and celebrity that constituted Los Angeles, it would come as no surprise that a story like this had stayed broadly off-radar. By the time any prisoners got suspicious and started to ask questions of their contacts on the outside, Lock and Ty's mission should be complete.

Coburn had also told them that a decision had been made to keep knowledge of their task within as small a circle as possible. Not even the Marshals team transporting them had been informed of their true status. The only person within the prison who had been told was the warden, Louis Marquez.

Lock sat back up and craned his neck a little further, the cuffs digging into his wrists, the chain round his midriff, which linked to his cuffs and leg restraints, biting into the side of his abdomen. Straining like this, he could glimpse the huge purpose-built buildings where the inmates lived, and where three-quarters of them were destined to die. On one side of the prison lay the gigantic X-shaped Secure Housing Unit, four arms moving out from a central spur. Beyond that, Lock could see the equally vast rectangular blocks of general housing units, with the grassy recreation yards in the middle. This was where he and Ty would be. With Reaper. And a few thousand potential assassins, all of whom had been hardened by years of incarceration.

In the most obvious way it made the challenge seem next to impossible, but in another it made it easier. When escorting a high-ranking army general through a street bazaar in Baghdad, or ushering the British Prime Minister into a hotel in Belfast, the challenge was to stay alert because you never quite knew where the threat was coming from. Or whether it would come at all. But down there, Lock could safely assume everyone to be a threat, up to and including the man whose life he was charged with guarding.

He was set for an exhausting five days. But if that's what it took to bring to book the men who had ordered the murder of Ken Prager and his family, then so be it.

As the plane banked hard to the left, the ocean replaced his view of Pelican Bay Supermax, crests of white waves slamming into steep, perilous cliffs. Lock sank back into his seat.

The pilot's voice crackled over the tannoy, a robotic delivery not without an undercurrent of humour. 'Two minutes to landing, gentlemen. And I'd like to take this opportunity to thank you for flying the unfriendly skies with JPATS, America's least favourite airline.'

A few minutes later, they ducked in low under the clouds and slammed down hard on the runway. Lock lurched forward in his seat, the huge, bear-like Marshal sitting next to him putting out a beefy arm to prevent Lock's head from banging the seat in front. The plane taxied to the far end of the runway and juddered to a halt.

As soon as the pilot had turned off the engines, Lock was hustled towards the front of the aircraft and down the steps, Ty behind him. Raw salt air mixed with a light mist as they were led towards two separate unmarked Toyota Land Cruisers. The vehicles skirted round Crescent City itself and headed north-east along Lake Earl Drive.

Lock sat alone in the back of the rear vehicle, minutes away from one of the most dangerous prisons in North America, suddenly glad that Carrie couldn't see him. He'd called her from Jalicia's office, hoping to get the answering machine, but she'd picked up on the third ring. He'd kept the details of his and Ty's task as sketchy as possible. Witness protection. A five-day job. He'd said nothing about his reason for taking it on, or what it would actually entail.

He could tell that Carrie was doing her best to sound unconcerned.

'So your trip to San Francisco was worth it then?' she'd asked him.

'Guess so,' he'd said.

Lock had made a pact with Carrie that, despite her reporter's instincts, she wouldn't ask for too many details about his work unless he offered them up. And this was not a situation he thought it wise to tell her too much about.

There'd been an awkward silence.

'Ryan, are you OK?'

'I'm fine. Why?'

'I dunno, you sound distracted.'

41

'It's just been a long day is all.'

'This job, do I have anything to worry about?'

'No way. I'm gonna have Ty with me. We'll be fine.'

'OK then. So, see you in five days?'

'Carrie?'

There was the trill of a cell phone in the background.

'Other line. Gotta go. Listen, be safe, OK?'

And then she was gone, before he'd had the chance to tell her how much he was going to miss her and that he loved her. Sitting in the back of the Land Cruiser, he wondered if he'd ever get the chance to say those things. With a lurch of regret, he realised he should have said them while he'd had the chance.

Less than ten minutes later, they turned right past an unmanned guardhouse and into the Pelican Bay complex. They followed the road round to the left for a time. Finally, they stopped outside what Lock guessed was the processing area. The rear door opened and Lock stepped out. He stared up at the gun towers and electrified fences topped with strands of razor wire, his home for the next five days.

The Marshal standing next to him followed Lock's gaze.

'Welcome to hell, asshole.'

7

'Roll it up, Reaper.'

Reaper hopped off the top bunk in his cell in the Secure Housing Unit. He raised his arms above his head and stretched out his back. Usually there were at least four officers present when he went anywhere, now there were only two. Reaper took it as a good sign.

'Where am I going?' he asked Lieutenant Williams. As cops went, Williams was OK. He didn't yank anyone's chain unless they yanked his. And, rarely for a guard, he didn't hold a grudge.

'Just cuff up for me, would you?' Williams said, ignoring the question.

Reaper folded his arms. 'Sure. Once I know where I'm going.'

Williams ripped the top sheet from the stack of papers attached to the clipboard he was carrying and passed it through the food tray slot. Reaper bent his knees, crouched down and picked up the piece of paper. He scanned it and smiled before handing it back through the hatch.

'Don't know how you swung it with the warden, and I don't wanna know,' Williams said, making a show of putting the movement order back on his clipboard.

'Haven't you heard, Lieutenant? I'm a reformed character.'

'Yeah, right.' Williams chuckled. 'You got all

43

your stuff together?'

'Can you give me a couple of minutes?' Reaper asked.

'Be back in two,' Williams said, turning military-sharp on his heel.

Reaper listened as Williams and his fellow floor cop exited the electronically controlled door at the end of the corridor. Once it had clanked shut, he set to work gathering his belongings, which mostly consisted of books. Being locked inside a cell on your own for twenty-three hours a day, you had to find something to occupy your mind or you went crazy.

He'd thought about this day for a long time, five years in fact, but he never truly thought he'd see it. Not with his record of behaviour. Since being moved to Pelican Bay from San Quentin, Reaper had twice shared a cell. On both occasions something his cellie had done — like coughing too loud, or talking too much, or snoring — had frayed his nerves to the point where he'd had no alternative but to dispatch them. It didn't matter what colour their skin was either. He just didn't play well with others.

There had been other homicides too. On the yard. In the showers. In the early days of Pelican Bay, back when they still fed the prisoners communally in chow halls, he'd strangled an elderly Hispanic inmate to death with his bare hands for serving him cold coffee. Some of the killings he'd got in trouble for, some he hadn't. Getting into trouble didn't really matter to him anyway. Not when you were serving three life sentences without the possibility of parole. What were they gonna do? Give you another twenty years? The guards and the police and the whole system must have thought so too because they labelled most murders inside prison as NHIs, which stood for 'No Humans Involved'. Of course, kill an ATF agent, or order one to be killed, and that was different. Then they started talking about The Row, which had focused Reaper's mind for the first time in a long while, and had gotten him thinking about the future.

Reaper could hear Williams coming back. He took one last look round the tiny cell, picked up his box of belongings and stepped out into the narrow corridor.

Leading the way, he marched to the end of the corridor and the door opened. Two more corridors, two more doors, and he was outside. He could actually feel a breath of breeze on his face. He was out of solitary.

That was the first step. In five more days, if everything went to plan, he'd be out of this place entirely. Then his mission could really begin.

8

The things I do for my country, Lock told himself as he stood facing the wall of the prison's tiny reception area, his fingers touching the whitewashed concrete, his legs spread wide as a prison guard squatted beneath him with a flashlight.

'OK, now reach down there with your left hand and spread your cheeks,' came the officer's command.

Lock complied, consoling himself with the fact that men of a certain age in the United States actually paid a physician to endure this humiliation on an annual basis.

'Keister's clear,' said the guard matter-of-factly to one of his colleagues. Then he turned back to Lock. 'You can pull up your pants now.'

Before their handover to the US Marshals Service, Ty, who figured that over half of the kids he grew up with in Long Beach were currently serving time somewhere in the nation's prison system, had brought Lock up to speed on some of the prison lingo. Keister was slang for your anal cavity, also known as a prison purse. The keister was the hiding place of choice for drugs, or money, or, more commonly, prison-manufactured improvised weapons, also known as shanks.

Lock turned round. In front of him, two more correctional officers were puzzling over his paperwork. The guard who'd just cavity-searched him nodded towards Ty. 'You and your homeboy here might have come in together, but once you're on block together you might want to keep your distance. The white cons frown on any of their number hanging with a black.'

By 'frown', Lock knew that the guard meant 'would murder in cold blood'. The racial segregation strictly enforced by the prisoners was also something he and Ty had discussed. It would make communication difficult but gave each of them access to two separate powerful groups. If Lock's cover was blown, or a hit on Reaper was imminent, Ty was more likely to hear it from the black prisoners. Lock's first warning would likely be a knife in the back while taking a shower.

The two guards staring at the clipboard were still deep in conversation. Finally, they looked over to Ty. 'OK, Johnson, you're A-block, unit 8. You too, Lock. But be aware of what you were just told. You guys associate in here and something jumps off, that's down to you.'

The older of the two guards chipped in. 'Stick with your own kind and you'll be fine.' He paused. 'Probably.'

★ ★ ★

In cell 845, Reaper was sitting cross-legged on the top bunk, deftly crocheting what looked to Lock like a multicoloured beanie hat. The crocheting was a surprise, Reaper's appearance slightly less so. Even sitting down, Lock could

47

tell that he was vast. Rather than his decade in prison having withered him, it had only succeeded in putting even more muscle on his bones. The image that flashed into Lock's mind was that of a Great White Shark patrolling the vast ocean in a remorseless death-quest. And he was stepping inside a cage with the beast.

Six feet four tall and two hundred and fifty pounds, with a huge barrel chest and freakishly big biceps, everything about Reaper seemed inflated. Atop broad shoulders, a square head sported a walrus moustache. His eyes were dark grey, bordering on black. Like many of the original members of the Aryan Brotherhood, he could have stepped straight from the pages of one of the Louis L'Amour dime-store westerns the gang so respected.

When Reaper looked up, Lock's focus shifted from the man himself to his environment. Unlike the other cells, which Lock had passed with the floor cop who was escorting him, Reaper's home was bereft of pin-ups. Instead, it looked like the place had been recently vacated by some strange hybrid of domestic goddess — Martha Stewart, say — and Eva Braun. On the walls were tacked needlepoint samplers, and stacked at the end of the top bunk was a neatly folded array of knitted sweaters.

Reaper carefully placed the crochet hook and the hat on the bunk next to him. 'Who the hell's this?'

'This here's your new cellie.'

'Reaper don't share his house with no one. Least of all not some punk-ass fish bitch.' He turned back to his crocheting. 'Find him somewhere else.'

The young floor cop hitched his thumbs into his utility belt. 'One more word from you, Reaper, and you can go back to the SHU.'

Reaper jumped down from the bunk and landed softly on the concrete floor. As he did so, the floor cop moved his right hand to the oversized can of pepper spray on his belt.

Reaper glanced at the bottom bunk, although 'bunk' was a rather grandiose word for what amounted to a solid concrete slab that he was using to store his collection of books, which ran the gamut from jailhouse classics such as *Mein Kampf* and Nietzsche's *Beyond Good and Evil* all the way to the slightly more practical *Stitch 'N' Bitch: The Knitter's Handbook*. Lock reflected that somehow in these surroundings even the title of a book on knitting could take on a sinister edge.

Reaper's gaze, steady and unflinching, honed no doubt by years of prison face-offs, shifted to Lock. 'You can sleep on the floor.'

The floor cop stepped out on to the walkway and waved to the other correctional officer situated in the control pod a few yards away. 'Good to close 845.'

A second later, the barred door of the cell slid back into place, sealing Lock inside with Reaper.

* * *

One tier down and two cells along, Ty's reception was proving a little warmer. In fact, he felt like the prodigal son returned to the fold. His new cellie grasped both of Ty's hands and burst into a warm laugh. 'Look who it ain't. I heard a rumour you were heading to these fair shores. Never thought you'd be my cellie though.'

Ty threw his meagre possessions on the bottom slab and looked at the three-hundred-pound colossus who filled most of the rest of the space. 'How you doin', Marvin? How's your mama?'

'She good. Her kidneys are bad. Too much salt.'

Given the neighbourhood that Ty had grown up in, and the fact that most of his graduating class in high school had proved criminally precocious by graduating a few years ahead of schedule to juvenile hall, he'd anticipated meeting a few old faces.

Marvin had fallen in with a street gang known as the Crips, one of the two major black street gangs in California, the other being the Bloods. He was known in Crips circles as Lil Dawg, which demonstrated that even organised criminal gangs don't always lack a sense of humour.

Marvin enveloped Ty in a hug. 'You finally gave up on that war hero shit, huh?'

Ty shrugged. 'Guess so. What you here for?'

'Some trumped-up bullshit, that's what.'

Ty let it go. Ask any of the inmates whether they were guilty or not and they would tell you they were innocent, or that there had been some misunderstanding, most of which involved either guns, drugs, or a combination of both. There was no point arguing with them.

Ty sat down, and Marvin began to regale him with a list of old faces from the neighbourhood and their current status, which divided evenly into the dead and the incarcerated. Far from being disappointed that the one person he'd grown up with who'd gone on to live a productive life was now in jail, Marvin seemed delighted to see Ty. It was as if in some perverse manner Ty was some kind of statistical aberration. Which, in a way, Ty knew he was. As Marvin rattled off the names of their old friends who weren't dead, what particular part of the California penal system they now called home, and what sentence they were currently serving, Ty grew more depressed.

'So, who do I need to watch out for in this unit?' he asked when Marvin finally paused for breath.

'Every motherfucker in here is a bad ass. You come in here as a murderer, that don't make you jackshit.' Marvin stopped. 'Not that I'm saying you're jackshit. I mean, with you being in the military, you've probably capped more mother-fuckers than anyone else down in this place.'

Ty humoured him with a smile. 'Something like that.'

'Tell you who we do got on this unit right now though. Came in today in fact. Just before you got here.'

Ty shrugged a 'who?'

'That Reaper motherfucker. Just got moved in here from the SHU.'

'Who's he?'

'Not someone we want on our unit,' said

51

Marvin, with a sniff reminiscent of a suburban housewife who didn't approve of the new neighbours.

'That still don't tell me who he is.'

Marvin looked Ty straight in the eye. 'He's the guy that you and your homeboy are supposed to be babysitting.'

'What the fuck you talking about, Marvin?'

'How much they paying you, Tyrone? Because whatever it is, it ain't gonna be enough.'

Ty sighed. 'How'd you know?'

'Reaper has been locked down in the SHU for years. All of a sudden he's out on the mainline and you and your buddy come riding into town on some bullshit manslaughter charges no one's heard about. Never try to con a convict, Ty.'

Ty thought of Lock, and his ashen face when he realised who had been murdered along with his family. He turned to Marvin. 'I'm gonna need your help to make sure nothing happens to Hays.'

'And you're asking *me*?'

Ty took a breath. 'Yeah, I am.'

'You know what that motherfucker is in here for? Killing two little black girls and their papa. Those little girls could have been our sisters.'

'I've been in the military, right?' Ty said.

'I know that.'

'Well, sometimes you find yourself on some strange sides.'

Marvin glanced round the cell. 'No shit, Tyrone.' He paced to the edge of the cell door and back again.

'I'm asking you as a friend.'

Marvin puffed out his cheeks, then exhaled. 'OK, here's how we're going to play this. I'm gonna make sure that we got your back on the yard. You do what you came here to do. But as for your homeboy and Reaper, if it jumps off, they're on their own. And, man, in *this* place it don't take much for the shit to jump off.'

9

'ID, please.'

The blue-blazered security guard standing in the lobby of the Federal Court building in downtown San Francisco reached out a hand as the young white woman with the thick mane of blonde hair and baby bump squinted at him through the sunlight.

'Excuse me?'

'I need to see some ID,' he repeated.

'Oh, I'm sorry,' she said, rifling through her bag and finally coming up with her California driver's licence. The name on it was Jessica Summers, but her real name was Freya Vaden. To her associates, and those closest to her, she was known simply as Chance.

The guard glanced at the licence for less than a second and passed it back to her. 'Thank you, Ms Summers.'

Chance handed over her bag to be passed through the scanner and walked through the metal detector. The detector alarm sounded, bringing a call for a 'female assist' from a male supervisor.

'Ma'am, if you could step to the side.'

'Oh, I'm sorry,' Chance said, her hands moving to rub her swollen belly.

'Latisha, could you come check this lady for me?'

As Chance waited to be searched, she checked

54

out the lobby and the steady procession of people in and out. Through the glass windows and doors of the entrance she could see a gaggle of TV news people. Next to them was a phalanx of heavily armed US Marshals, all of them here for the opening of the trial of six members of the Aryan Brotherhood on conspiracy charges.

A female courthouse guard stepped out from behind the scanner. Standing behind Chance, she performed a cursory pat-down.

'When you due, honey?'

'I'm only fourteen weeks, long way to go,' Chance said, smiling.

'This your first?'

Chance nodded.

'I could tell. You got that glow about you. Now, I just need to wand you, OK?'

The female guard reached back and grabbed a hand-held metal detector as Chance held out her arms. As the guard wanded her chest there was a beeping sound.

'Underwire bra?' the guard asked matter-of-factly.

Chance looked at the floor and blushed.

'OK, you go on ahead now,' said the guard. 'Oh, and good luck.'

'Thanks.'

Chance gathered her bag and took a left towards the bank of elevators. She rode the elevator all the way up to the floor where the trial was taking place, then made her way towards the courtroom. A cheerful-looking black guy sporting the same blue US Marshals security jacket as the guards downstairs opened the door for her as she approached.

She ducked past him and into the courtroom. For a moment, she worried that proceedings would stop and people would turn to look at her. But no one did. It only worked like that in the movies anyway. The reality was that for most big trials court staff, attorneys, members of the press and members of the public flitted in and out of the courtroom all day.

Chance took a seat at the back, near to where she guessed the media were. Opening her bag, she pulled out a yellow legal pad and a pen and began sketching the layout of the courtroom.

At the front of the courtroom a woman was on her feet. Chance recognised her from TV coverage as the lead prosecutor, Jalicia Jones. Jalicia was making some long speech, which Chance ignored, focusing instead on the men in the dock. Greying hair, the occasional pair of reading glasses, offset by old-school moustaches and beards — they looked like an eccentric gathering of grandfathers. Chance knew, though, that this was the leadership of the Aryan Brotherhood. Each sat with an accompanying armed guard. Two more armed guards, US Marshals, flanked the judge's bench on one side of the court and the dock on the other.

Chance noted where everyone was positioned, along with the weapons being carried, plus all the entry and exit points. Then she flipped the page and started to sketch the layout of the courtroom in relation to the rest of the building.

By the time she'd finished sketching, half an

56

hour had passed and a large LCD monitor was being wheeled in on a stand. Chance closed her pad and put it back into her bag. She'd have to wait until a break to leave now, plus she had her own reasons for wanting to stay a little longer, especially for this part of the proceedings.

Jalicia had wandered over to the jury. Chance took a while to study them. A couple of blacks. Three Hispanics. The rest were white, by the looks of them your typical middle-class San Franciscans. Wow, thought Chance, the guys in the dock didn't stand a hope in hell.

Jalicia was speaking to the jury. 'Ladies and gentlemen, what you are about to see is extremely graphic and disturbing. This was the footage mentioned in my opening statement, which was sent to my office prior to the initial indictments being made. It shows Agent Prager of the Bureau of Alcohol, Tobacco, Firearms and Explosives being tortured and executed, alongside his wife and teenage son. What I will prove beyond a reasonable doubt is that these murders were ordered by the men you see in the dock today as part of an ongoing criminal enterprise. Remember from my opening statement that to order someone else to commit a crime makes them as guilty as if they had pulled the trigger themselves.'

Jalicia sat down, and the lights were dimmed. Chance noted how dark it became in the room. Not dark enough, though. Not with those big old windows running one whole side of the room.

She leaned forward to watch what was on screen. Partly because that's what everyone else was doing, and she didn't want to stand out. But mainly because she'd never seen herself on screen before.

10

After dinner, which Reaper had consumed in silence, Lock watched his new companion embark on a punishing regime of physical exercises. Midway through a series of combination push-ups and squats known as burpees, Reaper, his torso slick with sweat, glanced up at Lock and spoke for the first time since Lock had informed him why he was here.

'So you're a bodyguard, huh?' Reaper asked.

'Something like that.'

'*My* bodyguard?'

'That's how it's going to work.'

'That so? Well, let me tell you something, the one thing I don't need around me is another guard.'

Lock lowered his voice, aware that while the block of cells was a cacophony of shouts and grunts as inmates worked through their own exercise routines, someone might be listening in. 'Well, you're stuck with me for now.'

Reaper got to his feet, rubbing away at the rivulets of sweat streaming down his body with a towel. 'That's what the last two guys who shared a cell with me thought.'

Lock had anticipated that an inmate like Reaper might not take too kindly to his presence.

'Just so we're clear, I don't intimidate that easy,' he said, standing right in close to him. 'Plus, you do anything to me, and you can forget whatever deal you've cut with the US Attorney's Office.'

'Might not be me you have to worry about. Only one thing that cons hate more than a snitch.'

'And what's that?' said Lock.

'A snitch's bitch.'

Lock jammed his thumb hard into Reaper's neck just below the angle of his jaw. He applied just enough pressure to get his attention.

'Listen to me, you piece of shit, you keep this up and you getting on to that stand won't be an issue, because I'll kill you myself. Now, I don't like you, and you don't like me, but for the next five days we're stuck with each other, so you do what I tell you to do, when I tell you to do it, and we'll be just fine.'

Reaper's face was flushed. Lock dug his thumb in a little bit harder.

'You got me?'

Reaper forced a nod. Lock gradually reduced the pressure, then let go, prepared for some sort of counter-attack. If Reaper had been criminally unstable before his incarceration, who knew the state of his mind now, especially given his near-suicidal demand to return to the mainline?

Reaper stepped back and massaged his neck. 'You scare easy, Lock. All I'm saying is I've had a lot of years down on my own, so it's not going to be easy to share a cell again. We're gonna need some rules.'

'Agreed,' said Lock. 'And my first rule is, your books sleep on the floor, not me.'

'Fine, but no going near my shit unless you ask first.'

'Well, I'm not big into handicraft,' Lock countered, nodding towards Reaper's crocheting. 'Anything else?'

'Keep the cell clean. And don't be running off your mouth about shit that doesn't interest me.'

As a list of dos and don'ts went, this wasn't any more extensive than many of the people Lock had protected.

'I hear you. I was in the military long enough to cope with sharing confined quarters.'

'Same here,' Reaper said. 'But the Bay's a little different. First, you got the toads. You gotta watch out for them.'

'Toads?'

'Toads, Blacks. Negroes. Then you got your Nortenos and Surenos. You getting this? Nortenos are the Hispanics from northern California, Surenos are from the south. The ones from Mexico are the Border Brothers. They associate separately on the yard, but they all fall under the control of the Mexican Mafia.'

'That's the gang they call La Eme?'

'Nice to see you did some homework, Lock. Yeah, La Eme got their shit down cold.'

'I thought they were tight with the Aryan Brotherhood too.'

'They're allied to whoever doesn't draw any heat on them. Remember, out on that yard and in the unit, all that matters is that you stand with your own. Check all that black and white together bullshit at the door. Don't matter who you are, who you roll with, or who you're talking to. In Pelican Bay, you're in the jungle.'

11

That night Lock was troubled by images of Ken Prager's family in their final moments. Every time he shut his eyes, their terrified faces crowded in on him. Lock tried to force them out, but it was no use. As soon as he began to drift off, they were back. The look on Ken's face was the most haunting. It was the look of a man who had sacrificed not only himself but those closest to him. A man who had been walking a tightrope, only to have it cut by some unseen hand.

Finally, Lock gave up on trying to get to sleep, and lay, eyes open, staring at the barren concrete walls of the cell. He should be back at home in New York, lying next to Carrie, Angel asleep at the foot of the bed. Instead he was spending the night in an eight-foot-by-twelve-foot concrete cell with a stone-cold killer who'd already made plain the fact that Lock was an unwelcome intrusion.

Given that sleep was proving impossible, Lock used the relative calm and quiet to think through what lay ahead. In some ways the task he'd been handed was simpler than other close protection jobs he'd embarked on. For one, the time frame was finite. Five days. By the time morning arrived, in a few short hours, they'd be at the start of the second day.

The second advantage Lock possessed, if it

could be called an advantage, was that he knew the threat was both clear and present. The Aryan Brotherhood would be coming after Reaper. That was a given. The only two questions that remained were *when* and *how*.

With Reaper having insisted — idiotically, Lock thought — on being placed back in the general population, the most likely scenario would be a strike in one of the public areas. That said, Lock couldn't categorically rule out an attack in the cell. In some ways, the confined quarters of the cell would be an ideal venue for assassination. There would be nowhere to run. Nowhere to hide.

There was also the problem of bathing to consider. In addition to the stainless-steel sink and toilet bowl bolted into the wall of each two-man cell, the unit had a communal shower area. Showering would have to be kept to a minimum. Reaper wouldn't like it, but tough.

Lock got up and walked to the cell door. Bars ran vertically from floor to ceiling. The building itself was two storeys. They were on the upper tier. There were a dozen cells on each tier, all facing out towards a central reinforced-glass-fronted control pod. Lock could see what the prisoners referred to as the bubble cop sitting inside the pod, leafing through a magazine and eating candy, his position giving him a one-hundred-and-eighty-degree view of every single cell door.

Looking down from behind the cell door, Lock estimated that from the top of the five-foot guard rail to the floor of the unit was maybe twenty feet. Not enough to definitely kill a man if he happened to fall over it, but enough to make sure he didn't make court. Lock made a mental note to ensure that Reaper stayed on the inside of the walkway at all times,

On the floor level were some blue hexagonal tables and chairs, all of which were bolted to the floor. In fact, since he had arrived, Lock hadn't noticed any furniture or fittings in areas that would be used by the inmates which weren't similarly secured.

On a wall that lay parallel to the front of the cells were four pay phones, wall-mounted at equal distances from one another.

There was a single blue reinforced door that led out of the two-storey cell area and into a waiting area. On one side of the waiting area was the entry point to the block's control pod. On the other side was another glass-fronted office. Lock had also noticed at least one single-man restraint cage. Next to that was the door that allowed entry directly on to the yard.

Undoubtedly, the yard would be the most challenging environment, but Lock had only seen it in passing. No doubt tomorrow he'd get a better look. For now, he had to try again to get some sleep. He returned to his bunk, closed his eyes, and within minutes he was back in the lonely, blood-soaked clearing with the blazing cross at its centre as it filled with screams of abject terror.

★　★　★

Lock was woken a little after six by the squeaky wheel of the metal food trolley as it rolled along the walkway outside his cell.

'Chow,' said Reaper, handing him the first of two trays passed through a slot in the door by a black prison orderly.

'We eat every meal in our cells?' Lock asked him.

'Uh-huh,' Reaper grunted, spooning some powdered egg into his mouth.

'Even on the mainline?'

Reaper put down his spoon. 'Used to eat outside the cells in a chow hall, but so many dudes got killed that now they use the chow halls for storage.'

Either side of them, the heavy barred doors of the cells started to clank open and inmates began to filter out. Reaper put down his tray, stood up and grabbed his towel. He was wearing loose blue cotton prison-issue pants and not much else.

'Where do you think you're going?' Lock asked him.

'Hit the showers,' Reaper said.

'Oh no you're not,' Lock said, putting his own tray down and sliding off his bunk.

'What? You think you're my mom?'

'Mom, nursemaid, babysitter, all rolled into one, that's me,' said Lock. 'Don't you think we should see what kind of a reaction you get on the yard before you wander off to take a shower?'

Reaper sighed. 'You're taking this kinda seriously, aren't you, soldier boy?'

'And so should you, if you want to stay alive.'

While Lock finished breakfast, Reaper settled for washing himself in the sink. As he ate, Lock mulled over Reaper's overwhelming confidence. He couldn't decide on its source. Was it a macho veneer acquired over years spent in prison? Or did it go deeper? Did Reaper know something that either Lock or Jalicia didn't?

Lock took his place at the sink as an orderly came back along the tier and collected the breakfast trays.

'So, what now?' Lock asked Reaper, unsure of what kind of day lay ahead.

'It's Sunday, right?' Reaper asked him.

Lock had to stop and think about it. Already, the confined quarters were starting to distort his perception of time. 'Yeah, that's right,' he said, pushing away the thought that Sunday mornings were usually reserved for walking Angel in Central Park with Carrie.

'Then we got no work,' said Reaper, 'just play. And I tell you what, soldier boy,' he went on, looking around the stark confines of their cell, 'this sure as hell beats solitary.'

Their cell door shuddered and began to roll open.

'Yard time,' said Reaper. 'Let's go meet the neighbours.'

12

As Lock stepped out on to the yard, bright sunlight caught him unawares, and he had to put his hand up to shield his eyes from the blinding glare. The yard itself was a large grassy space divided up with benches. A walking track ran round the perimeter, and beyond that was more fencing topped with razor wire. Beyond that was another yard and another set of cell blocks which emptied out into the same sub-divided central space. The entire yard fell under the watchful eye of a guard in the gun tower, who scanned the inmates from behind mirrored sunglasses while toting a Mini-14 rifle.

In addition to the guard high above them in the gun tower, there were cameras mounted at strategic points around the yard. There were also two guards on the yard itself, both armed with batons, tasers and large canisters of pepper spray. The yard had been constructed in such a way that, unlike some of the older prisons Lock had seen on TV, every inch of public space was open to scrutiny.

For the first few seconds, Lock could feel the heavy weight of the other inmates' stares, accompanied by an ominous silence. Then it was gone, as the inmates separated into their different racial groups: the black prisoners headed for the basketball court, the Hispanics settled themselves on some benches in the far

67

corner of the yard and the white inmates gravitated to another set of benches.

Lock nodded towards this group. 'Who are they?'

Lock's nod drew narrowed-eye stares from the white inmates.

Reaper stepped in front of Lock and put a massive callused hand on Lock's chest. 'Yard etiquette 101,' he said. 'First rule, you never stare at someone, you never nod towards them, and you definitely never point at anyone on the yard. Unless, of course, you want to fight them.'

'Point taken, but you still didn't answer my question,' said Lock.

'We're cool,' said Reaper. 'They're NLR for the most part.'

'NLR?' Lock asked.

'Nazi Low Riders.'

'Not Aryan Brotherhood?'

'No,' said Reaper, stepping away from Lock and pivoting back round, his eyes sliding across the yard towards three gargantuan white inmates standing on their own next to the fence, arms folded. 'Those three dudes over there are AB. Now, come on, soldier boy.'

Reaper began to walk. Conversations fell away to a series of whispers. The basketball game stopped. Even though no one stared, Lock knew that they were being watched.

Lock fell into step with Reaper. But rather than head towards his old comrades near the fence, Reaper was making for the larger group of Nazi Low Riders. Whatever the etiquette, the three Aryan Brotherhood members were now openly staring at Reaper.

'I hope you know what you're doing,' said Lock as they got within ten feet of the group of Nazi Low Riders.

The group parted and an older white inmate sporting a ratty moustache and a winged death skull tattoo which ran the length of his clavicle just beneath his throat stepped towards them.

He and Reaper clasped hands and then hugged.

'It's been a while, Phileas,' Reaper said to the man.

'Too long,' said Phileas, motioning for Reaper to take a seat on the bench next to him.

Across the yard, the three Aryan Brotherhood members were mumbling among themselves. One of them spat at the ground.

Lock had been right about one thing: Reaper had never intended to step back on to the mainline without a plan in place. However, he still had a job to do, and who was to say that Reaper's apparent defection from the Aryan Brotherhood to their rivals, the Nazi Low Riders, would be the last betrayal the yard would see?

Lock skirted around the benches so he was closer to Reaper, only to have a huge hand pushed hard into his chest. A Nazi Low Rider gang member sporting a swastika tattooed across the centre of his forehead stared down at him — no mean feat considering that Lock was six feet two inches tall.

'Where the fuck you going, dawg?' he asked.

Lock kept his gaze as even as his voice. 'Just

watching my cellie's back, brother.'

'Well, do it somewhere else.'

Lock stood his ground, but kept his hands down by his sides. His posture was loose and unthreatening. 'Sorry, I can't help you there, dawg.'

Lock's challenge had the desired effect. The man took a step towards him. Lock brought the palm of his right hand up hard and fast, finding the man's throat and snapping his head back. Lock followed this up by slamming his knee into the man's groin. The Nazi Low Rider folded like a bad hand of poker.

One of the guards patrolling the yard started towards them, his hand on his canister of pepper spray. The guard in the gun tower, swivelled his weapon in Lock's direction.

Lock stepped back, ready to fight some more.

Phileas, who'd been talking to Reaper, turned to the man who'd been pole-axed by Lock. 'Knock it off,' he said. He tapped Reaper on the elbow. 'Let's take a walk.'

He and Reaper headed off to the track that circled the yard. Lock fell in behind them.

As he did so, the man he'd just attacked got to his feet and grudgingly put out his hand. 'They call me Eichmann,' he said, by way of introduction. 'I keep an eye out for Phileas.'

'Lock,' said Lock, shaking Eichmann's hand. 'Come on, let's not fall behind here.'

'What the fuck you talking about?'

Reaper and Phileas were already level with the three members of the Aryan Brotherhood. If they decided to rush Reaper there would be less than twenty yards to cover. Maybe Phileas had suggested that he and Reaper take a stroll for the express purpose of getting Reaper in close enough to the hit squad.

'I'm talking about the Three Stooges over there by the fence,' said Lock, staring straight ahead.

'Don't worry about them,' said Eichmann. 'We got the numbers on this yard now.'

'Sometimes it doesn't come down to numbers.'

'So what does it come down to?'

'The element of surprise,' said Lock, heading straight for the three members of the Aryan Brotherhood.

Eichmann followed Lock as he zeroed in. When he was within five feet of them — a distance at which they would have to move towards him in order to strike a blow — he stopped. All three were under six feet tall, but what they lacked vertically they more than made up for in terms of sheer dumb muscle.

Lock greeted them with a nod. 'Gentlemen.'

'What you want?' the Aryan Brotherhood member in the middle asked him, the blood vessels in his neck bulging.

'I was going to ask you pretty much the same thing,' Lock said. 'You keep on sneaking romantic little glances over in our direction, and it's kind of creeping me out. If you could stop doing it, I'd appreciate it.'

'Hey,' said the one in the middle, 'this is our yard.'

Lock glanced over his shoulder at the dozen or

so Nazi Low Riders assembled on the benches who were staring with menace at the three Aryan Brotherhood members. 'Not any more it ain't.'

The Aryan Brotherhood member in the middle took a step towards Lock. Lock raised his hands, palms open, shifting his right foot back a little and keeping his eyes on the man's hands.

Like some kind of conjuring trick, there was a sudden flash of metal in the man's hand, and he lunged towards Lock with the shank. But Lock managed to catch his wrist. Behind him he could hear the shouts of the guards and other inmates. The two other Aryan Brotherhood members rushed towards him, but Eichmann blocked them, taking a few solid punches for his trouble.

Lock lowered his body to give himself some leverage, turned the man's wrist, and snapped it with a dull crack. The blade fell from his hand, landing in the dust. Lock used his hold on the man's broken wrist to pull him slowly down towards the ground.

The guards were close now; Lock could smell the oxygen-suffocating odour of pepper spray. He let go, and took a couple of steps back.

A baton crashed into his side. Then the guards rushed past him and Eichmann to deal with the three Aryan Brotherhood members, ordering them to the ground. All three finally complied, one taking a blast from a guard's taser first.

Lock and Eichmann rejoined the group of Nazi Low Riders as more guards arrived, herding everyone back towards the confines of the unit. Lock was worried that he would be pulled from the group, but the guards seemed more concerned with restoring order. At the main door leading back into the unit, he watched as the three Aryan Brotherhood members were hustled through a gate in the chain-link fence and out of the yard.

Lock caught Reaper's eye,

'What was that about?' Reaper asked him.

'Something my old man taught me,' Lock said.

'And what's that?' Reaper said, rubbing the back of his neck with one giant shovel of a hand.

'Always get your retaliation in first.'

13

The screen door of the rented single-storey house slammed behind Chance as she emerged into the early-morning sunlight. She stood there for a moment collecting her thoughts. She was dressed in an outfit guaranteed to deduct at least twenty IQ points from any heterosexual male: cut-off Daisy Duke shorts, a pink Hello Kitty T-shirt, white cotton ankle socks and a pair of black kitten-heel sandals.

The pit bull that Chance had won from a Hell's Angel in an all-night poker game barked a warning from its metal-framed run which ran the length of the house. She had planned to sell it on to a guy she'd met who was into dog fighting, but in the end decided to keep it, figuring it would prove a deterrent for inquisitive neighbours. So far she'd been proved right. In the month she'd been renting the small whitewashed bungalow, no one had been to her front door, not even the mail man.

She climbed into the red pick-up truck parked in the drive, tossed her briefcase on to the passenger side of the bench seat and reversed out on to the street at speed. Within ten minutes she was roaring down the on-ramp and merging with the early-morning traffic on Interstate 5 South. She kept her speed at an even sixty as she headed out of Los Angeles.

She flicked on the radio, catching a Jimmy

Buffett tune mid-chorus. Jimmy was singing a song called 'We Are the People Our Parents Warned Us About'. It was one of Chance's favourites.

Chance rolled down the windows either side of her as traffic ahead of her slowed to a crawl. The breeze felt good on her skin. In the lane next to her a businessman in a BMW saloon was staring at her. She raised her sunglasses and winked at him. The poor sap lost all concentration and looked up just in time to avoid rear-ending the car in front of him. Chance spotted a gap in the outside lane and zoomed into it, leaving the BMW driver in her dust.

Men. Always thinking with their dicks.

Leaving Orange County the traffic cleared, and she started making good time. The meeting was set for eleven o'clock and she couldn't afford to be late.

In the end she made it with an hour to spare, taking the off-ramp twelve miles shy of San Diego and following the directions on her GPS according to the coordinates she'd been given.

The rendezvous point was down a dirt track at the back of a vacant lot. The track dead-ended at what looked like a disused auto repair shop, Chance parked the truck and went to take a look around.

The building was squat and low. There were two large sliding doors. She heaved one open and stepped inside. The place smelled of motor oil and tobacco. A bench ran the length of the back wall. A stack of truck tyres was piled against a barred window.

Chance heard a vehicle approaching, its gears grinding. She ducked outside to take a look.

A yellow rental truck parked up and a man in his late fifties sporting salt-and-pepper hair and a pair of old-school Rayban Wayfarer sunglasses hopped out of the cab. He was wearing khaki combat trousers, a white T-shirt and black boots.

He stopped when he saw her and looked her up and down. Her outfit was definitely having the desired effect.

'Hi,' she said, flicking back a strand of blonde hair from in front of her face.

'Well, if this don't beat all,' he said. He had more than a hint of a Southern accent, Georgia maybe. Or Mississippi.

'You bring everything?' Chance asked him.

'Oh, I got *everything*,' he said.

What an asshole, thought Chance.

'Can I see it?'

'Sure, it's in the back of the truck.'

She followed him to the rear of the truck. He fiddled with a padlock then opened up doors at the back. He climbed in the back and helped her up. There were three plywood coffins there.

'Nice touch,' said Chance.

'No one's going to open one of these coming back from Iraq on a military transport plane,' the man said,

'You mind if I take a look?' she asked him.

'Go right ahead, honey.'

She prised open the lid of the first coffin and took a look inside. She took out an M-4 assault rifle and checked it over.

The man shifted his weight from one foot to

the other. 'It's all here. Everything you asked for. Now, did you bring the money?'

Chance nodded, replacing the lid. 'You help me get this stuff loaded first?'

'Sure thing. Tell you the truth, I'm glad to be getting rid of it,' he said, rolling up his sleeves to reveal a black sun tattoo.

They set to work moving the coffins from the back of the hire truck to her pick-up. Chance could tell that the man was surprised by her physical strength. 'You sure you should be lifting stuff?' he asked her.

Chance smiled sweetly. 'Dude, your belly's bigger than mine. What do you think Pilgrim women did when they were pregnant? Sit home and eat bonbons?'

He laughed and they carried on.

As they lifted the final coffin he told her to be careful. 'This one's got that real special delivery.'

Chance felt her heart quicken. 'The pressure plates?'

'Calibrated to the weight you asked for.'

Slowly, they manoeuvred the coffin from the truck and slid it along the bed of the pick-up. Then Chance covered all three coffins with a green tarpaulin.

'The money's here,' she said, walking round to the front of the pick-up, opening the passenger-side door and grabbing the briefcase. She flipped open the two catches and held the contents up for inspection.

The man smiled at the thick bundles of hundred-dollar bills. His tongue flicked across his lips.

She looked past him to the rear of the truck. 'Damn, that tarpaulin's come loose. Could you fix it for me?'

'Be my pleasure, honey,' he said.

She put the briefcase down on the ground and reached back into the cab of the truck, grabbing a loaded Glock 9mm. 'You're so sweet,' Chance said, levelling the gun at him and firing two shots into the man's back from less than ten feet away. He took a step, his body twisting round. Then his legs folded and he fell, face down. She closed in on him, firing two more rounds into the back of his head.

Satisfied he was dead, she got back into the red pick-up, picked up her cell phone and called Cowboy, one of the two men she trusted most in the world. Along with his friend Trooper, Cowboy was a dedicated Aryan warrior. They had been by her side through the toughest of times, and in a world where trust was in short supply she knew they would stand by her come what may. They had proved as much when they'd helped her resolve the Prager situation.

Cowboy answered on the first ring.

'I got it,' she said.

'Any problems?'

She stared in the side mirror at the man's body lying flat, blood puddling out around him.

'Nope,' she said. 'Plain sailing.'

14

A blue-steel light filtering through the bars of Lock and Reaper's cell announced the dawn of a new day. Along with the other inmates in the unit, Lock and Reaper had spent the remainder of the previous day confined to their cell. Having been escorted from the yard, the three members of the Aryan Brotherhood had failed to reappear. Lock guessed they had been transferred either to another unit or solitary, and not before time.

Regardless of the reason, and even with them gone, Lock knew there was no way he could afford to relax. The Aryan Brotherhood was a powerful organisation whose tentacles stretched out beyond their immediate membership, and its leadership wasn't about to give up without a fight.

Finishing up a breakfast of fluorescent pink ham, bread, butter and an apple, washed down with milk, Lock put down his meal tray and nodded towards the stack of books on the floor. 'Mind if I take a look?'

'Go right ahead. You might learn something.'

Lock flicked past Reaper's well-thumbed copy of *Mein Kampf* and settled instead on an equally dog-eared edition of Sun Tzu's *The Art of War*. He held it up. 'Keep your friends close and your enemies closer?'

Reaper looked up. 'It wasn't Sun Tzu who said that.'

'Who was it then?'

Reaper laid aside his food tray and hopped down from his perch. 'Michael Corleone in *The Godfather*.' He plucked the book from Lock's hands and held it up. 'No, what Sun Tzu said was this: 'Engage people with what they expect. It settles them into predictable patterns of response, occupying their minds while you wait for the extraordinary moment — that which they cannot anticipate.''

Reaper seemed to be reciting the passage from memory.

'And what does that mean?' Lock asked him.

Reaper hopped back up on to the top bunk with a grace that belied his age. 'You'll know it when you see it.'

'An extraordinary moment?'

Reaper chuckled to himself. 'Oh, it'll be extraordinary all right.'

Lock felt a ripple of concern. Since he'd stepped into the cell, Reaper hadn't come across as a man worried for his life. He also seemed to be finding great amusement in a secret only he was privy to. The more Lock thought about it, the more suspect Reaper's testimony seemed to be. There was a game being played, but he wasn't sure it was the game Jalicia and Coburn thought it was.

Lock was torn from his thoughts by the sound of cell doors being opened on the ground floor of the unit.

'OK, gentlemen,' shouted Lieutenant Williams, standing with his hands on his hips, in the centre of the floor. 'Showers. Two cells at a time.

And just so you know, if there's any more trouble in this unit, you'll be back on lockdown.'

Inside their cell, Reaper wagged a finger at Lock, and smirked. 'You hear that, soldier boy?'

Half an hour later their cell door opened and, stripped to the waist, Lock and Reaper stepped out on to the tier along with two Hispanic inmates from the cell next door. Lock signalled for Reaper to hang back but Reaper pushed past the two smaller Hispanics and made his way towards the showers, which were at the far end of the unit. Lock took his time, keeping an eye on the two Hispanics as they followed Reaper into the showers.

Reaper soaped up and set about washing himself. Lock and the other two inmates did the same.

Reaper closed his eyes and let the hot water cascade across his face. 'Lock, will you stop looking at my ass.'

The two Hispanics sniggered and traded a look, then glanced over at Lock.

Lock stared at them. 'What the fuck are you looking at?'

His challenge seemed to do the trick, as they quickly looked away.

Lock washed up as best he could with the gritty prison-issue soap, keeping an eye on the door leading into the showers. He thought about what Lieutenant Williams had just said about no one being allowed out of their cells if there was any more trouble.

They dried off, dressed and headed back up to their cell. Twenty minutes later, once everyone in the unit had been given the opportunity to get cleaned up, the unit's cells were opened one at a time and the general housing inmates filtered out to work within the prison or to attend class. Lock and Reaper were left to last, which was fine by Lock.

Together, they stepped out on to an empty tier and walked down the stairs. Waiting for them at the bottom was Lieutenant Williams, who motioned them to follow him out on to the yard.

'You see that?' Williams said, pointing to the chain-link fence that encircled the yard area.

Lock noticed that every piece of metal on the fence, every attaching link, was slashed with a dash of purple paint. The colour was starting to fade though, ravaged no doubt by the sea air and wind.

Lieutenant Williams nodded towards a tin of paint and two brushes sitting next to the fence. 'I want you to paint over every slash of purple that's already there,' he said.

Reaper shrugged. 'Want us to count the bricks in the unit when we're done?'

'Watch your mouth, Hays,' Williams said, marching back towards the unit.

Lock stared at the fence for a moment.

'They mark all the pieces that someone might break off and use as a shank,' Reaper explained. 'If there's no paint where there should be, it's easier to see.'

Of course, thought Lock, a piece of metal from the fence provided the basic material for a very deadly weapon. It took a lot less energy to drive metal into someone's body than plastic.

* * *

By the time lunch was called, dark patches of sweat had formed under Lock's prison blues, and the inmates from the unit were starting to filter back from their work details and classes. First back were some of the white inmates. Phileas led this group, with Eichmann next to his boss. Behind them came a group of black inmates, Ty among them. Ty split from them, and nodded for Lock to join him. Lock rested his paintbrush on the edge of the can of purple paint and got up.

Reaper shot him a look that was loaded with anger. 'Where the fuck are you going, Lock?' he hissed.

Lock noticed that Reaper wasn't the only one looking at him as he joined Ty. The other white inmates were openly staring as Lock caught up with Ty next to the wall.

'What's up?' Lock asked Ty.

'The Aryan Brotherhood have given the contract to the Mexican Mafia, and they've kicked it down to the Nortenos,' Ty whispered.

'Thanks. You hear anything else, you let me know.'

15

'The Nortenos have taken over the contract on you,' Lock said, digging his fork into a piece of mystery meat on his lunch tray.

Reaper shrugged. 'Figures. But we've got bigger problems than that.' He slammed down his tray. 'What were you doing back there talking to that toad on the yard? I damn told you the rules, soldier boy.'

Lock eyed Reaper coolly. 'Those are your rules, not mine.'

'Wrong, they're the yard's rules,' Reaper said, 'To us, someone who associates with the blacks is worse than a snitch, worse than a child molester. Now, I warned you, but you had to do it your way, and now you're going to have to deal with the fall-out.'

'Your concern's touching, but I can handle myself.'

'We'll see,' said Reaper.

★ ★ ★

An hour later, he and Reaper were out on the basketball court. Lock looked around at his companions. With their low brows, dumb-muscle bulk and yellowing, crank-rotten dentistry, Lock wasn't sure this was what people meant by the term 'master race'.

Behind them, the black inmates, Ty among

them, had taken the benches in an orderly handover. Distance was maintained between the two groups as they did so. It occurred to Lock that every group on the yard operated as its own personal escort section. If these guys hadn't been such lousy criminals, they might have made halfway decent close-protection operatives.

The whites had divided into two teams, Lock finding himself on the same team as Reaper but up against Phileas. Not ideal. It would have been easier to keep an eye on Reaper if he'd been up against him. The court, mid-game, would be a good place for a hit too. Lots of movement buying vital seconds before any guards on the yard or, more crucially, in the gun tower noticed anything was happening.

At first all went well, the mid-afternoon heat ensuring that a brisk pace, with lots of baskets and fouls that bordered on common assault, quickly slowed the game to a walking pace. Lock went up against Phileas, dribbling the ball round him and catching an elbow in his abdomen for his trouble. As Lock doubled over, Phileas stole the ball and headed for the basket. Reaper stuck out a foot to trip him but Phileas feinted left and scored a deft two-pointer which sparked whoops of delight from his team-mates.

After fifteen minutes of barely contained mayhem, Phileas, the gnarled leader of the Nazi Low Riders, called a time-out and both teams gathered under the basket to catch their breath. Reaper scraped a hand across his stubble, then grabbed the ball and was off, moving down court at a steady clip. Lock jogged after him, as did Phileas, the proper game seemingly over.

Reaper passed the ball to Lock, then started to wander back down towards the inmates.

Phileas caught up with Lock. 'Come on then, soldier, let's play a little one on one.'

Lock bounced the ball, eyes flicking back down the court to Reaper.

'Don't worry about your cellie,' Phileas said. 'He can take care of himself. Believe me.'

'I never doubted it.'

Phileas lunged for the ball, but Lock shifted back, keeping it just out of his reach. Phileas narrowed his eyes and half-turned so he was focused on the group of black inmates moving slowly from the benches, ready to head back into the unit.

'The toad you came in with,' Phileas said.

Lock's hackles rose as he heard his friend being abused for the second time that day. Under any other circumstance, Nazi Low Rider shot caller or not, the guy would be choking to death on his own tongue. 'His name's Tyrone.'

Phileas shrugged. 'You name your pets?'

Lock tensed as Phileas dived in again, taking the basketball with the tips of his fingers, dribbling it four more steps, setting up for the shot, then stopping, both hands on the ball.

'We want him dead. And we want you to do it.'

'Forget it,' Lock said, moving round so his back was to the hoop and he had a clear view all the way down the court to Reaper, and beyond to the black inmates and Ty.

'Time to wet your steel, soldier,' Phileas said as Lock watched Ty bumping fists with the other black inmates. 'Next yard, Lock. You kill him or we kill you.'

16

It was early morning when Chance once again shuffled through the metal detector in the lobby of the Federal Building. This visit, she'd still worn an underwire bra but also a crop top, which emphasised the fact she was pregnant. The metal detector beeped and she was asked to stand to one side. It was a different female guard this time, which came as a relief. The woman wanded Chance with the handheld detector, which sounded as it passed over Chance's chest and lower abdomen. Then she moved on to patting her down.

As the female guard moved her hand over Chance's belly, Chance winced.

'You OK?' asked the guard.

'Sorry, I'm just a little tender there.'

Chance could read the female guard's discomfort. She finished the search by moving her hands away quickly down Chance's legs and checking the soles of her shoes.

'OK, ma'am, you have a nice day.'

Chance slipped away towards the bank of elevators and headed up to the tenth floor. There, she walked briskly towards the disabled bathroom. She locked the door behind her, pulled off her jeans and panties, lowered the toilet seat and set about retrieving the package of cellophane-wrapped C4 explosive and detonator cap from inside her vaginal cavity. She placed the package in the sink, pulled her panties and jeans back on, and slipped off her bra. In less than ten seconds she had pulled the length of wire from her bra, which she now stuffed into her bag, taking out a newly bought cell phone as she did so.

With all the components in front of her, she set to work. In less than five minutes the IED was assembled and placed behind the toilet. She crossed to the sink and carefully washed her hands, using a brush she'd brought with her to remove any remaining residue from under her fingernails.

She left the bathroom, caught the elevator back down to the lobby and left via the revolving glass door on the opposite side of the building from which she'd entered.

A few blocks from the courthouse, Chance clambered into the cab of her red pick-up truck. Her old friend Cowboy was driving, his trademark black-velvet-brimmed Stetson pulled down low, obscuring emerald-green eyes. Next to him sat Trooper, two hundred pounds of muscle topped off by a mane of long blond hair which always reminded Chance of the actor Mickey Rourke in that movie about the down-at-heel wrestler.

Trooper put an arm round her shoulder. 'You OK?'

'Fine,' Chance said, enjoying having them both near her again.

Cowboy signalled before pulling out into traffic. 'You get it placed?'

Chance smiled across at him. 'Sure did. Now all I have to do is make a phone call.'

17

A chilling breeze cut across the yard as Lock and Reaper set back to work marking each piece of metal in the chain-link fence with a slash of purple paint. With Phileas's ultimatum still ringing in his ears, Lock was thankful that, like the day before, they had been released last from their cell in the unit.

Reaper dabbed a splodge of purple on to his brush. 'Today's the day, huh?' he said to Lock.

'What day's that?'

'Day you pop your cherry inside here.'

Lock rolled up his cuffs. 'We'll see.'

'Listen, man, I'm sorry about Phileas, but you talk to a toad on the yard, this is what happens.' Reaper ran his brush across a metal end wire secured to one of the posts. 'And you can't say I didn't warn you.'

'I'm not laying a finger on Ty.'

'Then you're gonna have to face the consequences, my friend,' Reaper said, reloading his brush with paint, then sketching the outline of a man's face in the dirt.

Lock paused for a second to study the outline, picking out a strong chin, aquiline nose and hooded eyes — the unmistakable features of the current President.

'Didn't think you'd be a fan of his,' Lock said.

Reaper stopped to admire his handiwork. 'I ain't,' he said sourly, 'although he's done great things for our movement, that's for sure.'

Lock didn't stop to dispute that with Reaper. Ever since the country elected its first African-American President there had been a surge in two things: gun sales and membership of white supremacist groups.

Seemingly lost in thought, Reaper dabbed a little more purple on to the end of his brush and drew a circle round the President's head, then painted in a couple of lines to form crosshairs.

'Nice touch,' Lock said, grabbing the white plastic handle of the paint tin and holding it up. 'We're out. You want to go see if you can get us some more?'

Reaper took the tin and got to his feet. 'Sure thing. You don't want to come with me?' he added sarcastically.

'Not this time,' Lock said, watching Reaper swagger across the yard.

As soon as Reaper was out of sight, Lock walked to the end of the fence they'd already worked on and pretended to be checking over each purple slash. At the same time he angled his body so that he had his back to the guard in the gun tower.

He hunkered down on his haunches and with his paintbrush in his left hand set about unhooking and then twisting off a piece of wire connected to the terminal post. After what seemed an eternity it came away in his hand, and he pocketed it. Then he dabbed at where the chain-link had been with his brush and set to work on another piece. By the time Reaper emerged from the unit building with more paint,

Lock had managed to prise away three pieces.

He turned and walked back along the fence towards Reaper, who raised the tin of paint in salute before looking from Lock to the far end of the fence.

'What you doing down there, soldier boy?'

'Just making sure I hadn't missed anything,' Lock said. 'If a job's worth doing, it's worth doing well, right?'

Reaper smirked and tugged at his walrus moustache. 'If you say so.'

They set back to work. Now all Lock could do was pray that one of the guards noticed the missing pieces of the fence before it was too late.

18

Shouts and curses bounced off every surface in the unit as, one by one, the inmates were taken from their cells, cuffed and ordered to lie face down on the floor. Once secured, a search team of three guards stepped into each cell and systematically tore the place apart, upturning mattresses, tearing pictures from the walls and throwing everything else on to the floor of the cell.

Up on the tier, Lock lay on his bunk, his hands clasped behind his head, and listened to the commotion with a quiet feeling of satisfaction.

Reaper's head appeared above his. 'Think you're real cute, don't you?'

Lock stared right through him. 'No idea what you're talking about.'

Reaper's legs swung over the edge of the bunk, the soles of his feet directly above Lock's chest. He pushed off with his arms and landed on the floor of the cell.

'Where'd you hide 'em?'

'Where'd I hide what?'

'Those pieces from the fence you must have snuck when we were painting it.'

'That what all this is about?' said Lock, getting to his feet.

Reaper stepped towards him so that inches separated them. Lock stood his ground.

'The deal was I got back to the mainline or I didn't testify.'

Lock spread out his arms. 'You're on the mainline.'

'I spent five years in the SHU, cooped up in a cell. No yard time. No phone calls. Nothing to do but go crazy. I ain't doin' it any more. So, I want you to tell me where those pieces are.'

Lock's eyes slid to Reaper's hands. He tensed, waiting for him to make a move. There were often pinch points with a principal, usually revolving around trivial issues such as them asking the bodyguard to carry their luggage, or to get them coffee at three in the morning. This was slightly different.

'You think this'll get you out of stabbing your buddy?'

Still Lock didn't react.

Reaper blinked first, stepping back and beginning to search the cell. 'They find them in our house and it's bad news for you and me both.'

Lock knew Reaper was lying. The warden could have found half a kilo of coke, a keg of Bud and a Playboy Playmate in the cell and Reaper would still be heading for sunny San Francisco in less than two days' time.

From outside the cell came the slamming of heavy reinforced steel doors and the barked orders of cops as they moved methodically through the unit. Lock was counting on them hitting this cell soon, and finding the three pieces of metal fence he'd secreted well enough to make it look like he'd made an effort to hide

94

them, but not so well that they wouldn't find them.

The pieces were his ticket to the warden's office, where he was going to suggest that it was time to move Reaper out, as well as him and Ty.

'Well, what do we have here?'

Lock stayed where he was as Reaper sucked the blood from a couple of tiny cuts on the end of his fingertips where the metal taped under the bunk had caught his hand. Then Reaper ducked his head under, and less than thirty seconds later came up with the three hasps of metal.

Shouldering past Lock, he crouched down by the cell door. There was a gap at the bottom. Less than half an inch. He waited until all the guards were inside cells and batted the metal under the door. The pieces scooted across the walkway and fell down on to the floor of the unit. If they made a sound when they landed, Lock didn't hear it over the cacophony of orders and protests.

There was a shout, and below Lock's cell the guards gathered round the three small pieces of chain-link. The guard who'd spotted them first glanced up, his index finger pointing at three cells on the second floor from where the metal might have been ejected. Then he shouted up to the cons gathered at those doors: 'Smart move, assholes.'

Reaper stepped back to his bunk, his fingertips still red. He dug out a sharpened toothbrush he'd shown Lock before and handed it to Lock. 'Take it, because believe me, you're gonna need it.'

'I need to speak to the warden,' Lock said to the young floor cop who was the first to reach his cell, knowing that such a request, made in the open, where other inmates could hear, was a high-risk manoeuvre.

'What's the matter? Coffee too cold? Your pillows too hard? Sheets not got a high enough thread count?' The cop was clearly still pissed at the missing metal, which had disrupted the day's routine. Like any other large institution, Pelican Bay was, by necessity, all about routine.

'Just tell him, OK?'

Reaper clapped a meaty paw on to Lock's shoulder. 'Yard time, soldier boy. No avoiding it.'

Lock knew that all he could do now was tough it out.

★ ★ ★

When he found himself standing at the door that opened on to the yard, Lock felt as though he was standing in one of the tunnels leading into the Coliseum, a gladiator waiting to emerge blinking into the sunlight, knowing that there were only two possible outcomes: victory or death.

Out on the yard, the white inmates immediately took one set of benches in the corner furthest from the block. Lock scanned the other groups: to his left, the group of Nortenos eyed the white inmates; on the other bench were the black inmates, Ty at the centre.

'They know something's up,' Lock said, stalling for time.

The eyes of every white inmate swivelled towards him.

A metal shank appeared suddenly in Phileas's hand. Sharper than the jagged-edged toothbrush, a razor-sharp tip with barbs running all the way up it, so that it would do even more damage coming out than going in. 'No time like the present,' Phileas said, the inmates standing around Lock fading away like snow in the Sahara.

Only Reaper remained standing next to him. 'What the fuck you fools doin'? He walks across the yard alone, the toads'll know something's up for sure.'

The mist of bodies moved back in.

'We all stay real close,' Reaper continued. 'Do it on the way back in.'

'No,' said Lock. 'If I'm gonna do it, let me do it now.'

★ ★ ★

Ty watched as Lock broke away from the group of white inmates and headed straight for the dozen black inmates sweating it out across the yard.

'They're getting ready to make a move,' Marvin muttered in his ear.

Ty could sense it too. It was like a change in air pressure. It had built all the way up to the lockdown when the metal pieces on the fence had gone missing. Their disappearance had to be down to Lock. His way of trying to contain Reaper, or make sure that no one got to him.

'You ready?' Marvin asked.

'I'm good,' Ty said, aware that his lips were barely moving.

By now, Lock was less than fifteen feet away, and he had been joined by a phalanx of white inmates. Phileas was on his left, Reaper on his right.

Ty rose. He and Marvin started towards the white inmates.

The yard fell silent. Ty could feel everyone's eyes on him as he kept walking. The Nortenos were already moving from their bench in anticipation of what might happen, hands by their sides, relaxed, not looking to engage but readying themselves should they have to.

They were within ten feet now. A few more steps and Ty would be close enough to the white inmates to prompt a rush from them.

Ty's eyes fixed on his target. Using a technique Lock had taught him, he began shading Phileas's body grey, leaving only the main target areas of head and groin red. You focused on the red areas; the rest took care of themselves.

Two of the guards on the yard had stopped what they were doing and were looking up. One had his radio keyed, keeping it open.

To his right, Ty saw one of the black inmates break ranks, pushing off hard and running full pelt towards the white inmates. The next second he sensed the blur of movement that was Marvin making his move — the physical equivalent of the side of a mountain slipping into the sea. Then it was on, and they were toe to toe on the yard.

19

Ty threw the open palm of his left hand into Phileas's face, following up by slamming the elbow of his right arm at his nose. Phileas's torso shifted back, but his feet stayed planted. A fist flew into Ty's chest, landing hard close to his solar plexus. The air punched out hard from his chest, but he kept fighting, throwing a knee up into Phileas's groin. Then another. And another. Phileas groaned. His head came down, earning him another knee, this one finding his face.

Ty's height gave him leverage and he set about using every inch of it. Blood clotted in the dust as he continued to rain in blows on the older man. Then what felt like an express train clobbered the side of his head and he was on the ground. There was no sensation of falling. One minute he was standing, the next he was looking up at the bloodied face of Phileas, smiling down at him through broken teeth, and raising a foot, which crashed hard into Ty's nose, snapping the cartilage.

'Toad motherfucker,' Phileas said as Ty covered his head and prepared to take the blows.

★ ★ ★

Lock had moved hard right to avoid direct engagement with Ty. Glancing back, he saw Reaper on his shoulder — for a big man who'd spent a large part of his life in a small box, he moved *fast*. The other white inmates clustered round them in a tight phalanx.

The shank was down by Lock's side. Time to do something about that. He slowed his pace fractionally and the front of someone's foot caught the back of his heel. He was ready for it so he didn't fall, but he did stumble, and as he grabbed someone behind him to steady himself, the weapon tumbled from his hand.

Ahead of him, he could see Ty giving a good account of himself. Marvin was getting the worst of it from one of the Nazi Low Riders who had him pinned to the ground and was throwing punches with bowling-ball-size fists at Marvin's head. The remainder of the black inmates were also pressing in to get some of the action. A couple rushed to Marvin and Ty's side while the rest pivoted hard left towards Lock and his group.

On the periphery, the two guards on the yard drew their canisters of pepper spray from their hips, stepped back and let loose at the edges of the melee in a futile attempt at delaying the inevitable.

There was a flurry of limbs as the two groups clashed in a mass of roundhouse kicks and brutal punches. Lock found himself facing a black inmate about his own height but twenty pounds heavier with the word 'Thug' bannered in blue ink across his forehead. Lock stayed low in an effort to minimise the target area offered to his opponent, then stood and slammed his right shoulder as hard as he could into the centre of

Thug's chest. Tear gas swirled around the yard, and Lock stepped back, noticing as he did so that the mass engagement had broken into small clusters of two or three bodies.

Blood spurted in a regular pulse from the neck of a black inmate to Lock's left as two of the Nazi Low Riders went to work, one pinning him down while the other stabbed him repeatedly in the face and body. The stabber paused and grinned at Lock before plunging his shank back into his prostrate victim.

Lock looked round for Ty, then caught another whiff of tear gas which stung his eyes and blurred his vision.

Staying low, he charged Thug, coming up hard again, this time with an elbow to his opponent's chin. It was a clean connection, right on the button, and Thug's legs buckled under him. Lock helped him along, sweeping the hapless black inmate to the floor by grabbing his prison blues around the collar and bringing his right leg hard into the back of Thug's knees. Lock gave him a final kick in the head for good measure, keeping the arc of his foot low, and started to skirt round the bodies.

Amid the mayhem, he'd lost sight of Ty.

★ ★ ★

Wisps of tear gas clung low to the ground, lending a near-medieval tinge to the scene as Lock glimpsed half a dozen guards in full riot gear opening a gate into the yard and rolling on through. Wielding tasers and batons they went to work, weeding first through those inmates closest to the fence.

'Get down on the ground now!'

'Do not move!'

Most inmates offered only token resistance, two or three minutes of close-quarter combat having sapped the energy of all but the fittest. After taking a couple of baton strikes to their bodies to demonstrate their continuing machismo, they followed orders, rolling away from opponents and kissing the dirt, bruised fingers laced tight behind their necks.

As the guards moved in, Lock spotted Ty. Next to Ty, Marvin was lying motionless on the ground, clots of red dirt flecked on the ground around him. Ty was still going at it, giving a good account of himself, throwing palms and elbows at Phileas with alarming speed and ferocity. Phileas was backing away, his face swollen.

Lock couldn't resist a smile as Ty grabbed Phileas by the back of his neck, using his spare hand to gouge at his eyes — a classic piece of Krav Maga, where total destruction of your opponent was prized over looking good.

'Get down on the ground!' the guard nearest to Ty yelled.

Do it, thought Lock. Just do it, Ty. Give it up. But Ty was too far gone, too consumed by the massive dump of adrenalin brought by combat.

Lock half-turned and caught a baton to the back of his knees. His legs folded and the ground came up to meet him. His hands pressed the dirt as he pushed himself back up, but another blow, this one to his back, sank him, just as he caught a glimpse of Ty astride Phileas, the guy barely moving.

★ ★ ★

Up in the gun tower, a lone guard surveyed the yard through the scope of his rifle. Save for one corner of the yard, all the inmates were lying face down. The riot officers moved among them, assessing who needed medical attention and who needed restraints.

To his left, though, a black inmate still had one of the whites pinned down. A riot officer blasted a cone of pepper spray in the black inmate's direction, but the black inmate had pulled his shirt up over his face, shielding himself from the worst of it.

The guard's finger moved to the trigger of his gun as the inmate advanced on the guard. Picking a spot behind and to the left of the inmate, he squeezed the trigger.

Lock heard the sharp crack of the shot and watched a puff of dust from the warning shot rise near Ty. He looked up towards the gun tower, but right then two members of the riot squad moved in front of him, their heavy black boots blocking his vision.

A few seconds later came the crack of a second shot, and the yard fell silent as Ty hit the ground.

20

Jalicia watched as Bobby Gross, lead defence attorney for the Aryan Brotherhood leadership, swept into the San Francisco courtroom, his entourage of a dozen other attorneys and assistants trailing in his wake. As he approached the table where she sat with her three-person prosecution team, he stopped, ran a hand through his carefully blow-dried head of hair, and pursed his lips. Jalicia suspected that he probably spent more time in front of the mirror in the morning than she did.

'Can I help you with something, Bobby?' Jalicia asked, fully aware of how much Gross hated being called by his first name.

He leaned in towards her. She could smell his breath. Minty fresh. 'Tick tock. Think your boy's gonna make it?' Gross was all smiles, a football coach riling his opposite number before the big game.

Behind Gross, his clients, the six members of the Aryan Brotherhood leadership, were being led in by their escort of US Marshals. They seemed to be in high spirits, laughing and joking among themselves. Most of them had been in prison for over thirty years, and it showed in the motel-tan pallor of their skin. Several wore reading glasses. All were dressed in a preppy smart-casual uniform of chinos and business shirts, buttoned to the neck — all the better to hide biceps that could crack a steel-reinforced walnut, not to mention the patchwork of shamrocks, swastikas and Nazi lightning bolts inked across their torsos and arms. The only tattoo none of them could conceal was the one that identified their membership of the AB — the shamrock inked on to the third knuckle of their right hand.

Their nicknames were jokey, bordering on cartoonish: Pinky, Sherlock, Duke, Shark, Gringo, The Monk. They looked like the senior members of a *Deadwood* appreciation society who'd taken the construction of their respective personas just a little too seriously.

Jalicia gave them and then Gross a confident smile. Every day since she had informed Gross about her star witness he'd tried to needle her about Reaper's appearance.

'My witnesses are all fine,' she said.

'Not what I hear,' Gross said. 'Seems there's been a little incident up at Pelican Bay.'

Jalicia's heart jumped into her throat. 'I know,' she lied.

The door behind Gross and his team opened and Coburn stalked in with a couple of men she recognised as members of the US Marshals team that had transported Lock and Ty up to Pelican Bay. Jalicia excused herself and made her way across to them.

'Something's happened?' she asked.

Coburn spread his palms to the floor. 'Take it easy. Reaper's fine.'

She ushered Coburn and the two US Marshals out into the corridor, away from the

105

prying eyes and ears of the Aryan Brotherhood leadership and their hotshot attorneys.

'OK,' she said. 'Give it to me from the top.'

'There was a riot on the yard,' Coburn said.

'They tried to get to Reaper?'

'Reports are confused about precisely what happened. The California Department of Corrections just released some of the footage from their CCTV system.'

'But Reaper's OK?'

'A little bruised,' offered one of the Marshals.

'What about Lock?'

'He put a couple of other inmates in the medical wing,' Coburn said. 'They've stashed him in solitary confinement with Reaper for safe keeping.'

'Reaper's gonna love that,' she said.

'Better pissed off than dead,' Coburn said.

The look on Coburn's face suggested that there was something he wasn't saying.

'What is it?' Jalicia asked.

'It's Lock's partner. The guard didn't know he was one of us.'

'Which guard?'

The two Marshals looked away.

'The one in the gun tower,' said Coburn.

'Ty's been shot?' Jalicia said.

'He's breathing. But we don't know how bad he is.'

Jalicia massaged her temples. 'Give me a minute, would you?'

She took a deep breath, then another, trying to push away her shock at what had happened to focus on the real dilemma: what to do with

106

Reaper. There was nothing she could do about what had happened at the prison, but she could still deliver her star witness's testimony.

'OK, listen. I'm going to try and get the judge to halt proceedings temporarily. Give us some time to sort out this mess.'

'You think he will?'

'No, but it's got to be worth — '

There was an ear-shredding boom, and the floor under Jalicia's feet rippled with the shock waves of a massive explosion. She was lifted up by the blast, then deposited on to the ground with a thump as clouds of dust turned everything around her grey. Fire alarms wailed in protest. She swiped at her eyes, aware of gritty powder clogging her nose and throat.

Jalicia shook her head, trying to figure what the hell had just happened, then began to crawl forward on her hands and knees. Looking up, she saw flames curling round the door of a bathroom twenty feet ahead of her. She turned round, still on all fours, and headed back in the direction of the courtroom. The dust thrown up by the explosion mingled with an acrid black smoke from the nearby fire.

Stay calm, Jalicia.

She kept moving, her hand eventually finding thin air where it should have found floor. She leaned forward, reaching down to see if the space led to the first tread of a staircase, or whether it was simply a hole. She lowered her hand into a void, and quickly withdrew it.

The dust was beginning to settle, but the smoke from the fire continued to billow around her. She backed up a little, keeping her face as low to the ground as she could. She could hear a man's voice close by.

'Jalicia?'

It was Coburn.

'Over here,' she said, realising the absurdity of what she'd just said. Even she hadn't a clue where 'here' was.

'You OK?'

'I think so.'

A beam of light punched through the colloidal mix of dust and smoke off to her left.

'You see the light?' Coburn said. 'I want you to come towards it.'

Jalicia began to crawl towards the light. Her knees and elbows ached, and there was an insistent high-pitched whine drilling into her head, but she kept moving.

'Keep coming. You're almost there.'

The news spurred her on. A few moments later she felt a hand on her shoulder as Coburn pulled her back up on to her feet, then propelled her through a doorway and into a stairwell. Cops and US Marshals were moving up, towards the top floors, against a tide of bodies heading down.

Two flights down, she signalled to Coburn to stop. Hands on her knees, she stood for a moment and caught her breath. She glanced up at Coburn. 'Thank you.'

'No trial without our lead prosecutor,' Coburn said, clamping a hand on to her shoulder. 'You good to start moving again?'

Jalicia straightened up, studying the heavy bags under his eyes, his grey-flecked hair turned white by the dust. 'Yeah.'

In the lobby, the blue-blazered security guards were busy trying to get as many people out of the building and away from the immediate area as possible. Coburn split from Jalicia to go and talk to a San Francisco Police Department sergeant. A few moments later he was back.

'You want the good news or the bad news?'

Jalicia glanced around at the people still pouring from the stairwells, their faces blackened by the smoke on the higher floors. She was still shaken from the explosion and badly in need of a caffeine hit. 'There's good news here?'

'All the defendants are accounted for. The Marshals are moving them to a secure facility until we can get the trial up and running again.'

'So what's the bad news?'

'There's been another bombing.'

Jalicia felt her stomach churn. 'Where?'

'The Federal Courthouse in Los Angeles.'

21

Blood vortexed across the room, splattering the far wall of the medical centre's triage area. Ty opened his mouth to scream. Despite the intense pain in his stomach, he thought quite calmly, abstractedly almost, *That ain't good*.

He lay back as a woman's face hovered above him. She was Asian. And really pretty. And somehow human in a way he'd forgotten, even in this short space of time, people could be. He tried to open his mouth again, this time to speak. Something bubbled at the corner. He reached his hand up and the tips of his fingers came away red.

'Take it easy, Tyrone,' the woman said. 'I'm going to give you something for the pain.'

Ty felt a jab in his hand, like a cat scratching him, and a few moments later his arm went cold, and then there was a warm feeling, and he didn't feel quite as bad.

He licked his lips, his tongue tasting iron behind the salt.

'Am I gonna die?' he asked, realising the absurdity of the question. As if anyone was going to answer yes.

'I don't think so, but we have to get you stable.'

Ty grimaced with the pain. *Fuck*. No one had told him that getting shot hurt this much. Another hot spike of agony stabbed through his shoulder. He could feel tears, hot and wet, forming in his eyes.

'Jesus, make it go away,' he groaned.

He tried to focus, to think of something. Anything.

He'd heard the first shot. But he'd been so lost in the violence that he hadn't even considered stopping. Even though he realised now that the guard in the tower had no way of knowing who he really was, he somehow, stupidly, hadn't believed that the first warning shot was just that, a warning.

Man, he'd been dumb. He'd gotten so far into playing the part he'd forgotten who he was, and now he was paying the price.

He felt himself grow weaker, a warmness spreading through his body. He tried to clasp his hands but felt his fingers fall away from his palms. His spine, arched with pain a second ago, gave way, folding into the mattress beneath him.

He closed his eyes, consciousness drifting from him. As his eyes closed, he prayed that he'd be able to open them again at some point.

★ ★ ★

The riot squad had moved the main culprits into different parts of the prison's Secure Housing Unit. Lock had found himself in a cell next to Reaper. The cells could hold two inmates but such was the nature of the population in this part of the prison that almost all of the cells were single-occupancy. These men tended to express

111

their distaste at having to share by killing their cellie.

Lock stared out through the perforated Arizona doors of his cell at a blank wall. Having Reaper back in the SHU had been part of his plan. Ty getting shot hadn't. There was no word yet as to whether his friend was dead or alive, and no way of knowing either. The idea of Ty being dead made his stomach churn to the point where he thought he might throw up.

Reaper's voice came from the next cell: 'Hey, Lock.' His tone was super-upbeat, like he and Lock were wealthy neighbours who by some stroke of fate had ended up in adjoining suites at the Four Seasons in Maui.

'What is it?'

'Wanna know something? You did real good out on that yard. Man, you would have made a great member of the Aryan Brotherhood. Shame about your toad buddy, though!'

'His name's Tyrone,' Lock said through gritted teeth.

'Bet he's up there sitting on a cloud right now eating watermelon and chitlins.'

Despite his best professional instincts, Lock felt a surge of rage. If there wasn't a wall between them he'd have ripped Reaper's throat out. But there was a wall, and he wasn't about to give Reaper the satisfaction of knowing that his taunts were having an effect.

'Ty's tough. He'll come through.'

'Hmm,' Reaper said. 'That's too bad. Man, some of those tower cops can't shoot for shit.'

'Tell you what, I'll paint a target on your back

112

and you can go running round outside and give 'em some practice.'

'Ooh, do I detect a hint of hostility from my so-called bodyguard?'

Lock moved from the door back to the bunk and climbed up. He ached all over. Even his bruises had bruises.

He himself had been shot before. Once. A single shotgun round in the chest, courtesy of a two-man assassination team he'd been chasing down who'd rigged a door. It had hurt like hell, even though he'd been wearing an anti-ballistic vest.

Reaper lowered his voice to barely a whisper. 'Hey, I never asked for your help. But seeing as we're both here, let's not forget what's at stake. If I don't make that trial, no one's going to be held to account for snuffing your buddy Prager, and this whole exercise will have been one big waste of everyone's time.'

22

Water slicked the floor of the blackened shell of what had formerly been a restroom in San Francisco's main courthouse. Jalicia stepped through what remained of the door, followed by Coburn. Shards of ceramic toilet and basin lay scattered in every direction. There was a handbag in the far corner of the room.

Jalicia picked her way through the debris towards the stall where the device had detonated. There was still a smear of blood against the wall. Both stall panels had been blown away, and the toilet itself had been reduced to a porcelain stump. Water gurgled from the bottom of it.

'How the hell did someone get past security with a bomb?' Jalicia asked.

'The guards here usually look for weapons,' Coburn replied, 'not high-grade plastic explosives. Plus, whoever placed the device planted it on a floor the public have access to rather than next to one of the courtrooms or a secure area.'

'How did they detonate it?'

'We'll only know that when forensics can tell us if it was on a timer or if it was set off by remote.'

Jalicia squared her shoulders. 'If they think they can intimidate us into dropping the case, they can forget it.'

She watched as Coburn kicked out at a piece

114

of ceramic tile, peeled from the wall by the wave of the blast. The smell of raw sewage seeping up from exposed outlet pipes was starting to get to her. She took a step towards the mirror. It used to run the length of the wash basins; now only a few fractured pieces remained on the wall, throwing back a circus-freak reflection of her sharp features.

'We push them, the Aryan Brotherhood push back. That how we play this?' Coburn asked.

She turned to face him. 'No. The AB push us, we knock them the fuck down. *That's* how we play it.'

'They might come after you as well.'

'I ever tell you about my great-grandmother, Coburn?'

'I'm guessing you're about to. Mind if I make myself comfortable?'

'She grew up in the Deep South during the civil rights struggle. When the high school in her home town was forced to integrate by the federal government, she was one of the first black students to attend. She told me about walking in that first morning. The local police just stood by while a bunch of locals abused her and the other black students. Spat on them until they were drenched in it. Kicked at them. Called them every name under the sun. It was so bad they had to turn back and go home. But she told me that the worst part was the next day when she had to force herself to go through it all over again. But she did it anyway.'

'This is a little bit more than a bunch of rednecks,' Coburn said.

115

'These guys are better armed, that's all,' said Jalicia, walking back out of the bombed-out restroom, the click of her heels echoing down the halls of justice.

★ ★ ★

Bobby Gross was out on the sidewalk, covered from head to foot in a thin layer of grey dust. Jalicia approached him as he fumbled a cigarette into his mouth with a trembling hand.

'I have a message for your clients,' she said.

He cupped a hand round the tip of his cigarette while he lit it. 'That so?'

Jalicia reached up and plucked the cigarette from his mouth, tossing it on to the ground and grinding it to dust under her heel. 'Tell them they're not going to stop this trial.'

She walked back to where Coburn was nose to nose with a US Marshal. Behind her, Gross had recovered his composure sufficiently to start haranguing her from a safe distance. 'My clients could have died in there, Jones,' he bellowed.

Jalicia tuned Gross out, instead focusing on Coburn and the US Marshals clustered round him. 'I want this trial up and running again as soon as possible,' she announced. She glanced back at the building, where smoke was billowing through the windows of the upper floors. 'We're going to need a change of venue so let's get a list of possible federal courts that might be able to accommodate us as soon as possible. We can meet later this afternoon to go over them.'

23

Lock rubbed at his wrists, and settled down in a chair next to Ty's bedside. Ty's face was covered by an oxygen mask and he had a line running into his wrist that was connected to two separate IV drips, while a monitor sketched his pulse and blood pressure in luminous green against a black grid. The prison warden, Louis Marquez, stood with Lock and watched the rise and fall of Ty's chest.

Minutes passed. Lock watched the ventilator as it moved up and down, the monitor's steady rhythm. Ty's usual scowl was gone, replaced by an expression devoid of tension. He looked like kids did when they slept. Untroubled.

'If I'd had my way, Reaper would never have left solitary confinement,' Marquez said. 'But the US Attorney's Office wanted his testimony.'

Lock's jaw tightened. 'And they're still going to get it. I'm going to see to that personally.'

One of Pelican Bay's numerous medical staff, a petite Asian-American woman whose name badge read Dr Lau, walked into the bay. She checked Ty's chart without acknowledging either Lock or the warden.

'How bad is it?' Lock asked her.

'There's some tissue and nerve damage, and we've had to pull the slug out of his shoulder, but he's stable.'

Lock looked over at Marquez. 'Shouldn't you

be getting him to a civilian facility?'

'We're pretty experienced in dealing with violent trauma injuries here,' Dr Lau said. 'Get plenty of practice.'

Lock turned to her. 'He'll be OK though, right?'

'There are no guarantees, but, for someone who's been shot, I'd say his prognosis is good. As long as he doesn't pick up a secondary infection he should be fine.'

'What you plan on doing with Reaper?' Lock asked Marquez.

'Well, I'll tell you something, son. I never thought the day would come when I'd say this about an inmate, but I want him out of my goddamn prison. So I plan on shipping him down to San Francisco as soon as I can. Let the goddamn US Attorney's Office deal with him. If they can.'

'Maybe now they'll take our original advice,' Lock said, 'and stash him in a safe house.'

'You know he'll try to escape, don't you?' Marquez cautioned.

'You seem pretty sure about that.'

'Soon as I heard that he wanted back on the mainline, that's what I thought. Of course, having you here kind of cramped his style. That's probably why he asked the Nazi Low Riders to screw around with you and your buddy.'

Lock thought about this. It made sense that Reaper was behind the Nazi Low Riders' order to attack Ty. It was a way of getting Lock and Ty out of the way, without appearing openly hostile to Jalicia.

'Let me know when you're going to make the transfer and I'll ride along to make sure I deliver Reaper to the prosecutor personally,' Lock said.

Lieutenant Williams stuck his head through the curtain. 'Warden?'

'What is it?'

Williams hesitated as he looked from the warden to the uncuffed Lock, who was still wearing the prison blues that identified him as an inmate.

'Go ahead,' Marquez said. 'You can speak freely.'

'Someone just blew up the Federal Building in San Francisco.'

Ty's heart rate stayed constant on the monitor, while Lock's jumped. 'How bad is it?'

'Bad,' Williams said. 'Half a dozen dead. Plenty more injured. They've hit the Federal Court building in Los Angeles too.'

'Same people?'

Williams shrugged a 'who knows?'. 'Group calling itself the White Aryan Resistance Movement has claimed both.'

Marquez nodded grimly. 'Boy, they really don't want him testifying, do they?'

'Can you give me a minute?' Lock asked Marquez.

'Take as long as you need.'

He nodded at Williams, the two men left, and Lock was finally alone with Ty.

Lock reached out and touched his partner's hand. 'Tyrone, listen . . . '

Ty's left eye flicked open. He reached up and struggled to pull the oxygen mask to one side so he could speak. Lock helped him with it.

'Can you not touch me and shit?' Ty croaked. 'Don't want anyone getting the wrong idea.'

Lock felt relief. First that Ty was conscious, but more critically that he was giving Lock grief, which meant he had to be feeling better.

'What the fuck you doin' here anyway?'

'Good to see you too, Tyrone.'

'They didn't get you then?'

'Excellent piece of deduction seeing as I'm sitting here with all my limbs intact.'

'Shit. I was counting on not having to split the fee.' He pushed himself up to a sitting position. 'You get me some water, brother?'

Lock filled a glass from the water jug on the table next to Ty and passed it over.

'How d'you feel?'

'Like I been shot.'

Ty reached back to adjust the position of his pillows but winced with the pain. Lock did the honours.

'You want me to get someone?'

'Maybe that cute little Asian doctor,' Ty said, lowering his voice. 'We got a vibe going.'

'You can't be feeling that bad.'

'They didn't shoot me in the dick.'

Lock glanced down the bed, made a 'I got bad news' face.

'Man, you'd better be fucking with me.'

Lock stood up. 'Just get better, Ty.'

Ty waved him back. 'You ain't even given me a sit rep.'

Once Ty had promised to take it easy, Lock

filled him in as best he could on events since the riot on the yard.

'Good call heading to the court with Reaper. I don't trust that motherfucker one little bit. Even by convict standards, he's a snake.'

'The question is, what kind?'

'Guess we're all gonna find out when he takes that stand.'

Lock got up. 'I gotta go.'

Ty raised a clenched hand. They bumped fists.

'I mean it about that guy,' Ty said. 'Watch your back.'

24

Jalicia and Coburn took their seats in a meeting room within the 9th Circuit Court of Appeal Building in downtown San Francisco. The cell phone of Manny Lopez, the US Marshal in charge of court security, chirped. As he shrugged an apology, the cell phone of the man sitting next to him, an FBI field agent by the name of Peter Breedlove, blasted out the James Bond theme tune. Flushing, Breedlove scrambled to answer it.

He listened for a few moments, then said, 'When?' He covered his cell phone with one hand. 'A bomb threat was just phoned in to the Santa Ana Federal Court building by someone claiming to be from the White Aryan Resistance Movement.'

'They give a code word?' Coburn asked.

Breedlove looked irritated. 'No one heard of these guys until today.'

Jalicia, sitting at the head of the table, put a line through the Santa Ana Court building, which lay third on the list compiled by the US Marshals Service. 'So, where do we go from here?'

Coburn cleared his throat. 'The trial doesn't have to stay in California, does it?' he asked.

'Nope,' said the judge who'd been hearing the case. 'As long as it's in a state covered by the 9th Circuit. What were you thinking, Agent Coburn?'

'Well, we can safely assume, even from early reports, that it's the same group, and that they're active in California. After all, California is the Aryan Brotherhood's home turf.'

Bobby Gross, who'd insisted on being party to the discussion, loosened his tie. 'Let's not jump to any conclusions as to who's responsible,' he said.

Jalicia noticed that the vein in his neck was pulsing.

'Oh, come on,' said Manny Lopez. 'Who else wants this trial stopped bad enough to bomb at least two Federal Buildings?'

Gross stood up. 'I will not tolerate — '

'Regardless of who's responsible,' Coburn said, smoothing his hands across the conference table, 'I think everyone can agree that California's too dangerous right now.'

There was a general murmur of agreement.

Jalicia leaned forward. 'You have somewhere in mind?'

'I think the more remote we go, the better. A smaller community than Los Angeles. That means if anyone shows up who's out of place it's going to be one hell of a lot easier to spot them.'

Breedlove, the FBI agent with the 007 fetish, nodded. 'Makes sense to me. It's too easy for these people to blend in at a big city court facility.'

'Then I have just the place,' Coburn said.

★ ★ ★

Ten minutes later, across the bay in Oakland, Chance snatched up her cell phone and heard

123

the man on the other end of the line say, 'It's playing just like you said.'

Chance's heart began to pound. Hers had been an educated guess about what would happen after the explosion. When she'd heard that six people had been killed her heart had sunk. Not because she felt bad for them — most of them were either black or Hispanic — but because she thought they might stop the trial entirely, which could set things back weeks if not months. What she'd been counting on was the bloodthirstiness of the prosecutor, and Jalicia Jones hadn't disappointed.

'They're moving it?'

'Yup.'

There was the sound of voices in the background. Chance was about to end the call when the man on the other end of the line said, 'Be right with you.'

She could hear the man talking to someone, then he came back to the phone. She smiled at the thought they had someone right there in the belly of the beast.

'Yeah,' said the man. 'They're moving it to Medford in Oregon. Hope that works for you guys.'

'Don't worry,' said Chance, 'we'll make it work.' She paused. 'What about Reaper? When's he arriving?'

'It's gonna be tight. They're moving him tomorrow. Soon as I get more details, I'll let you know.'

25

Wearing his regular civilian uniform of Nike sneakers, blue jeans from Gap and black sweater with a protective vest thrown over the top of it, Lock stopped in front of Reaper's cell. Lieutenant Williams and the two other guards charged with transferring Reaper to the team of US Marshals outside the prison stood behind him. The early hour had been chosen so that Reaper would leave the prison under cover of darkness and arrive at the court around daybreak. His testimony was expected to take the whole day, with cross-examination running into a second.

Lock had spent the last few hours with Ty, who was staging a strong enough recovery for his own transfer to a civilian medical facility to be scheduled for later that day. He'd also, at long last, spoken to Carrie, who'd initially chewed him out over his lack of contact, then about his stupidity in taking on the job in the first place. Given that the Aryan Brotherhood trial, courtesy of the bombings, was now national rather than just California news, she was already in the air and on the way to the new trial venue in Medford, Oregon, to cover the story for her network. He was looking forward to seeing her, but determined to remain focused on finishing the job he'd started.

Reaper was dressed and waiting for them.

Offering his hands up to be cuffed, he checked out Lock's new look with a smirk. 'Well, don't you scrub up nice.'

Smiling back, Lock reached through the hatch and ratcheted Reaper's cuffs a notch tighter on his wrists. Reaper's smirk dissolved. He pulled his hands back, walked to the back of his cell, picked up a book and returned to the door. The bubble cop in the pod that controlled access to the cells pressed a button and his cell door opened.

Reaper took a step out into the corridor. The movement of a prisoner had brought the inmates in the cells around him to the Arizona doors which fronted the cells in this section of the prison. Eyes pressed against the half-inch holes which perforated the doors in place of the more traditional bars.

Lock took the book from Reaper's hands — *The Art of War* — and handed it to Williams, who flicked the pages before returning it to Reaper.

'JPATS are usually a little light on in-flight entertainment,' Reaper said by way of explanation.

Reaper glanced down at his legs, presumably anticipating having leg restraints put round his feet. But Lock had already advised that they forgo this particular measure during Reaper's transfer. If there was an attempt on his life, which looked more likely than ever given the bombings, they would have to get him out of the situation. If that was the case, a protectee who couldn't run would likely get everyone killed.

126

Lock put a hand on Reaper's elbow and with a 'Let's go' guided him back along the spur of cells that led into the centre of this section of the SHU. Most of the cells were occupied by white inmates, but overcrowding after the riot had ensured a sprinkling of Hispanic and black prisoners. It was like walking past the lions' enclosure at midnight. Eyes peered, yellow and unblinking, from the depths of every cell, lips peeled back over teeth. Then came the low roar of threats designed to get the prey's blood pumping — all the faster for it to bleed out.

Lock and Williams positioned themselves on Reaper's left so that they stood directly between Reaper and the cell doors. Even with the doors sealed, and with no bars, it wasn't unheard of for prisoners to use improvised darts tipped with a filed-down metal disc from a sprinkler head, dipped in their own faeces and then propelled through one of the half-inch holes in their cell door using the elastic from shorts, to take out a guard or other enemy.

A final threat was hissed low in Spanish from a nearby cell before the door at the end of the corridor clicked open and Lock led Reaper's escort out into the hub of the SHU, then along a wide linoleum-floored corridor towards the sallyport — a confined double-doored space used to control entry to and exit from the SHU.

There, Reaper was signed out by Lieutenant Williams. Reaper then twisted his head back round and took a long look down the corridor. The gesture unsettled Lock. It was as if Reaper was saying his goodbyes, although surely he wasn't naive enough to think that he wouldn't be trading his cell at Pelican Bay for another somewhere else.

Paperwork completed, they moved out of the SHU and into the wide expanse of open ground known in the prison as No Man's Land. Even at this hour, with all the inmates tucked up inside their cells, No Man's Land was lit up like a Christmas tree. Concealed cameras must have tracked their every move because yards before they reached them the gates rolled back to allow them free passage.

Then they were moving through the three razor-wire-topped fences, the middle one charged with enough juice to kill someone on contact. A caged exit ensured safe passage into a second sallyport, where again Williams had to sign Reaper out.

Reaper rolled his neck, closing his eyes as he worked out the kinks of tension.

The gesture gnawed away at Lock. A good half of close protection work was visual awareness and reading body language. There was something off about how Reaper was acting. On the journey across the yard Reaper's prison stroll had morphed almost seamlessly from a tight, contained prison shuffle into a languid stroll.

Lock had seen Reaper feign indifference as he strolled on the yard with Phileas, and had taken that for what it was: a show of bravado designed to dissuade a potential attacker, the strutting of an alpha male. This was different. Surrounded by tension, Reaper, who now had his nose buried in his book, seemed utterly relaxed.

26

The Marshal in charge of transferring Reaper to Oregon shook Lock's hand, the firmness of the grip sending a jolt of pain spearing up Lock's arm. 'Thanks for everything, but we can take it from here,' he said as Reaper was placed in the middle vehicle of a three-SUV convoy for the short drive from the prison to the Crescent City airport.

'I could use the ride,' Lock said, firmly.

'Sure you could. But I'm not sure we can use you. Listen, we do high-value witness and high-risk prisoner transfer every single day.'

Lock met the comment with a tight smile. 'Not like this one. If you want me to stand aside, that's fine, but you'll need to speak to Jalicia Jones at the US Attorney's Office first. She's the one who contracted with me.'

The Marshal glanced back at the waiting aircraft, and hesitated.

'Listen, embus and debus, making sure that a specified person gets from point A to point B safely, is what I do,' Lock said quickly. 'I'll leave any heroics to your guys, but it can't hurt to have a fresh pair of eyes with you.'

Lock stepped in closer so his next words with the Marshal wouldn't be overheard. 'I'm not sure Reaper's dealing from the top of the deck. And seeing as I've spent the best part of a week smelling the guy's farts, wouldn't it make sense to have me riding shotgun next to him?'

The Marshal's gaze slid from Lock to a correctional officer in the gun tower high above them. 'OK, but remember who's calling the shots.'

★ ★ ★

Landing at Crescent City's airfield may well have been stomach-churning, but take-off must have brought a whole new dimension of bowel-loosening terror to the cabin of the twin-engined Cessna. From where Lock was seated, the procedure seemed to involve gunning the twin engines to a point where the tyres were almost spinning, then taking off the brakes and hurtling down the absurdly short stretch of runway before hanging Road Runner-style in mid-air as they left dry land, and praying for an up-current. Lock figured that a giant catapult would have done a similar job, but with less of a carbon footprint.

Once they were airborne, Lock's stomach began to settle. The journey along Lakeshore Drive to the airfield had been tense. Moving location always was, whether you were escorting the President or a felon.

There was a sudden bump as the plane hit some turbulence. Lock, having secured a seat by the window with no one next to him, with Reaper across from him, stared out, but all he could see was clouds.

Up ahead, Reaper was still in high spirits. 'Hey, Cindy-Sue,' he called, 'can I get a beer and some pretzels back here?'

The Marshal ignored him.

'A blow job would be good too,' Reaper continued.

Lock swivelled round in his seat so that he was facing Reaper, at the same time pulling off his right sneaker and removing one of his socks, which he balled up in his fist. He stood up, crossed the aisle and pushed Reaper back down into his seat with the palm of his left hand. As Reaper opened his mouth to protest, Lock jammed the sock into Reaper's mouth as hard as he could, his spare hand pincering Reaper's throat.

'Now, are you going to sit there like a good boy or not?'

Reaper's eyes flared with rage but he nodded. Lock pulled the sock back out.

Immediately, Reaper shouted to the Marshal at the rear of the plane, 'Hey, he can't do that!'

Lock leaned in closer. 'Understand this, you piece of racist, trailer-park trash. I don't work for the cops, or the Marshals Service, or the United States Attorney's Office. I'm a private contractor, and right now I'm off the clock, working on my own time, so the only person I have to answer to is me. Now, back there was your turf. Everything from here on in is mine. I've kept my end of the bargain, which was to keep you breathing, and now you're going to keep your end, without any more games or dicking anyone around. And if you don't, you're not going to have to worry about The Row at San Quentin because I'll open the door of this plane and toss you out of it. You got me?'

27

Chance nudged the red pick-up truck through the gate and on to the service road, turned off the engine and waited. A few minutes later the wind started to pick up, the boughs of a stand of nearby Black Oaks beginning to bend as a helicopter came in to land.

She got out of the pick-up and shielded her eyes with one hand. She could just about make out Cowboy in the pilot's seat, his face shaded by the brim of his black Stetson. Trooper with his mane of hooker-blonde hair sat next to him in the co-pilot's seat.

As Cowboy cut the engine and they clambered from the cockpit to greet her, Chance felt a wave of relief. From now on in they'd be together. No more solo missions.

She watched as Trooper pulled out a pack of American Spirit cigarettes and fumbled in his pocket for a lighter, an expensive-looking Zippo with the number 88 engraved on the front plate — each eight standing for the eighth letter of the alphabet, the two Hs together shorthanding the phrase 'Heil Hitler'.

Cowboy hard-stared him. 'Operation's started. You smoke that, you make sure and bag the butt.'

Trooper flicked up the Zippo and lit his cigarette, finding a free middle finger to flip Cowboy the bird.

'I ain't joking,' Cowboy said.

Trooper sucked the freshly lit cigarette into his mouth and chewed down on it — one of his many gross-out party tricks acquired during too much time spent with outlaw biker gangs.

Chance laughed. Cowboy and Trooper fought like family, worse sometimes. 'No arguing now, boys,' she said, giving first Cowboy and then Trooper a hug.

Cowboy took a step back and stared at her. 'Nice job on those buildings.'

Chance felt herself blush. 'Wasn't nothing. This is gonna be the difficult part.'

She ushered them back over to the pick-up and spread out a recon map on the hood. It showed the airfield and surrounding area. She stabbed at a point on the map, then pointed in the direction of the stand of trees, which would obscure the helicopter from the area beyond. 'We'll wait in there,' she said. 'Now, help me get this gear unloaded. We don't have long.'

* * *

No sooner had they dug into their respective positions and settled in to wait than a Medford Police Department cruiser appeared at the gate at the far end of the airstrip. Chance raised her M-4 to her shoulder and peered through the scope for a better look as the front passenger door of the cruiser opened and a female deputy waddled out and sprang the padlock securing the gate.

Chance guessed they were here to ensure that

nothing was amiss before the Marshals team from the court arrived to collect Reaper from the aircraft. It wasn't a big deal. They'd drive round, see nothing, wait for the Marshals transfer team to arrive, then leave. All they had to do was sit tight.

Chance took another peek through her sights. The gates were rolled open but the female patrol officer was stood stock still, staring directly to her left. Worse, she was waving to her colleague inside the vehicle. He clambered out and joined her. Chance strained to hear what was being said, but they were too far away. Whatever it was, though, it wasn't good, because the male cop started to walk in their direction while the female patrol officer ducked her head back into the car to get on the radio.

'Shit,' said Chance, crawling on her side into the brush and motioning for Trooper, who was on her right, to start moving round so that he would be in a position behind the male cop if he made it this far.

Chance's mind was racing. If he came over, he'd get shot, they'd have no alternative. And then their operation would be mortally compromised. They'd have to go for the extraction they'd originally planned, and that would make this seem like a picnic.

Once she was happy she couldn't be seen from the road, Chance got to her feet. Her breathing was heavy and her back was killing her. She started to skirt round to her left. On the way she began to discard her cammo gear. She stripped down to bra and panties. That would work fine.

She grabbed a handful of dirt and rubbed it over her face and into her hair. Then she headed back towards the service road.

★ ★ ★

One minute, Patrol Officer Michelle Hulsey was watching her partner, gun drawn, head towards the line of trees, the next, a woman appeared on the edge of the airstrip screaming her head off. The woman was semi-naked and seemed to be in some distress.

Hulsey saw her partner turn round and wave Hulsey out of the car and towards the woman. 'See what she wants,' he shouted.

It figured, thought Hulsey, with no little resentment. She had to be the one to deal with the hysterical female. She put her head down and walked towards the woman.

'Ma'am, are you OK?'

'You've got to help me!' screamed the woman.

Hulsey was close enough to get a better look at her now. Something was off. Slowly, it formed in her mind what it was. The woman's face was dirty, like she'd been dragged through the undergrowth, but the rest of her naked flesh was clean.

Hulsey's hand slipped to the butt of her service weapon just as she heard a gunshot behind her. She spun round and saw her partner hit the ground. His legs were on the edge of the road, the rest of his body splayed on the grass. Whatever had just happened, it was going to require back-up — and fast.

She started backing up towards her cruiser, fumbling for her gun. But the woman had already pulled out a handgun, seemingly from nowhere, and was pointing it at her.

'If you want to live, do exactly what I say.'

'Whatever is going on here — ' Hulsey stuttered, putting her hands up slowly.

'That doesn't include talking, bitch.'

Two men wearing full camouflage gear, including tactical body armour, stepped from the trees carrying automatic rifles. One of them was wearing a black cowboy hat; the other had long blond hair. Matter-of-factly, they began to drag her partner back towards the trees, leaving a smear of blood on the grass.

The woman spoke again as she advanced towards her. 'What have you called in so far?'

Hulsey's mouth was dry. She had to will herself to form words. 'Nothing.'

'Good. So now we're going to get back in that car of yours, and you're going to get back on the radio and say that it checked out fine. And remember this. One false move and you're dead, OK?'

28

Dawn nudged against the darkness, revealing curls of black clouds set low against the unforgiving frontier-industrial landscape of Medford, Oregon. Lock's motivational talk had quietened Reaper right down, and there was no talking between the Marshals either.

Hollywood might script dramatic courtroom assassination attempts, Lock reflected now that the flight was coming to an end, but both he and everyone on board knew that their real challenge lay in the transfer between airplane and courthouse.

Lock got up from his seat and made his way over to the Marshal in charge.

'What do you have on the ground for the transfer?'

'Six Marshals in three separate vehicles.'

This made sense to Lock. One vehicle would have Reaper in it. One would be out in front scoping out likely trouble and clearing a path through any traffic. The third would, if they had any sense, contain a counter-attack team in case anyone was stupid enough to give them any problems.

'The Marshals evenly split among the vehicles?'

'No, we got three in the CA vehicle. Transfer vehicle just has a driver. We'll make up the numbers in it when we land. Anything else you want to second-guess me on?'

Lock's reply was cut off by the captain on the intercom. His message was brief: no weather report or thank you for flying JPATS, just a curt 'Buckle up, we're making our final approach in about a coupla minutes, gentlemen.'

Lock fastened his seat belt as the plane looped round to the east. From his window he could see the postcard-size airfield below. It was surrounded by dense woods. On the ground he could see three black SUVS — no doubt the transfer vehicles — rolling up towards the entrance.

Then, much further back, not even within the confines of the airfield itself, he saw a helicopter. It was small, black and, judging from the hardware mounted either side of the cockpit, very definitely military.

Then he spotted something else. A patrol car, recognisable by the lights and number painted on the roof, parked in tight to the perimeter fence. And crouched behind it two figures holding what even at this height were clearly heavy-duty assault rifles.

Lock unclipped his belt, stood up and waved the Marshal in charge over.

'What the hell is it now?' the Marshal said.

'Did you order a helicopter as a back-up transfer vehicle?'

The Marshal looked at Lock like he was crazy. 'No. Why?'

'Because there's one down there.'

'Probably some black ops shit. This place gets used for all kinds of stuff.'

That didn't explain why a helicopter was in plain sight *outside* the airfield.

'What about your CA team? Where are they?'

The Marshal was clearly losing patience. 'In their vehicle, I'd guess.'

What he'd just seen still made no sense to Lock. Again and again in his career, saving the principal's life had come down to one simple mantra. Look out for two things: the absence of the normal or the presence of the abnormal.

'Then who the hell are those guys?' Lock said, pointing out the two figures crouched behind the patrol car, automatic weapons trained on the runway.

The Marshal followed the trajectory of Lock's finger and froze. 'I've no idea.'

There was a hiss of noise from the intercom, then the captain's voice: 'Final approach, folks. Hold on tight.'

29

'Abort the landing!' Lock bellowed as he and the Marshal raced towards the cockpit door. The Marshal made it there first but Lock pushed past him and grabbed the door handle. It wouldn't turn. 'Get this plane back up in the air!' he shouted. He stepped back and took a kick at the door, but it didn't budge. He guessed that no amount of kicking would do the job, JPATS aircraft doors having been specifically designed to resist such attempts.

'It's Brody,' shouted the Marshal. 'Let me in.'

There was a whirr beneath them and a hard clunk as the landing gear went down.

The Marshal pounded on the door. 'You need to get us back up in the air.'

The cabin door opened and a shaken co-pilot stood there. He had a Sig P250 in his hand, no doubt a precautionary measure in case Reaper had somehow overthrown his guard.

'What the hell's going on?' he demanded.

'We got a problem on the ground. Abort the landing,' the Marshal barked.

Lock could see the trees below rushing in on them fast. Dead ahead, a police cruiser was making its way on to the runway. The two armed figures who'd been standing behind it were now nowhere to be seen.

'It's too late,' the co-pilot replied. 'Get back to your seats, now!'

They were almost on top of the trees; then, for a fraction of a second, they were below them. Lock and the Marshal turned round just as the plane's wheels made contact with terra firma. The jolt sent both of them tumbling back down the aisle. Lock grabbed an arm rest to steady himself as the pilot slammed on the brakes.

Through the window next to him, Lock could see the police cruiser driving parallel to them, a female deputy at the wheel. The look of terror on her face told him everything he needed to know about the situation they'd just landed themselves in.

★ ★ ★

Chance was shouting instructions from a prone position on the rear bench seat of the police cruiser.

'OK, now slow down.'

Hulsey took her foot off the gas. The plane sped past them, revealing the three SUV transfer-convoy vehicles five hundred yards away on the apron.

'Now, lower the rear window.'

'Please, don't do this,' Hulsey pleaded.

'Lower the goddamn window, bitch.'

Hulsey did as she was told, her fingers trembling.

Chance grabbed the RPG launcher from the footwell and took aim at the rear SUV parked on the apron. She pulled the trigger, the recoil throwing her back on to the seat. Clawing her way back up, she watched as the SUV took a direct hit, the impact of the grenade twisting the frame and punching the SUV over on to its side.

So much for the counter-attack team, she thought.

Beyond her, Chance could see Cowboy and Trooper making their move, emerging from their positions and laying down covering fire as they made their way towards the two remaining SUVs. Rounds pinged off the vehicles. She spotted Trooper stopping to reload as Cowboy let off a three-round burst from his M-4. She smiled as Trooper finished the reload, his moves sharp and balletic, so at odds with his shambolic appearance.

The passenger door of the lead SUV opened and a Marshal appeared in full tactical gear. Trooper, lying flat on the floor in a sniper position, took aim and shot the Marshal full in the face from a hundred yards. The Marshal's mouth caved in on itself, dragging his nose and eyes with it.

Chance grabbed a fresh RPG round from her backpack and rearmed the launcher. It took her a moment. In front, Hulsey was yammering into her radio: 'Officer down, officer down! Back-up requested immediately!' Chance ignored her. The pleas were already redundant; not even a factor. The Marshals on the ground and the pilot of the plane would already have communicated to the authorities in Medford and beyond that there had been a different sort of welcoming committee than the one they'd anticipated.

She finished reloading and looked at the digital timer hooked to the front of her bra. They had three more minutes.

Reassured that they were on schedule, Chance hefted the reloaded RPG launcher over her shoulder again and aimed for the lead vehicle.

She hit it dead centre. Another Marshal emerging from it took the full force of a front panel of the vehicle as it was blown from the carcass. His arms were ripped from his shoulders and arced behind his back and up into the air, landing just a few feet from her.

Chance threw the launcher back into the vehicle, opened the driver's door and pulled Hulsey out by her hair, leaving her on the runway. Then she clambered into the driver's seat, threw the cruiser back into drive and took off after the plane.

★ ★ ★

In the cabin, all Lock could hear was the sound of explosions on the runway behind them. The plane was slowing dramatically, and behind him the remaining Marshals were scrambling to the windows, trying to get a visual on the unfolding chaos. Better than anyone else on the plane, Lock knew there was only one objective in a situation like this: get the hell out of it.

Lock stormed the short distance back down into the cockpit and pushed past the still open door which was swinging back and forth on its hinges.

'OK, we need to turn this thing round and get back up in the air,' he said, assuming command.

Brody, the Marshal in charge, was standing

behind him, his face pale. 'We have armoured vehicles on the ground, we can still make the transfer,' he said, doing a bad job of trying to inject an air of authority into his voice.

'What the hell do you think those explosions we just heard were?' Lock demanded.

'I'll need clearance from air traffic control,' said the pilot.

Lock put a hand on the pilot's shoulder and squeezed hard, trying to snap the guy back into the real world. 'Do you have fuel, and is there enough runway behind us if we turn round?'

The pilot looked at Lock like he'd just been asked for the square root of pi.

The co-pilot seemed to be faring slightly better. 'We've got enough fuel to get up but not to go anywhere.'

'Enough to circle for ten minutes and get back down again?' Lock asked.

He checked the gauge. 'Sure.'

'And what about taking off? We got enough runway between us and those trees back there?'

'I think so.'

'Good.'

The pilot was still staring wall-eyed at Lock. 'But we need clearance.'

Lock did the only thing he could under the circumstances: he opened the palm of his hand and slapped the pilot hard enough across the face to pull him back to reality. 'Forget the clearance and do your job or we're all going to die. Do you understand me?'

The pilot rubbed his cheek, his pupils dilating, the sting of the slap aceing the shock he was already in. He nodded, and turned his attention to the controls in front of him.

Lock turned to Brody. 'You going to second me here?'

Brody hesitated as the nose of the plane slowly swung round, giving them a head-on view of the twisted, smouldering wreckage of the SUVs. Then he squared his shoulders. 'Let's do it.'

★   ★   ★

Chance flicked on the lights and siren, then buried the gas pedal of the cruiser. The plane was turned towards her now, but it had come to what looked like a temporary stop. Behind her, Trooper and Cowboy had jacked the remaining Marshals Service SUV, Cowboy executing the driver on the runway as they did so. The female cop had suffered a similar fate as she'd tried to crawl her way across the debris-strewn runway.

Chance skidded to a halt next to the door side of the plane and waited. She could see men's faces at the windows peering out. No sign of Reaper though. He'd be last out.

She started as the twin engines growled back into life, a warm tide of gasoline-air blowing her long hair from her blackened face. The whine of the engines grew more insistent, rising in pitch and volume, then the pilot slipped the brakes and it was careering down the runway.

She slammed down on the gas, one-eightied the cruiser and took off after the plane. But it was a losing proposition. Even though the aircraft wasn't the fastest thing on three wheels,

145

it was still more than a match for the piece-of-shit Crown Vic she was helming.

She gestured frantically at Trooper and Cowboy in the SUV, who took the hint and drove their commandeered SUV directly across the flight path, reaching the centre of the runway near to what she imagined would be the take-off point of the JPATS plane.

★ ★ ★

Lock and Brody were thrown forward again as the pilot jammed on the brakes. Lock grabbed the edge of the console and hauled himself up. They were closing in fast on an SUV parked in the middle of the runway. He braced himself as best he could for the impact that would surely come.

★ ★ ★

Chance caught up with the plane just as it came to a shuddering halt only yards from the SUV, boxing it in at the rear. Reaching for her rifle, she ran to the front of the plane. She could see the pilot, his face ashen.

She raised her M-4 and sprayed the front of the cockpit with a three-round burst. The engines whined again as the pilot slumped dead against the controls.

She felt a surge of triumph. Reaper was going nowhere.

★ ★ ★

In the cockpit, Brody and the co-pilot were also hit. The co-pilot had taken a bullet to his right thigh and Brody was bleeding from the side of his face, his body armour having spared him more serious injury. Two of Brody's colleagues dragged them back into the main body of the aircraft while the remaining Marshal stayed close to Reaper, who hadn't moved through the whole ordeal.

Lock reached down and relieved Brody of his weapon.

One of Brody's colleagues stared at him. 'What the hell are you doing?'

Lock checked the weapon. 'Deputising myself. From here on in, you do what I say.'

30

'You don't have the authority to do that,' the Marshal said.

'Listen, Sparky, we're immobile and sur-rounded by a hostile group of heavily armed combatants. Now, I could go hide under one of the seats if you like. Or I can try to get us all out of this alive.'

Lock looked quickly out of one of the windows. At least three heavily armed individu-als, including the woman. He checked his watch. They were five minutes into the contact already. No matter how gung-ho the ambushers were, they weren't going to be able to stick around indefinitely.

Lock looked at the escort who was with Reaper and jerked his thumb in the prisoner's direction. 'Get him on his feet. Whatever anti-ballistic gear we have spare, put it on him.'

'What are you gonna do?' he asked.

'Test a little theory I've been chewing over.' Lock paused, then looked directly at Reaper. 'It strikes me that if the people outside with all those heavy weapons wanted Reaper dead, then right about now they'd be filling the fuselage with a lot of holes. Which means they want him alive.'

'So why does he need the body armour, then?'

'You'll see,' said Lock as the Marshal hauled Reaper to his feet.

'Got it all figured out, don't you, Lock?' Reaper sneered.

'You tell me. Are they here to kill you or help you escape?'

Reaper fell silent.

'Yup, thought as much,' Lock said.

★ ★ ★

Chance was beginning to worry. There seemed no clear way into the aircraft. She yanked at what she thought might be a baggage hatch, but it wouldn't budge.

They should have brought tear gas, she thought. Something to flush the Marshals and Reaper out with.

She kicked out at one of the tyres, then crouched under the body of the plane and shouted up at the door, 'You have ten seconds to hand him over. Do you understand?'

★ ★ ★

The woman's voice was muffled by the fuselage, but the words were audible.

Reaper was having an anti-ballistic helmet screwed on to his head by one of the Marshals. It was like fitting a baby bonnet on a linebacker.

Lock crossed to the door. 'OK, but you have to give us more than a ten-count.'

The woman's reply was curt and to the point: 'Ten . . . nine . . . '

The Marshal suited Reaper up as the countdown continued. When the woman hit zero there was silence. Then a volley of automatic fire burst through the undercarriage, ripping out the stuffing from one of the seats at the rear of the plane. Everyone froze.

'So if they want him alive so much, what was that about?' the Marshal asked.

'It's called playing the percentages,' Lock said, grabbing Reaper and frogmarching him towards the door at the front of the plane. 'OK, no more firing, I'm bringing him out,' he shouted, jabbing a finger at one of the Marshals to open the door. 'But you have to move back from the aircraft. Right now.'

'We'll pull back, you send him out.'

Lock stayed with Reaper and motioned for the two Marshals to get their weapons and move to the exit-side windows.

'OK,' he shouted. 'As soon as we see you move back, I'll send him out.'

★　★　★

Chance pulled the patrol car away from the plane. Every second that passed, their options were narrowing.

The door of the plane juddered open, the stairs unfolded, and there stood Reaper in all his glory. It was enough to make Chance catch her breath.

But then, as Reaper took the first step, she saw that he wasn't alone. There was a man with him. The man produced a Glock, shoved it in Reaper's face, and with his free hand pushed the cuffed Reaper down the rest of the stairs. At the bottom, he stopped and pressed the gun hard into Reaper's mouth.

'You seriously think I'm going to hand you this piece of shit?' he shouted.

Behind Chance, Cowboy and Trooper had fanned out, trying to find an angle, but Reaper's sheer size precluded a clean shot at the man who was now propelling him across the runway.

Then the man stopped.

'You want him so bad, you come and get him.'

★   ★   ★

Lock had to concede that Reaper made for one hell of a human shield. It was like standing behind a Stryker armoured vehicle.

One of the attackers, a man wearing a cowboy hat, darted out from behind the hijacked police cruiser. Lock flicked his borrowed Glock away from Reaper's mouth and let off a single shot which bounced off the runway three feet to the guy's left, then put the gun back to Reaper's head.

'Come on, you pussies, come and get him. I can do this all day.'

Another male attacker with long blond hair appeared, this time from the other side. Lock hauled Reaper in closer to him, pivoted round and got off a shot which went high and wide.

In the distance, a symphony of sirens could be heard, getting louder.

'The question is, how long you got?'

★   ★   ★

Chance could hear the sirens too. She could even pick out the trail of flashing red lights. She clenched her fists, furious. They could stay, fight their ground, but ultimately they'd be overwhelmed, and the mission would be a failure. Or they could walk away now, and try again.

She took a deep breath, filling her lungs. She exited the patrol car, grabbing the grenade launcher on her way out.

Cowboy and Trooper screeched to a halt next to her in the black SUV they'd jacked from the Marshals. They screamed for her to get inside as she raised the launcher and sent a final defiant message roaring towards the JPATS plane.

★ ★ ★

Lock pushed Reaper down on to the ground as the RPG round whistled over them. A wall of fire soared into the sky as it made contact with the plane, the fuel tank engulfing the entire fuselage in flames. He hated to think what it was doing to the men inside.

Looking up, Lock saw the jacked SUV slamming out on to the service road beyond the perimeter of the airfield. He pulled Reaper back to his feet and smiled into his stony face.

'Looks like you're gonna have your day in court after all.'

31

The police cruiser edged its way slowly down the street like a Halloween-styled homecoming parade float. Rorschach-style blood spatters patterned the windshield. The bodywork was peppered with shrapnel and bullet holes. One of the tyres was shot out so badly that sparks were flying from the rim. Behind the cruiser followed, at the same funereal pace, a convoy of police and Emergency Medical Service vehicles.

With no view through the windshield, Lock hung out of the driver's window to get a better view of the terrain ahead, his right foot alternating between the gas pedal and the brake. He brought the car to a halt beside the steps of the Medford courthouse and got out, his randomly purloined body armour and smoke-blackened face giving his appearance a post-apocalyptic makeover.

'All ashore that's going ashore,' he said.

He opened the rear door and hauled Reaper out, shoulders first. In addition to his usual restraints, Reaper was sporting the previously threatened piece of cloth jammed into his mouth to stop him from talking.

Reaper hit the sidewalk like a sack of potatoes. Lock put out his hand and helped him to his feet. A couple of Medford cops went to help Lock but he waved them away with a gruff 'Back the hell off.'

153

He shoved Reaper hard in the back, propelling him up the stone steps. At the top, Jalicia stood among the open-mouthed crowd with the rest of her prosecution team. Lock kept Reaper moving until the final step, when the front of his right foot happened to clip the back of Reaper's left foot and he sprawled face first directly in front of Jalicia. As Reaper tried to look up, Lock placed his boot on the back of his head, forcing his face back down on to the stone.

'Everyone else who was on the plane is dead,' Lock said. He glanced down at Reaper. 'All apart from me and this piece of shit.' He dug into his pocket, pulled out a set of keys for Reaper's cuffs and leg restraints, and handed them to Jalicia. 'Here's your witness.'

The shock was etched on Jalicia's face. 'Everyone's dead?'

'There was a welcoming committee waiting for us at the airfield.'

'How the hell could they have known where he was coming in?'

The question had crossed Lock's mind ever since he'd spotted the assault helicopter. There was only one answer: they had someone on the inside.

But who? One of the Marshals? A guard back at Pelican Bay? Someone in local law enforcement? It was a pretty wide field. Without knowing who the group who'd ambushed them were, narrowing it down was going to prove next to impossible.

'I don't know, but they were well prepared.' Dust caught at the back of his throat. 'Pardon me,' he said, turning his head in Reaper's direction and spitting some of the runway grit from his mouth. 'One more thing you should know. I gave them ample opportunity to kill this piece of shit, and they didn't take it. For whatever reason, they wanted to take him alive.'

Two cops rushed in to scoop Reaper up from the ground.

'Now,' Lock said, 'if you'll excuse me . . . '

Carrie was standing ten yards away, in a knot of other media people, with her cameraman. Lock looked at her as she brushed back a strand of blonde hair from her eyes, which were blue and earnest as she talked to another reporter. She turned and saw him. Her features softened as she made her way towards him.

As she reached him, she raised an eyebrow. 'Straightforward mission, huh?'

Lock shrugged. 'It was when it started.'

He reached out and placed his hands either side of her face, his thumbs stroking her cheeks.

She smiled. 'It always is with you.'

He leaned in and kissed her softly on the lips. It felt fantastic.

★   ★   ★

They walked slowly back to the mini-van Carrie's network had provided. Lock took her through the whole story, starting with the conference room in San Francisco. She'd already heard about Ty and had good news for Lock: 'They're moving him down to a hospital in San Francisco later today.'

155

Lock felt the slabs of tense muscle in his back and neck ease a little. 'That's good.'

They both fell silent for a few seconds. Lock was anxious about what was coming next. He'd taken on what had proved to be a near-suicide mission, and kept Carrie out of the loop. The guilt about it had weighed on him all the while he'd been inside the prison, only outweighed by the dour determination he'd felt to bring the killers of Ken Prager and his family to justice.

'Ken Prager was my friend,' Lock said. 'I had to do what I could to help bring these guys to justice.'

'Loyalty's a fine quality,' Carrie said, avoiding eye contact.

Lock's heart sank.

'I don't know, Ryan. I mean, if I had a great story to chase, I wouldn't want to have to ask your permission. That's one of the things I like about you. You're not threatened by my career. You respect my independence.'

That much was true. In his downtime between jobs, Lock was quite content to walk Angel in Central Park, hit the gym, then shop for groceries and cook dinner. Carrie often teased him that barring his adrenalin junkie tendencies, he'd make someone a great wife one of these days, and he laughed along with her. Maybe it was a generational thing but he'd never bought into any macho bullshit about a woman's place being in the kitchen. He was happy to be with a woman who didn't take any crap, and who'd built a life for herself.

'I'm sensing a 'but' here somewhere,' he said.

'I just don't know if this is working out between us,' Carrie said.

Lock sighed. He wasn't about to plead for another chance. Not because he was too proud, but because, in his experience, once a woman had made a decision about a relationship there was rarely any going back. They were harder than men in that respect. Yet he wasn't quite ready to give up on what they had.

'Does it change anything if I say that I don't think I've ever missed anyone before like I missed you these past five days?' he asked.

Carrie looked away again. He could sense her softening.

'How do I make it up to you?'

'There is one thing,' said Carrie, watching as Reaper was finally bundled from view by a phalanx of law enforcement.

'Name it,' said Lock.

'Help me get an interview with Reaper.'

32

The guard opened the holding cage and Reaper stepped out. Jalicia nodded for him to free his shackles. Layers of body armour, some of it still slicked with the blood of dead US Marshals, jutted out from his bulky frame. He looked, thought Jalicia, like a cross between the Terminator and a Kevlar-encased Egyptian mummy.

'Get him out of that stuff,' she said, holding up a black plastic Nordstrom's suit carrier. She unzipped it and held it up for his inspection. 'A lot of people died to get you here, so you might want to make the effort to look presentable.'

Knowing that an inmate in prison blues was already a couple of credibility points behind a witness who was dressed in civilian clothes, Jalicia had brought Reaper the change of clothes: a single-breasted dark grey suit, a crisp white shirt still bearing the crease marks from its packaging, and a suitably conservative blue tie.

'Thank you,' Reaper said, showing no after-effects of the events surrounding his transfer.

'I hope it fits you.'

Reaper checked the label on the collar. 'Should be fine.'

Jalicia cleared her throat. 'Lock thinks those people back at the airfield were trying to free you from custody. He says this whole thing with you agreeing to testify is a sham.'

Reaper ran his fingertips over the silk of the dark blue tie, then tilted his head down so that he was looking straight at Jalicia. 'Lock thinks a lot of things,' he said, sounding world-weary.

'Is it true? Once I get you on that stand out there, are you going to punk me, Frank?'

Judging by how his mouth folded in on itself, the use of his first name seemed to pinch Reaper. Maybe it was a long time since he'd heard it. His pupils shrank to pinpricks of black. 'I could tell you 'no'. Or I could tell you 'yes'. But we all know that convicts lie, right? So the only way you're really going to know is when you start asking me questions in front of that jury.'

Jalicia stepped back, determined not to let him see that he was getting to her. 'That's not much of an answer,' she said.

'It wasn't much of a question,' he fired back.

'I'll see you on the stand. Remember to speak nice and clearly.'

Jalicia turned and walked out of the holding area. In the corridor, she leaned against the wall, closed her eyes and counted to ten, slowly. She was going to get through this, she told herself. This case was going to make her career.

The voice of the Aryan Brotherhood's lead defence attorney snapped her back into the present.

'Are you praying, counsel?'

Judging from his broad grin, he seemed to have recovered his composure after the bombing at the courthouse in San Francisco.

'What do you want, Gross?'

'I was going to offer you a final opportunity to save your blushes.' He moved in closer. 'My clients are prepared to name the individuals who killed Agent Prager and his family.'

It was Jalicia's turn to smile. 'They could have done that right at the start and saved us a lot of grief. Not to mention dead bodies.'

Gross shrugged. 'It's how the game gets played. You wait for the clock to run right down.'

'What are they looking for in return?'

'You drop the death penalty,' Gross stated.

'Let me get this straight. First, your clients order the murder of a federal agent and his family. Then they bomb a Federal Courthouse to stop their trial. And, finally, when they're out of chances to take out the main defence witness, all of a sudden they want me to show mercy. So they get to go back to what they were doing anyway, and all of this was for nothing?' She took a step forward herself so that she was inches from Gross's smug features. 'No deal.'

'You're letting your emotions cloud your judgement,' said Gross.

He had a point, but Jalicia wasn't willing to concede that to his face. Deals like this were the currency that kept the conveyor-belt of what passed for justice in America oiled and operational. Of course, Gross had a reputation for using last-minute carrots like this to put prosecutors off balance, but she was minutes away from testimony that had the potential to bring the Aryan Brotherhood to its knees. No, this was too big a win for her. There would be time later to hunt down the people who pulled the trigger on Prager and his family.

If Gross sensed her initial doubts, he was careful enough not to press too hard. 'Think about it, counsel,' he said. 'You wouldn't want to pass up an opportunity you might regret later.'

★ ★ ★

Inside the courtroom, Lock, a protective hand on the small of Carrie's back, found a couple of seats near the front. After the massive adrenalin rush from combat at the airfield, he was on the inevitable comedown. His concern about Reaper's true motive and a grilling by the FBI hadn't helped his mood much either. The only ray of light was that he seemed to have gone some way towards patching things up with Carrie.

As they took their seats, she touched his hand with hers. The tenderness of the gesture gave him reassurance that he hadn't blown it entirely.

'You think he'll testify?' she whispered to him.

'Oh, he'll take the stand. The guy's got an ego to make Simon Cowell blush. It's what he'll say that worries me.'

'You know, since the bombing in San Francisco I've been doing some checking into these white supremacist prison gangs. Nazi Low Riders. Aryan Brotherhood. Texas Circle.'

Lock had a sudden flashback to the prison yard at Pelican Bay and Ty lying in the middle of it, face down, in the dirt.

'And?' he asked her.

'It's not quite as cut-and-dried as everyone would like to believe. Even within each gang

161

there always seem to be two opposing forces pulling against each other.'

'Which are?'

'Well, on the one hand you have the criminal enterprise part. Stick together for protection, then extend that to other inmates, and start bringing trade into the equation — drugs, for instance. I'd call those guys the pragmatists.'

'Pragmatists? Now there's a five-dollar word.'

'You know what I mean, Ryan. These are the guys who tattoo on a swastika when it might as well be a dollar bill.'

Lock nodded, remembering Phileas, whose predatory business instincts and nose for a deal would, under different circumstances, have made him a fortune on Wall Street.

'But then there's usually another side.'

'You got a five-dollar word for them as well?'

'More of a ten-dollar phrase. I'd call these guys the true believers.'

'So where does that leave Reaper?'

'I'd say he's a believer, and part of that is a whole code-of-honour thing.'

Lock did a bad job of hiding his cynicism, the smirk crawling across his face.

Carrie held up her hand. 'Hear me out.'

'I'm a-hearing,' said Lock in his worst pastiche of a Southern accent.

'You said that guys like Reaper were into all those Louis L'Amour westerns.'

'Ate 'em up.'

'That's where the Aryan Brotherhood take one of their other nicknames from, right? The Brand. They got that from a Louis L'Amour story.'

'Far as I know.'

'Well, the Brand, the original Brand, in those stories they lived by a code of honour which included no harming of women or children.'

Lock swivelled round so that he was facing Carrie. 'Can I talk to reporter Carrie rather than love-of-my-life Carrie?'

Carrie eye-lifted her consent.

'I know what you're saying, but where does that leave Ken Prager and his family? The Aryan Brotherhood didn't seem to have a code when it came to them.'

'That's what I'm saying. The Aryan Brotherhood breached the code.'

On cue, the door at the back opened and Reaper shuffled in, his appearance transformed by the suit and tie. He nodded a series of polite hellos, first to the judge, then to Jalicia and the prosecution, and finally to his former comrades, who glared at him from the dock.

'So what is he then, Ryan?' Carrie asked.

Lock studied Reaper as he settled himself into the dock, his eyes startlingly dark and unblinking, his head held high. 'He's a chess player,' he said. 'And as far as he's concerned, you, me, Jalicia, Coburn, his former buddies sitting in that dock, we're all just pieces on his board.'

33

By the time Reaper was finally sworn in, it was gone three in the afternoon. Jalicia's heels left a puncture trail in the thick brown carpet as she walked towards him. Compared to the courtroom in San Francisco, the one in Medford, with its brown-on-brown colour scheme, felt claustrophobic and oppressive.

'For the record,' she began, 'could you state your full name and place of residence?'

Reaper showed his teeth, like a talent contestant who'd spent too much time practising in front of the mirror for his TV debut. 'Frank Hays. But most folks call me Reaper. I live a little outside Crescent City, California.' He turned to the jury and gave them the same smile. 'More specifically, the Secure Housing Unit at Pelican Bay State Prison.'

'Thank you, Mr Hays. Can you tell me, do you know any of the defendants? And, if so, how do you know them?'

Reaper glanced at the defendants, his former comrades, his expression not changing, although there seemed to be an extra twinkle in his eyes. 'I know all of them from doing time alongside them in prison.'

'Which prisons, Mr Hays?'

'San Quentin back in the day, Corcoran, Chino, bunch of other places,' Reaper replied, reeling off some of the grimmest prisons in

California and beyond. He turned to the jury again. 'If it's got bars and a gun tower, I've probably seen it.'

Jalicia walked back to the prosecution table and shuffled through some papers, ready to signal a switch of gear — time to get down to business.

'Many inmates who've been accused of being a member of the Aryan Brotherhood have claimed that there is no such organisation. In your experience, is that the case?'

'Lady, it's like that Brad Pitt movie: the first rule of the AB is you don't talk about the AB. Least not with outsiders.'

'So it does exist?'

Reaper looked over to where the six defendants were watching him intently. 'Oh yeah, it exists.'

'And you were a commissioner in the AB?'

Reaper's head swivelled to the jury again. 'You just promoted me. There's only three commissioners, all sitting over there. I was what they call a shot caller.'

'Thank you, Mr Hays, I stand corrected. But while incarcerated in Pelican Bay Supermax, you were *the* Aryan Brotherhood shot caller for that institution.'

'Yeah, I called the shots.'

'And what does that mean in reality?'

'It's like being one of the head honchos at one of those Fortune 500 companies. Any major decisions that had to be made went through me.'

Jalicia angled her body towards the jury. Predominantly white, with a sprinkling of blacks and Hispanics, they still looked drained by what had happened in San Francisco but now they were all leaning forward slightly, taking in everything Reaper was saying.

She turned back to him. 'What kind of decisions? Could you give me a for instance?'

Reaper studied the ceiling as if he was dredging up an example. 'Like, say, if someone wanted to attack one of the toads. By which I mean the blacks.'

There was an audible shuffle of discomfort in the courtroom. Reaper looked at Lock.

'That would have to be sanctioned by you first?' Jalicia asked.

Reaper smiled, still looking in Lock's direction. 'Exactly.'

'And what about decisions made elsewhere in the organisation? Would you be apprised of those?'

'The big ones, sure.'

'Such as the decision to have someone killed?'

Reaper shrugged, super-nonchalant, like he and Jalicia were discussing what to pick up from the store for dinner. 'I'd get to hear about it.'

Jalicia could feel the defence attorneys tense in anticipation of the next question. She took the decision to back off a little, go round the block one more time, make sure the jury were in no doubt about the nature of the Aryan Brotherhood.

'What was the term used by this organisation for giving the go-ahead to have someone murdered?'

'Someone was going to get killed, they had to be green-lit.'

'Green-lit? Like the Hollywood term for deciding to put a movie into production.'

'Except we usually tried *not* to make a big production out of it.' Reaper smirked.

'And these killings would take place inside prisons?'

'Sure. And on the outside too.'

Jalicia allowed her face to register a degree of surprise, even though she knew where this was leading. 'But how would that even be possible if the members of this gang, yourself included, were all incarcerated?'

'You don't have to actually pull the trigger yourself, you know. Ain't that what this whole deal's about?'

Jalicia took a breath, and stepped towards him. 'If you could just answer the question.'

'Let me see how to explain this to you.' Reaper put the palms of his hands together, the tips of his fingers resting against his lips. 'OK, so say we decide someone who's on the outside needs some killing. We look at who is about to be paroled, or who we already have on the outside. We get a message to them and that's how it's done.'

'And this would be a member of the organisation or an associate?'

'Usually an associate.'

'And why would someone who had recently been released from prison commit murder in the first degree, risking further incarceration, possibly a capital or life sentence, merely on your

167

say-so, or the say-so of the Aryan Brotherhood?'

Reaper clasped his hands together. 'Real simple. The one thing we can be sure of is that this person is headed back into prison at some point. If they haven't carried out their mission, then next time they step on the yard we kill 'em.'

Jalicia wanted to hammer this one home so that even the slowest member of the jury would be able to grasp it. 'So, if they don't commit the murder, as soon as they step back inside a jail or penitentiary, you'll have them killed.'

Reaper looked over at the jury, and smiled. 'Yeah, that's about it.'

★   ★   ★

The lights were dimmed in the courtroom as Jalicia played the jury the DVD recording of Prager's forced mutilation at the hands of his son. She kept a close eye on them as they watched it. At certain points a couple of the female jurors covered their eyes. In the dock, two of the AB members nudged each other and snickered. To Jalicia's disappointment, the jury didn't catch it.

When it had ended and the lights rose again, she got out of her chair and approached Reaper.

'As far as you're aware, Mr Hays, none of the men in the dock today were present during what we just saw?'

'Them being in prison, I guess not.'

'As we established before the recess, though, the Aryan Brotherhood have contracted out

168

murders to people on the outside. That's correct, isn't it?'

'We outsource stuff like that, yeah,' Reaper replied.

'And is it your belief that the murder of Agent Kenneth Prager and his family was a task outsourced by the men here today?'

A mis-step. Gross was on his feet before she hit the word 'task'. 'Objection. It's not a matter of what the witness believes. We're supposed to be dealing in facts here.'

Before the judge could overrule, Jalicia switched into damage limitation mode. 'Mr Gross is quite correct. I withdraw the question.'

Gross looked deflated that she hadn't put up more of a fight.

'Thank you, Ms Jones,' the judge said.

Jalicia stepped towards Reaper again, noticing how his dark grey eyes tracked her every move. 'Mr Hays, until you decided to testify in this case, you were a member in good standing of the Aryan Brotherhood, is that fair to say?'

'Yes, I was.'

'But when you heard about the death of Agent Prager and his family you were sufficiently troubled by it to contact my office.'

'That's correct.'

'And why was that?'

'Listen, don't get me wrong, Prager was a federal agent. And he was undercover, which makes it ten times worse. He was an enemy combatant — I believe that's the phrase these days, ain't it?' Reaper looked at the jury. 'But his wife, and their boy . . . ' He turned back so that he was facing the public gallery, Lock included. 'No one in this court might understand this, 'cept maybe those six over there, but I joined the Aryan Brotherhood because we lived by a code. It wasn't much, but it was something. You folks out there, living your little suburban lives, paying your taxes, saving up for that big-screen TV so you have even less excuse to talk to your wife or the miserable brats you're raising to be good little consumers, none of you might understand this, but to join the Aryan Brotherhood meant something. The code of the Aryan Brotherhood meant something.'

Jalicia could sense that Reaper was rapidly losing the sympathy of the jury.

'And that code included not harming women and children?' she interrupted.

Reaper shifted on his seat. 'Excuse me, but I was speaking. Isn't that why I'm here?'

'I'm sorry for interrupting you, Mr Hays, but if you could focus on the questions you're being asked.'

Reaper shifted his attention to the window, where sunlight streamed in. 'Pretty day. Don't get to see much of the sun up in the Bay. Good place for a prison though. What's that saying, 'out of sight, out of mind'? You can't get much more out of sight than Crescent City.'

Gross leaned over to one of his junior counsel and stage-whispered, loudly enough so that the jury would catch it, 'Or out of mind, apparently.'

'You said in your deposition that there was a letter you received a few days after the murders,'

Jalicia pressed on. 'You said that in that letter — '

Gross was on his feet again. 'Can someone remind Ms Jones that we are here to hear from her witness, not her?'

Before the judge could speak, Reaper interrupted, leaning as far forward in his chair as he could, lasering in on Jalicia. 'You asked me what I believed before that scum-sucking commie over there' — Reaper nodded at Gross — 'broke in. Well, I'll tell you what I believe. I believe, with all my heart, in the fourteen words. The words spoken by a true American patriot before the Zionist Occupation Government murdered him. The words abandoned and forgotten by so-called comrades-in-arms in that dock.'

Reaper was on his feet now, pointing at the six defendants. The two guards next to him struggled to get him to sit down, but it wasn't a fair match. They were both big guys, but Reaper had ten years of six hours' exercise a day on them.

'The fourteen words are: 'We must secure the existence of our people and a future for white children',' he bellowed, shoulders back, his torso military-straight.

He sat back down so hard that Jalicia could feel the floor beneath her feet vibrate. Then he started to cough violently. His shoulders hunched, he waved for his glass of water. One of the guards handed it to him.

As he raised the glass to his lips, it spilled from his grasp, bouncing off the edge of the dock and shattering on the floor. By now Reaper was

171

doubled over, his right hand reaching up to massage his left shoulder, then moving across to his chest. Finally, he keeled over, taking one of the guards down with him, still struggling for breath.

Disbelieving silence gave way to whispers of confusion. As the noise level in the courtroom rose in volume, the judge banged his gavel. 'Session adjourned. Clear the court.'

The six members of the Aryan Brotherhood in the dock craned forward expectantly. Across the room, Carrie held on to Lock's arm.

'What's wrong with him?' she whispered.

Lock shrugged. When it came to Reaper, it was anyone's guess.

34

Streetlights flickered into life as Lock emerged from the front of the Medford courthouse. Looking up, he could see a police sniper on a nearby rooftop, framed by the fading sunset. Lock crossed to where Carrie was standing with her cameraman, a bearded woodsman type sporting a flannel shirt and dungarees who'd been drafted in from a local affiliate station. Lock pulled her a safe distance from him and the other assembled members of America's media who clogged the sidewalk.

'He's fine,' he told her.

'What was it? He looked like he was having a heart attack in there.'

Lock shook his head. 'They ran an ECT. It wasn't a heart attack.'

'So what was it?'

'Some kind of anxiety thing.'

'A panic attack?' Carrie asked, disbelieving.

Lock shrugged. 'The excitement must have been too much for him. First time outside prison in ten years, half a dozen men across the court wishing him into the ground — who knows?'

'You think he faked it?' Carrie asked.

It was the first thing that had crossed Lock's mind, and he'd said as much to the paramedic who wanted to transfer Reaper to the nearest hospital for further tests. With Jalicia's help, Lock had won the day, and they'd stabilised

Reaper inside the court. But if Reaper had been faking, it was an Oscar-worthy performance.

'I don't know,' he said.

'So what happens now?'

'There's nothing physically wrong with him so nine o'clock tomorrow morning he's back on the stand.'

'Where they gonna keep him?'

Lock lowered his voice a notch. He'd been asked by Jalicia to advise on security until the Marshals Service could put in place proper replacements for their fallen comrades. 'A holding cell inside. It's best not to move him, although that's not what your buddies are going to be told.' He nodded in the direction of the press pack. 'We're going to move a decoy out. Muddy the trail a little.'

'What about the six defendants?'

'They're staying in a different part of the same building.'

'Isn't that risky?'

Lock took a step back, another sniper coming into focus on a different rooftop. A police helicopter buzzed low, chasing off a couple of television news helicopters that were hovering above the courthouse snatching some overhead footage before nightfall completely engulfed the scene. 'Right now, everything's risky.'

Carrie sighed. 'At least Jalicia got through most of what she wanted.'

'Oh yeah,' said Lock. 'Tomorrow's about tying up some loose ends and then the defence having their opportunity to pick it all apart, but as far as the jury's concerned the damage is pretty much done.' He looked at Carrie. 'Which is just as well for you.'

She glanced up at him, puzzled. 'What do you mean?'

'Well, it took one hell of a lot of persuasion, and I had to throw in my best friend almost being killed, but I got you the interview you wanted with Reaper.'

Carrie's mouth fell open. 'No way. Jalicia agreed?'

'Reluctantly, but yes. Coburn, Ken's boss from the ATF, showed up when I was talking to her about it. He thought that Reaper on the tube might get the bigwigs in Washington to start paying some more attention to the threat white supremacists pose to domestic security, which would mean more money for his budget.'

'And two bombed Federal Buildings won't do that?' Carrie said.

'Body count wasn't high enough, plus, as far as the politicians are concerned, it ain't real unless it's on primetime, right?'

Carrie smiled. 'And what does Reaper think about this?'

'Seems like he's turning into quite the attention-whore. Now he's started talking, no one can shut him up. He's said that nothing's off limits. You can ask him anything.' He paused. 'There are some conditions, however. It can't be broadcast until after the verdict. In fact Jalicia and Coburn don't even want it mentioned that you've done it until the jury are back.'

'That's fairly standard. Anything else?'

'You're not going to have a lot of time to prepare.'

'How come?'

'Because it's scheduled for tonight at midnight.'

'That means I have less than six hours.'

'Don't worry,' said Lock, leaning in to steal a kiss. 'You're like me.'

'In what way?'

He grinned. 'You always do your best work under pressure.'

35

It was two minutes to midnight in downtown Medford. With Lock behind him, Reaper walked into the blaze of TV lights, a prize fighter staking out his spot at the weigh-in. Still clad in his suit and tie, he looked more like an ageing rock star than an avowed neo-Nazi psychopath. He settled into the chair opposite Carrie as Lock and two US Marshals took up a position directly behind him.

Carrie flicked through her notes as the camera settled over her shoulder to capture Reaper's answers. While the interview was a major coup for Carrie, Lock had thought that it might also serve as a way of drawing out Reaper's true motives for betraying his former brothers-in-arms. But before they got to that, Carrie had told Lock she wanted the viewers at home to know exactly the kind of person Reaper really was.

'Mr Hays, why are you currently serving three life sentences without possibility of parole?'

Lock watched Reaper straighten in his chair, the muscles in his back tightening visibly as he did so.

'Like I said in court today, I was standing up for the most beaten-down minority in America today.'

'And who would that be, Mr Hays?'

'White people.'

'But you did commit a crime — several crimes, in fact.'

Reaper opened his mouth to say something, but Carrie cut him off with a wave of her hand. Lock tensed. Reaper was a man used to being heard.

'According to the record, Mr Hays, while serving as a Navy Seal, and with a once proud record of service to your country, you planted an explosive device in the vehicle of your commanding officer which killed both him and his two young daughters. Your commanding officer was African-American. Was that why you murdered him and his family?'

Jalicia had briefed Lock on some of this but the details had been left sketchy. He'd known that Reaper had served in the army, but not with such an elite unit. He'd also known about the murder of Reaper's commanding officer and his two daughters, and heard something about it being racially motivated.

Reaper lowered his head. 'The two kids were collateral damage. They weren't supposed to be there.'

'But you did intend to kill Lloyd Thomas?'

'Lloyd Thomas was an incompetent who climbed the ranks because of positive discrimination, because of the colour of his skin, and because of bleeding-heart liberals like you. As a result, men died. Good men.'

'Good white men?' Carrie prompted.

'Yes, they were white. White men like the ones who built this country. With their own blood and sweat. And now it's being torn from us, swamped by the mud people who want everything for nothing.'

There was a sudden crackle on the radio of a Marshal standing behind Lock. Carrie looked up from her notes in irritation. Lock turned round to see what was happening. The Marshal had his finger up to his earpiece, listening intently.

'We're going to have to finish this up later,' the Marshal said. 'We have a situation in the street outside.'

A sudden current of tension ran through the room. Everyone fell silent. Lock noticed Reaper's back straighten, as though he was getting ready for action.

'Kill the lights,' Lock said.

The cameraman hesitated, glancing at Carrie for approval.

'Now,' Lock ordered.

He did as he was told, reaching down to click off the three high-powered tungsten lights arranged in a triangle around Carrie and Reaper. Immediately, the room was plunged into semi-darkness.

Lock crossed to the door and flicked off the main light, reducing everyone in the room to shadows.

'If you move,' he said to Reaper, 'I'm going to shoot you.'

Crossing to the windows, he peered out. There was a black van parked in the middle of the street, surrounded by several police cruisers. Hunched behind the doors of the cruisers were four police officers, their service weapons drawn and trained on the van.

'What's going on, Ryan?' Carrie asked, stepping towards him.

Lock reached back with his left arm, pushing her away. 'Stay away from the window. That goes for everyone.'

He narrowed his eyes, trying to get a bead on the driver. It was difficult. The storm that had been building through the afternoon was now in full effect. Rain lashed the street, pummelling the sidewalk with heavy bullets of water which shrapnelled upwards in a thousand fragments or dug themselves into rapidly expanding pools of water.

The Marshal in charge handed Lock a pair of binoculars. He put them up to his eyes and racked the focus wheel between the two lenses with the pad of his thumb. It looked like a woman was in the van. Dark hair. Dark complexion. One of the cops was shouting instructions to her. Lock could just about guess from his body language and demeanour that he was ordering her to get out of the van with her hands up. But she wasn't moving.

Lock turned back to the US Marshal, who was right behind him, his finger still at his earpiece. 'What's the situation down there?'

'This van just ran the roadblock, then it stopped. Single occupant driving, as far as we can tell.'

'It's a woman?'

The Marshal met Lock's gaze. His expression suggested he was holding something back.

'Who is it?'

'Raise your hands where we can see them!'

'Toss the keys to the ground!'

'Keep your hands up and exit the vehicle!'

A litany of instructions. None of which she could follow. She looked down at her hands, which had been secured to the steering wheel with cuffs. Heavy-duty gaffer tape bound her tightly to the seat. After a hell of a struggle she'd finally managed to extricate her feet from the tangle of tape securing them, at an angle, to the gas pedal. Thank God, or she would have ploughed straight into the police cruisers racing towards her.

Jalicia's heart was pounding, and her shirt was soaked in sweat. She'd never been so terrified in her whole damn life.

★ ★ ★

Lock watched the van from the window of the makeshift TV interview room, then turned back to the Marshal and nodded in Reaper's direction. 'Let's get him back in a cell. Get on the radio and tell the people down there to fall back to the building. Also, get on your cell phone. We're going to need every single member of law enforcement we can round up down here. Tell them to bring every weapon they have, plus all their ammunition. I want every gun cabinet and rack within a ten-mile radius emptied.'

'It's Jalicia in the van, isn't it?' Carrie asked. 'What's going to happen to her?'

Lock took Carrie's hand. 'Dime to a dozen that van is rigged with explosives. There's nothing we can do for her. Not right now anyway.'

'But we can't just leave her,' she said, defiant.

'We can and we will,' Lock said, grimly. 'It's a come-on. The guys who've rigged the van plan on drawing everyone in. Then they'll blow it up. That gives them a window to get to their real target, which is this asshole here.' He hauled Reaper to his feet.

'And if you're wrong?' Carrie asked him, clearly unused to seeing this side of Lock, his ability to choose life for some and death for others.

'If there are no explosives then she'll be fine.'

'But what if they're on a timer?' Carrie pressed.

'Listen to me,' Lock said. 'These are classic terrorist tactics. It sucks, but we have to leave her. We don't leave her, a lot more people die.'

'OK,' Carrie said reluctantly.

'Goddamnit!' the Marshal erupted, staring at his cell phone. 'I can't get a signal.'

'Same here,' said one of the cops standing at the door. 'My radio won't work either.'

'They're using a jammer.'

Lock could see the beginnings of panic in Carrie's eyes.

'They can do that?'

Before Lock could explain that pretty much anyone with a credit card and an internet connection could purchase the technology to block communications these days, he froze,

182

aware of a sound beyond the keening of the wind and the splashing of the rain outside.

'Listen,' he said, and the room fell silent.

Lock concentrated hard, separating out first the atmosphere of the room, then the roar of the storm. What was left was a low, rhythmic thwump that was increasing in volume. Accompanying it in the skies above them was a point of light. The pinprick quickly expanded so that Lock was at first dazzled, then all but blinded by it.

He narrowed his eyes and brought up a hand to shade them from the worst of the glare, which allowed him a clearer view of a black helicopter turning so that it was side on to the building. A man was sitting on the floor of the cabin, his legs dangling out, his feet almost on the blade of the skid. He was clad in full body armour and holding an assault rifle. With his free hand he was feeding out ropes which twisted and dangled in the wind like tendrils of overcooked spaghetti.

Lock twisted round so that he was staring into the saucer-wide eyes of the Marshal, who'd joined him at the window.

'They're not our guys, are they?' Lock asked.

All the Marshal could manage was a slow shake of his head.

Mid-shake, the missile pod mounted at the front of the helicopter lit up with a fiery roar, punching out what Lock guessed had to be an RPG. It whistled downwards, leaving a ghostly yellow blaze burning across Lock's retina.

Less than a second later, the van holding Jalicia disintegrated in a fiery blaze of distended metal. The blast wave thumped so hard into Lock's chest that he and the others in the room were momentarily lifted off their feet and deposited ass-first on to the floor. The walls of the courthouse vibrated.

Ears ringing, Lock stood back up and went over to Carrie.

'You OK?' he asked her as she struggled into a sitting position.

'What the hell was that?'

'RPG.'

She gave him her reporter's stare. 'In English please, Ryan.'

'A rocket-propelled grenade.'

He looked back to the window. Down below, flames licked around the skeleton of the van, and he could see the charred outline of Jalicia's corpse slumped over what was left of the steering column. He tore his eyes away. By the time he looked skywards again, the light was gone. But up above them, the thump of the helicopter's blades slashing through the storm grew louder, drowning out the sirens below.

36

Lock moved fast. Dragging Reaper towards the door with his left hand, he unholstered his Sig Sauer 226 with his right. Carrie had kindly brought it to Medford for him, and it felt good in his hand. Solid. Reliable. Deadly. He pointed forward with it, motioning for the others to follow.

At the door, he turned to one of the younger Marshals who was toting an AR-15 semi-automatic rifle. 'Give me your side arm.'

The Marshal hesitated.

'Son, unless you can fire both of your weapons simultaneously, hand it over.'

The Marshal in charge shrugged a 'go ahead' and the younger man handed over his Glock 40 calibre. Lock took it, business end first, and palmed it off to Carrie.

'Thanks,' she said.

'Hey, what about me?' grumbled her camera-man.

'Just because you have a dick doesn't mean you can shoot for shit,' Lock said, staring at him.

Carrie set about checking over the Glock with the grace and speed of a career soldier. Lock had always regarded the ability to defend yourself as a more crucial set of skills for women than men, seeing as women were more often prey than predator. Hours on the range with Carrie had transformed her from merely competent to a crack shot who regularly scored higher than Ty — much to Ty's annoyance.

'But — '

Lock cut the cameraman off. 'She knows what she's doing, so do everyone a favour and get over yourself. Tell you what, you do your shooting with that camera you're toting. We come out of this alive, you might just snag yourself an Emmy.'

'What about me?' Reaper said. 'I can shoot.'

Lock yanked on Reaper's restraints, almost lifting the bigger man from the ground. 'No gun for you, but I'll give you a bullet any time you want one.'

'So where we going?' asked the Marshal in charge.

Lock poked at Reaper with the barrel of his gun. 'We're going to make sure that Elvis here ain't going to be leaving the building.'

★ ★ ★

The SWAT team sniper posted on the roof tossed his Styrofoam cup of lukewarm coffee to one side and peered into the blinding spotlight projecting from the front of the helicopter. He readied his weapon, all the while keeping his eyes on the powerful airborne spotlight bearing down on him, God-like, from a storm-ridden night sky.

He raised his assault rifle and leaned out from behind an air-conditioning unit. Still the light kept coming, the thump of the rotor blades drowning out the chaos of noise from the street below. He sighted a point at the very centre of the glare and fired off a round. Nothing. Just the light bearing down on him without mercy, the ever-increasing roar of the blades, and the chop of the air stinging his eyes.

A moment later there was another blast of fire from the helicopter and he was blown off his feet, shrapnel pinballing around him, cutting him to ribbons.

★　★　★

In the helicopter, Cowboy punched the air as beneath them the sniper's position disintegrated and a big hole opened up in the roof. He keyed his mike, which looped round the side of his face, finishing a few inches from his mouth.

'He's second floor, right?'

'Roger that.'

Cowboy climbed a little, steadying the helicopter over the rooftop. Behind him, Chance, her weapon drawn, clipped on to the ropes that had been slung over the runners, swung out of the helicopter and rappelled the short distance to the roof.

Trooper followed, zip-lining at speed to join her. While he provided cover, Chance placed the first charge next to the locked door of the rooftop stairwell, and ran back.

Cowboy gained some more height. A second later the charge detonated, the shockwave buffeting the helicopter. Spinning the copter round ninety degrees, for a moment he just caught a glimpse of Chance before she disappeared into the building.

Cowboy spun the helicopter back round and let loose a fusillade of .50-mil rounds towards a SWAT sniper position on the building opposite, which lay to his immediate right. That done, he took the helicopter down on to the roof. By the time they'd organised another effective firing position he'd be long gone.

He checked his watch. Ten minutes past midnight. At seventeen minutes past midnight he'd take off again. Anyone who wasn't on board by then was staying behind. That was the deal.

★ ★ ★

Chance and Trooper clambered down the stairwell, a couple of the higher treads blown away by the charge she'd planted. Lights flickered overhead.

A solitary jail guard ran towards them through the dust. 'Stop where you are!' he shouted, with all the authority of someone used to dealing with the unarmed.

Chance raised her M-4, found his outline easily with her night sights, and dispatched him with a single round, his anti-stab vest no match for a sub-sonic CQB round. His chest opened up, his intestines spilling out over his utility belt.

★ ★ ★

Lock and Reaper had reached the one-man cage where Reaper had been spending his downtime. Thirty seconds earlier there had been another two explosions, both of which had sent plaster dust cascading down on them. One of the guards opened the door.

'I'm going to need at least two more pairs of cuffs, and two more sets of leg restraints,' Lock barked.

'But he's already double-cuffed.'

'Just get me what I need.' Lock turned to the cameraman. 'You have gaffer tape on you, right?'

'Somewhere,' the cameraman said, digging into a bag slung over his shoulder and pulling out a thick roll of the silver insulating tape he normally used to secure cabling to the floor.

Lock took the roll and tore off a strip, cutting it away with his Gerber. He smiled at Reaper.

'What the hell you doin' with that?' Reaper asked.

'Giving you a taste of what Jalicia Jones had to endure just before your buddies out there snuffed her.'

'Paranoid, Lock?' Reaper sneered.

'Why didn't they kill you back at the airfield when they had the chance? Answer me that.'

Reaper clammed up, then another explosion rocked the building and light arms fire chattered above them. 'You can't leave me in here,' he said, looking around him at the metal cage.

'If they want you alive, they're gonna have to work for it,' said Lock, slapping some gaffer tape across Reaper's mouth and setting to work securing each of Reaper's hands to the top of the cage with the cuffs, and his feet to the bottom with the leg restraints.

Reaper kicked out at him but Lock ducked out of the way. Still, Reaper's knee glanced against the side of his head. The Marshal in charge pulled his baton. Lock grabbed it from him and swung back with it, bringing it down hard against Reaper's kneecap. Reaper's scream was muffled by the tape covering his mouth, but his eyes crinkled shut and he stopped fighting.

A moment later, Lock slammed the gate shut and sealed it with a large padlock. He stepped back to admire his work. Reaper stood there, his arms splayed out from his body in a crucifix pattern.

'You really think he's what they want?' Carrie asked.

'I don't think,' said Lock, 'I know. Now, let's get the hell out before Delta Force get here.'

★ ★ ★

Dead bodies littered the corridor behind Chance and Trooper as they made their way to the secure holding area, alternating who took point, folding in front of each other at every doorway, working their way quickly but methodically towards their target. Anyone they saw, they shot, including a woman dressed in civilian clothes who had pleaded for her life on bended knee, old-school style. Chance, wishing to conserve ammunition, had cut her throat with a Bowie knife.

'Let's hope they ain't moved him,' she said to Trooper.

She peered through a mesh-reinforced glass panel in a door that led into the holding area. The door was locked but the room beyond looked empty. She placed a charge and scuttled back, her face kissing the floor as the charge detonated. A few seconds later, the door came to rest at a forty-five-degree angle on its sole remaining hinge. Chance pushed it aside and stepped into the anteroom. A desk ran the length of one wall, its end section lifted up to allow access to another door. This door was also locked.

Chance checked her watch. The digital display was set to count down from five minutes, which was the time at which she'd estimated they'd have to start moving back to the RV point on the roof. Two minutes of the five remained.

She checked the door in front of them. Judging by the hinges, it opened inwards. She flicked her M-4 on to fully automatic, hefted it to her shoulder, fell into a modified Weaver stance and let loose with a burst of gunfire aimed at the lock. Trooper stepped forward, and each gave it a kick. The door flew open and they walked into a much wider corridor. Three doors faced them. One in the middle. One to their left. One to their right.

'Eeeny, meeny, miney, mo.'

The left. Chance nodded at it. She moved off to one side as Trooper tried the handle. It was open. They stepped in.

Reaper met her gaze. He was locked inside a steel-barred holding cage, each of his limbs double-cuffed to the bars. His mouth was covered to prevent him speaking.

On the front of the cage was an envelope

secured in place with gaffer tape. Chance ripped it away with a gloved hand and tore it open. Inside was a single sheet of paper. On it, scrawled in black marker pen, was a message.

Good luck getting him out of here, assholes.

It was signed *Ryan Lock.*

37

For a moment Chance just stood there, staring into the eyes of the man in the cage. He stared back at her. His expression was of a kind no one had seen in ten years. A softness came into his features and his eyes glistened with yearning. Chance felt a rock lodge in her throat, making swallowing painful.

Disregarding the seconds ticking away on her wrist, Chance reached in at the top of the cage and touched his hand in a gesture of comfort. Then she stepped back, freezing the man out and focusing on the task in hand.

She couldn't use explosives, that was for damn sure. Blow the lock on the door and she'd blow him up too. She sank down on to the floor and checked the bolts that anchored the cage to the floor. She wouldn't be able to shoot through them without a serious risk of catching a ricochet, but she had to weaken them somehow.

She turned to Trooper, who was gazing at the cage and its occupant with a world-weary 'What the fuck do we do now?' look of defeat, and pushed his shoulder, snapping him out of it. 'Get back up on the roof. Get the ropes, all the ropes, and tie them to the skids on the Little Bird. Then get up in the air.'

There was a slow-dawning realization in his eyes. 'Are you fucking nuts?' he said to her.

'Just do it. And tell Cowboy I'm going to need two more minutes.'

As Trooper ran out, Chance fired into the floor, exposing the joists beneath her feet. Then she jogged out of the room, working her way as fast as she could to the floor above.

On the stairs she had to stop to catch her breath, as she felt a fluttering inside her. The embryonic life inside her was urging her on, she told herself, giving her the kick in the pants she needed to finish the job she'd started.

She hauled herself up the stairs and tracked back, counting the same number of paces she'd taken on the floor below. She'd have to get the charge right. Get it wrong on the high side and Reaper would die. Use too little and there would be a mess but no hole.

In the end, the decision was made for her. There was only one charge left. She placed it, and hooked up the detonator. She spooled out several lengths of det cord, her thighs aching as she scuttled back in a permanent crouch. The clock was ticking though, and they were stealing time they didn't have.

★   ★   ★

Lock led the way out into the lobby, a marble-floored area with two banks of elevators. All the mayhem seemed to be contained above them. Explosions. Gunfire. A regular riot. He crossed to the smoked-glass windows that led out on to the street where EMS ambulances and cop cars crowded and confusion reigned. Local

194

law enforcement wasn't trained or prepared for an all-out airborne assault, especially somewhere like Medford.

Looking over his shoulder, Lock glimpsed the Marshal in charge in a heated discussion with a local cop sporting sergeant's stripes. Lock ignored them and pushed past, out on to the street. Carrie was on his heels, directing her cameraman to snatch some footage of the building as smoke billowed from the upper floors and flames spat from the windows.

Lock could just about glimpse the tail fin of the helicopter rising above the roof. He strained to see how many people were inside the cabin. It looked like someone was getting out of the building — empty-handed, he guessed. He crossed his fingers.

'Bye bye, assholes,' he said.

From inside the building there was another massive boom, and the windows that hadn't already been blown surrendered the glass from their frames. Lock ducked under a car, taking Carrie with him, as crystal splinters rained down on them from above, rendered invisible by the rain.

'You OK?' he asked her.

She exhaled, her cheeks flushed with blood, her blonde hair pasted against her face by the downpour. 'How come Katie Couric never has to deal with this shit?'

Lock smiled. 'Hey, it's not all rainbows and butterflies for her either. She had to interview Sarah Palin, remember.'

'Fair point.'

Lock backed out from under the car. The helicopter was still there. For a second, he thought there must be a problem with it, that maybe it had taken a hit from the couple of sheriff's deputies who, rather optimistically, were taking aim at it with handguns from the street. Then he noticed the ropes slinking their way down towards the roof.

He backed away from the building, distance giving him a better angle. The ropes were breaking-point tight — tighter, it seemed to Lock, than they would be with someone hanging from them. As the helicopter rose, inches at a time, they strained and twisted round on themselves, rolling the body of the helicopter from one side to the next. Any minute now, thought Lock, those ropes are going to snap and the sudden loss of tension is going to bring the whole thing crashing down.

The helicopter jolted. There was the sound of wood splintering, as if an old sailing ship were being wrenched from a weather-worn dock by the power of an angry sea. Then, rather than free-fall down, the helicopter righted itself and started slowly to descend back on to the roof.

Lock lost sight of it. He clenched his fists, torn between a desire to go back into the building and stay where he could see what was happening. He stayed put, and a few seconds later the blades of the helicopter rose again, more slowly than before. As it rose directly upwards, Lock could see people in the cabin. Three of them. The same number he'd seen when it arrived. No Reaper, then. Not unless he'd switched places with one

196

of them, which was unlikely given that he'd been left in the cage.

The grinding gears of a truck's engine behind him prompted Lock to turn round. An olive-green canvas-covered military transport truck was rolling down the street. Lock wondered why the hell the Marshals hadn't handed over this whole operation to the military in the first place. Jalicia might still be here if they had. They were too proud, that was why, and it was institutional pride, which was the worst kind as far as he was concerned.

Despite the mayhem and the local cops' best efforts, the street was still full of civilians. Their eyes were trained on the roof, on the departing helicopter. No more than twenty feet from Lock stood an overweight woman in a pink housecoat, mouth agape, her yellowing teeth a forceful rebuttal to the usual wonders of American dentistry.

'Holy shit,' she said.

Lock spun round, following her gaze. Up above them, the metal cage, complete with Reaper still shackled inside it, dangled twenty feet beneath the chopper, secured by the ropes tied to the helicopter's skids. The cage inched into the night sky. The four ropes, attached at either corner of the cage, twisted in the wind, but Reaper kept rising into the storm-blackened Oregon sky.

All around, people had stopped whatever they were doing and were staring. Cops. Civilians. Everyone. Lock felt a shiver of defeat run through them as the nose of the helicopter dipped and it started to coast smoothly away from the building.

Lock shielded his eyes against the glare of the Night Sun spotlight mounted on the nose of the helicopter. He could make out Reaper, his arms still spread, Christ-like, as he ascended into the heavens.

A voice crept into Lock's mind. Reaper's voice, but not his words. The words belonged to Sun Tzu, the ancient Chinese general. They were the words Reaper had recited from memory back in the cell they'd shared in Pelican Bay.

Engage people with what they expect. It settles them into predictable patterns of response, occupying their minds while you wait for the extraordinary moment — that which they cannot anticipate.

Then, like a cassette machine clicking off as it runs out of tape, the voice was gone, along with Reaper and the helicopter, which had travelled far enough that it had become just another distant point of light in a sky full of dead planets.

'The extraordinary moment,' Lock repeated softly to himself, his hand tightening so hard round the grip of his Sig that his knuckles turned white.

38

The cage inched towards the ground, pieces of wooden joist and chunks of plaster still attached to its base. The wait for the chopper to land had been interminable, worse than any time spent in solitary back at Pelican Bay, where seconds could stretch like an eternity. As it made contact with the earth, it toppled over. Reaper went with it, the tightness of the shackles that held him in place saving him from further injury. If Lock hadn't done his job so thoroughly, Reaper doubted he'd have a bone left unbroken by now. Above him he could see a couple of the ropes slacken and then fall back to earth as they were cut from the helicopter.

Reaper closed his eyes, the downdraught from the helicopter still roaring around him. Then he heard the engine being cut, and the sound of the rotors fell away. There were voices. Men's voices.

'Let's get it upright.'

'I got boltcutters in the truck.'

'Then go get 'em.'

'We're gonna need more than boltcutters. We're gonna need a blowtorch to get into the cage.'

Kids these days, thought Reaper. He licked his lips. 'Blowtorch will just weld it together, boys,' he said. 'You're gonna need a cutting torch. Something that runs at a ninety-degree angle. Oxyacetylene. Either that or an angle grinder

199

— you know, like people use for cutting off wheel clamps.'

When it came to engineering technology, Reaper doubted that anyone had the edge on him. A federally mandated right to information had provided him with a wealth of material over the last ten years, plus the kind of time not even tenured academics had to hone their knowledge.

'I got one of those in the truck,' said one of the disembodied voices.

'Then go get it,' Reaper said, now firmly in charge, the alpha male.

There was the sound of boots sloshing over soaking ground and then the cage was manoeuvred so that Reaper was upright.

Reaper could see her properly now. Wow, she was beautiful. A knock-out. And so strong, so commanding. He studied her face, searching out her features. Her deep grey eyes. So clear, so unswerving. Her delicate nose. Those high cheek bones which gave the rest of her face its nobility. Those who doubted that there was indeed a master race need only look at her face to have their objections quelled.

She smiled at him, that same look of shared understanding, then reached in again to touch his hand, pinching his palm between her thumb and index finger. 'You OK?'

'I could be on fire, but seeing you would make it all OK,' he replied, his voice as brittle as a three-pack-a-day smoker.

'I should have visited,' she said.

Reaper shook his head. 'You did what was

best.' His voice grew brittle again. 'You did good.'

'We'll get you out of there real soon.'

Reaper closed his eyes in acknowledgement, and to hide the tears he felt forming. He stayed like that as the men set to work.

Using the angle grinder, they had the cage door open in no time. Once they had one hand free from the cuffs, Reaper helped them with the rest, using a borrowed comb to spring the other cuffs. Then they set to work on the leg restraints.

Half an hour later, he stepped uncertainly from his cage. Chance threw her arms round him and he scooped her up, burying his face in her blonde hair. The men looked away, then busied themselves with other things. Finally, with the softest of kisses to her forehead, Reaper put her down.

'Let me introduce you around,' she said, suddenly formal.

Cowboy stepped forward, snapping a salute. 'An honour and a privilege, sir,' he said. 'Not many true patriots left.'

'That was some damn impressive flying,' Reaper said.

'I'm only glad I could be of true service.'

Trooper shook Reaper's hand. 'It's an honour, sir.'

Chance tapped his arm. 'Come on. We gotta go.'

'Man, she's bossy, ain't she?' Reaper grinned at Cowboy.

'You don't know the half of it, sir.'

Reaper looked at her with pride. 'Half a dozen

more of her in the movement and we'd have cleaned all the filth out of this country by now.'

'So where now?' he asked as they walked towards a pick-up truck parked at the edge of the clearing they'd used to land.

'Going to get you cleaned up. Then we have a private plane chartered tomorrow to get us out of the country.'

Reaper stopped in his tracks. 'Say what?'

'You don't think we should wait? I could try and move it up. We thought they'd be checking all immediate private charters. Plus, we have a couple of loose ends to tie up.'

'And where were we gonna go? Mexico? Argentina? Some other South American shit-hole? Hell, no. I didn't spend ten years down to turn my back on my country.'

'But if we stay here — '

He put an arm round her. 'You don't just light the fuse and then stamp on it. And you don't turn your back on your country in its darkest hour.'

'But the movement isn't strong enough yet.'

'It was strong enough to get me out. We have an opportunity here. This should be the start, not the end.'

'But — '

He silenced her with a look. 'Every day our rights as Americans are getting taken from us. One by one. We got millions of our people homeless and unemployed, getting kicked out of their homes and looking for some leadership. If we don't have the conditions for a revolution in this country now, then we'll never have them.'

He opened the door of the pick-up truck, then glanced back at the helicopter, where Cowboy was talking to the other men.

'You tell those men to remain on standby. I'm gonna have work for them to do.'

For the first time, he thought that she looked worried.

'All it's going to take is one big spark, and this country'll go up in flames. And this time, no one will be able to stop it.'

Chance looked up at him, her dark grey eyes wide. 'I knew you were gonna be like this.'

'How'd you know?' Reaper said, reaching out and putting his arm round her shoulders.

'I'm my father's daughter, ain't I?' said Chance.

Reaper smiled. 'You sure as hell are.'

39

Chance pulled the pick-up truck into the driveway of the ranch house and waited for her father to get out the other side. He took his time doing it, peering over the top of new sunglasses at the stand of trees masking the front of the property.

'Nice and quiet. How long you been here?'

'Rented it last month.'

'Landlord?'

'It's a woman. She spends most of her time down in Baja.'

'Huh.'

The pit bull started barking. Reaper walked over to its run and knelt down. It came over and licked at his hand through the wire mesh. 'I know how you feel, brother,' he said to the dog. Then he turned back to Chance. 'Some guard dog.'

Chance smiled. 'Never seen him do that before.' She turned towards the house. 'We'll have to go in the back way.'

He glanced at the front door. 'You rigged it?'

She nodded. 'There's an old fire road about four hundred yards back. I have another truck parked back there. Keys are in the ignition.'

He smiled. 'Man, I taught you well.'

'Fail to prepare, prepare to fail.'

They headed round to the back of the property. Chance opened the door and they walked straight into the kitchen.

'If you want to get some rest, there's a bedroom through there.'

Reaper stretched out. 'No, I spent enough of my life sleeping.'

Chance crossed to the refrigerator, reached in, came up with a six-pack of Coors and tossed it over. He caught it one-handed, ripped off a can and held it up against his forehead, just like in a commercial.

'You know how long it's been since I had me a cold one?'

Chance frowned, her throat tight. 'Ten years. Three months. And fourteen days.'

Reaper studied the floor. 'I'm sorry, Freya.'

She forced herself to perk up. Here was her father, a hero to the cause who'd sacrificed the best years of his life, and on his first day of freedom she was busting his balls.

'You've got nothing to apologise for,' she said.

'Wasn't a day went by that I didn't think of you.'

Her father ripped the beer open and offered it to her.

'I'd better not,' she said.

'That's right. I forgot. You been getting sick yet?'

'First couple of months. I'm over it now.'

Reaper sat down at the small circular kitchen table. He took a sip. 'You have no idea how good that tastes. Listen, I ain't been around and you're a grown woman, but the daddy . . . '

Chance could feel herself flush. 'One-night

stand. He was white. That's all you got to worry about.'

'I wasn't worried.'

'Hang on there for a second.' She walked into the living room, reappearing a moment or two later with a couple of Gap bags. 'I got you some clothes. Everything you asked for.' He started to empty them, laying out a selection of pants and underwear. He unfolded a couple of casual business shirts. 'Long-sleeved. Perfect.' It was the same uniform the members of the AB had worn to court — dress-down office casual, verging on the geeky.

'And nothing blue,' Chance added. 'I figured you might be sick of blue.'

Reaper drained the last of his beer. 'You got that right. I'm going to jump in the shower. Then I'm going to try on some of these brand-new duds.'

'I'll show you your room.'

In his room, the TV was on with the sound down. There was a live update from outside what was left of the Federal Building in Medford. The reporter was the blonde. It had to be that asshole Lock's girlfriend, Carrie something.

'Hey, turn it up.'

Chance picked up the clicker which was resting on the arm of a chair and maxed out the volume.

Onscreen, Lock's girlfriend was talking with someone back in the studio.

'So far, authorities are staying tight-lipped, but it's believed that the group which last night staged the most violent and audacious jailbreak

206

in America's history are also the same people responsible for the death of ATF agent Kenneth Prager and two subsequent bombings of the Federal Buildings in Los Angeles and San Francisco.'

The guy in the studio cut in. 'Let me interrupt you for a moment there, Carrie. Do the authorities have any idea who these people are?'

Lock's girlfriend shook her head. 'Not as yet. But they are saying that because of the tactics they deployed they believe at least some of these individuals are well equipped and highly dangerous, perhaps even former members of the military.'

Reaper clicked the mute button with relish. 'Big bang. Helicopter. Lot of guys with guns. That's all they've got.' He hit the button again.

'It's now clear that what we face in the hours and days ahead will be the largest ever manhunt to take place on American soil.'

Reaper clicked off the TV. 'With what I've got planned, they're gonna have bigger problems than finding little old me.'

Chance frowned. 'What you got in mind?'

'A holy war,' he said, solemnly. 'Blood flowing through the streets. It's gonna make '68 look like a picnic.'

Part Two

40

The van was gone, spirited away for forensic investigation. Four pads of melted rubber from its tyres marked out the rectangle where Jalicia had died. Spent shell casings and shards of broken glass lay scattered among tree limbs torn away by the storm. The building itself was still standing, though showing visible scars from the events of the previous night. Blinds dangled from glassless windows and charred, sooty tongues licked up its external walls where small fires had taken hold, discolouring the structure's normally white façade.

The media were here too, in even greater numbers than the night before, their satellite vans, honey wagons and production trucks making up a small village across from the Federal Building. Lock could see Carrie among them, delivering a piece to camera, still awake, running on the adrenalin of the night before.

Accompanied by Coburn, he stepped back into the lobby. The morning light had offered up one final surprise from last night's events, and he wanted to see it for himself.

They worked their way up the stairs towards the penultimate floor, which contained the prison's main holding area. Construction workers were already busy sifting through the debris and shoring up what was left of the roof and internal ceiling with heavy-duty props. Forensic

211

techs flitted among them, or stood chatting in huddles, seemingly unsure of where the hell to start.

This wasn't your typical crime scene, Lock reflected, where a single fibre or hair would offer up a debonair and otherwise flawless killer. This had been a bold, brazen, in-your-face massacre-slash-hostage extraction, the tactics copycatted from similar jailbreaks staged by groups like the Taliban.

'They're in here,' Coburn said, nodding towards a door on their left-hand side. 'I should warn you, it's pretty grisly.'

Lock shrugged. Seeing Ty shot on the yard and Jalicia's charred corpse sitting upright in the van hadn't exactly been a bundle of laughs. Grisly he was used to. Grisly he could cope with. It was losing that he struggled with.

And that, sure as hell, was what this felt like. Reaper had played all of them, yet he was the one who'd sensed it coming, and chosen not to be more strident about his concerns. You could call it gut instinct, or a sixth sense, but he knew that what it really was was the mind putting everything together, but not in a clear enough way that you could articulate it. You just knew that things were off, and he had known this ever since Jalicia showed him the footage of Prager, that they were all — her, Coburn, Ty, him — being drawn into a web. He had also sensed that Reaper's eventual escape wasn't an ending but more of a beginning. And that there was more to come.

'You ready?' Coburn asked him, pushing open

the bullet-pocked door.

'I'm ready,' Lock said, stepping through into the blood-soaked area where the six members of the Aryan Brotherhood had been held for the trial.

'Guess Jalicia got her wish in the end,' Coburn said, as Lock took in the carnage.

Against the back wall of one single holding cell the bodies of the Aryan Brotherhood lay piled up, their arms and legs entangled. The floor of the cell was slick with congealed blood. A forensic photographer hunkered down, clicking away with a digital SLR camera, capturing the scene for posterity. Even at this early stage, the bodies were starting to reek.

'Live by the sword, die by the sword,' Coburn said, almost respectfully.

Lock took his time, studying the heads, mouths gaping, eyes staring vacantly or with a measure of surprise. There was something off about this as well. Even raking the cell with an M-4 would have eaten up precious seconds. Revenge seemed too slender a motive for someone associated with Reaper.

'And dead men tell no tales,' added Lock, stepping in closer to the slaughter and counting off limbs. 'There are only five bodies.'

'What?' said Coburn, startled.

'Count 'em if you don't believe me. Someone's missing.'

The photographer manoeuvred round Lock, the camera still to his face. 'Yep, one of 'em made it,' he said, matter-of-factly.

Coburn looked startled. 'No one told me.

Where'd they take him?'

The photographer finally lowered the camera from his face. 'Craziest thing I've ever seen,' he said. 'They must have fired a couple of hundred rounds into that cell, but one guy crawled in under the other bodies, played dead. There was barely a scratch on him. Freaky, right?'

Coburn grabbed the photographer by the arm. 'Where is he now?'

The photographer looked down at Coburn's arm, clearly not appreciating the attention. Lock was spooked by it too. Coburn was upset about Jalicia — hell, so was he — but there was no point taking it out on some forensic tech who was only doing his job.

'The Marshals took him.'

'Where?' spat Coburn.

The photographer bristled. 'Take your hand off me, buddy, and I might tell you.'

Lock put a hand on Coburn's shoulder. 'Take it easy, huh?'

Coburn seemed to snap out of it. He mumbled an apology.

'They said something about shipping him back to the SHU at Pelican Bay, seeing as how it's the nearest Level Four facility to here.'

★ ★ ★

Lock walked back downstairs with Coburn, and sat out on the steps of the Federal Building with him. Coburn offered him a cigarette, which Lock declined.

214

'What the hell's going on here, Coburn?' Lock asked.

Coburn sighed. 'I wish I knew.'

'Bullshit. First these people kill Ken Prager, a federal agent.'

The muscles in Coburn's face tightened. 'He was undercover. What d'you think they were going to do to him? Throw him a party?'

'They took his family. Lured him out to the middle of nowhere so they could torture him and his family. Then they recorded the whole thing and mailed it to you. That seem like normal behaviour to you?'

'There is no *normal* when you're dealing with people like this, only levels of abnormal.'

'So why send Jalicia the footage?'

Coburn struck a match off the step and lit up. His face was lined and haggard, the grey hairs at his temples seemingly more numerous than when Lock first met him. Lock guessed he was still trying to come to terms with what had happened to Jalicia.

'I'd guess they were trying to send a message,' he replied after blowing out his first lungful of smoke.

'And killing Prager and his family wasn't sufficient?'

'If a federal agent gets killed in the forest and no one hears it, did it really happen?' Coburn asked rhetorically.

Lock sighed. It had been a hell of a twenty-four hours. 'They handed Jalicia a case. And if that wasn't enough, Reaper got in touch to make sure it moved ahead.'

'And then he pulled the rug out from under us. See what *I'm* saying, Lock? You're looking for some master plan here, when there isn't one.'

Lock thought it time to voice something that had been nagging away at him since he'd first met with Coburn and Jalicia. It made no sense to him then, but had seemed not to trouble anyone else, even though it left a huge cartoon question mark above the entire investigation.

'Prager was feeding back information to you while he was with the Aryan Brotherhood. So what was he saying? I mean, he must have known who these people were.'

'You think they'd still be out there if he had?' said Coburn.

Lock was incredulous. 'An investigation that went on for months and you don't know the identities of any of the people involved?'

'They were super-careful. Prager never visited their homes, never got their real names. Nothing. Not up until the end, when he confided some of it to Jalicia. We had a debrief planned for the night he was murdered. He was going to give us a lot of it then and we were going to pull him out.'

Lock wasn't convinced. He leaned in towards Coburn, trying for some kind of personal contact. 'Level with me here, Coburn. There's something you're not telling me.'

But Coburn turned away. 'Listen, Lock, this isn't your problem. None of this is.'

Lock thought of Jalicia, burned alive in the truck. 'That's not how I see it.'

'Clearly.'

'So humour me.'

'You've been an investigator, right?'

'For a time.'

'And how did you like it when other people started interfering in one of your cases?'

'I didn't. But then this isn't your case either any more, so we're kind of in the same boat.'

'You want to know what I think?' Coburn asked, looking at Lock properly for the first time since he'd lit his cigarette. 'I think they killed Prager and his family because they're sick fucks who didn't like the idea that they'd been betrayed by someone they thought was on their side. I think Reaper used his testimony to get himself out of the Bay so his buddies could try and spring him. When that was foiled they knew they'd already crossed a line so they gave it one more try to get him out. And I think that Jalicia was killed because she went after them in the first place, and to make matters worse, she's black. Revenge is motive enough without us needing to go any deeper. Listen, Reaper and his buddies are probably halfway to Argentina by now. The whole thing's a mess, but there's no great mystery here, so take my advice and leave it alone.'

Coburn ground out his cigarette with his boot, got up and walked away.

Lock watched him go, more convinced now than ever that Reaper's jailbreak was the beginning of something, not the end. But what? Knowing Reaper, Lock could be sure about one thing. Whatever it was, it was bad.

41

Cowboy and Trooper were eating a breakfast of pancakes and bacon at the small circular pine table in the kitchen when Reaper walked in sporting wrap-around sunglasses. His eyes were still getting used to long periods of natural sunlight. Chance drifted in a moment later, wearing white sweatpants and a fleece — the antithesis of the hellcat that had been on display the night before.

Reaper snuck a piece of bacon from a plate set down on the counter and popped it into his mouth. 'Damn, it's good to be free,' he said with a broad grin. 'Boys, I want to thank you. You've taken a lot of risks for me.'

Cowboy forked a square of pancake into his mouth. 'Shit, last night was fun.'

'You know,' Reaper said solemnly, 'there's money available if either of you want to get out.'

'No way,' Cowboy said, getting up to grab a beer from the refrigerator. 'I'm already looking at life in Leavenworth soon as I walk back on base.'

'Fuck it,' added Trooper. 'I've fought their goddamn war for 'em, now I'm going to fight one that I believe in.'

'OK then,' Reaper said, taking a seat at the table as Chance took a manila folder from under a cutlery tray in one of the drawers next to the stove top and handed it to him. He opened it and pulled out a small bundle of paper. 'The material is a little flung together but, believe me, this has been a long time in the planning. I know you guys have already helped my daughter with locating our second target. We have two reconnaissance missions. Both fairly straightforward but our window of opportunity is slim.'

Reaper selected a large glossy photograph, of a scholarly-looking elderly white man, and handed it to Trooper. 'Junius Holmes, member of the United States Supreme Court. Take a good look. He's famously a creature of habit. Right around now he trades his townhouse in Georgetown for a family home not too far from here. We need his daily routine, weekdays and weekends.'

'He carry a security detail?' Cowboy asked.

'That's one of the other things we need to figure. None of it's public domain. The Marshals have a unit dedicated to judicial security but it's stretched thin. Thinner since they've lost so many men here. But you and Trooper will have to assess that. Can I trust you to do that for me?'

Cowboy and Trooper nodded.

'Good,' said Reaper, picking out a second photograph, also of a man, but much younger, getting into a car outside a modest-looking suburban house. He was late thirties, early forties at most, white with sandy blond hair that ran to his collar. 'Glenn Love. He's a foreman at the San Francisco Department of Public Works, Bureau of Street and Sewer Repair.'

Cowboy and Trooper traded a look of bewilderment.

'Bear with me,' said Reaper, flicking to another picture, this time of the same house but with a woman packing two kids into a mini-van. 'This is Glenn's wife, Amy, and their two kids. This should be a slam dunk too. Families have a routine. We need to know what it is.'

'And once we know?' Cowboy asked.

'Details to follow.'

Reaper caught Trooper studying the floor.

'You got something to say, then say it, son.'

'Both men are white, and the second guy's got kids.'

'Just to set everyone's minds at rest, we're not out to hurt any kids. It's their father who's our target, and I don't plan on hurting him either, unless he leaves me no choice.'

'So, when do we start?' Cowboy asked.

Reaper smiled as he looked at his team, a team he was certain would do anything for him, whatever the circumstances. 'Now.'

42

Lock stood in the tiny wood-panelled reception of the motel just off North Riverside Avenue in Medford and slammed his hand down on the old-fashioned bell. The desk jockey, an overweight man in his early thirties with red hair, emerged from the back room.

'Good morning, sir, and how may I help you?' he chirped, his sunny outlook verging on the Canadian.

Jesus on a stick, thought Lock, the guy was acting like the town had just been awarded the Olympics rather than having just stood witness to a jailbreak worthy of one of the shittier Afghan provinces.

The desk jockey, his grin threatening to annex his jaw from the rest of his face, leaned forward, and Lock caught a whiff of day-old fried onions overlaid by breath mints. 'Sir?'

Lock propped his elbows on the desk and leaned in too, mirroring the man's body language. 'Are you OK?'

The man's grin ebbed at the edges. The look in his eyes suggested that he thought this might be a trick question. 'Yes, sir,' he replied nervously. 'Why do you ask?'

'Well,' said Lock, 'last night this town was lit up like downtown Basra, but you look happier than a pig in shit.'

The man shook his head slowly. 'I know.

Terrible. And in Medford of all places. But life moves on,' he added, perking up again.

'Sure,' said Lock, thinking that for quite a few people it wouldn't. He stood up straight again. 'Were you on duty last night?'

'Sure was.'

'One of your guests, a Ms Jones . . . '

The man looked blank.

'African-American woman. Late twenties. Tall. Good-looking.'

'Oh, yes. Very elegant lady. Very nice manners.'

'Quite,' said Lock. 'I need to know when you last saw her.'

The man stroked an imaginary beard. 'Let me see now. She came back in around nine o'clock to pick up her key. But after that, I don't know. I didn't see her leave.'

'She was murdered last night. The van that exploded outside the courthouse, she was in it when it went up.'

The desk jockey went pale. He opened his mouth, then closed it again. Evidently this isn't something covered in training, Lock thought.

'So you didn't see her leave?'

'No, sir.'

'Do you have CCTV cameras?'

'Just here in the office.'

Lock looked up. A single camera was mounted in the corner of the far wall behind the desk to capture anyone coming in or leaving. 'In that case, may I see the room she was staying in?'

At this, the man looked serious. 'Sir, are you with the FBI or something?'

'I can't tell you who I'm with,' said Lock,

taking a chance. 'But I need to see that room.'

'Do you have some identification?'

Lock leaned over the counter. 'What's your name?'

The man's eyes flitted beyond Lock to the door. 'Dale.'

'Dale, do you love your country?'

'Yes, sir.'

Lock made a show of pushing back his jacket so that the holster holding his Sig was in plain sight. Not that he looked down, or even acknowledged that he'd done it, but Dale's eyes were growing wide. 'I'm very glad to hear that, because there are people out there right now who definitely don't. And I need to find them, fast. And you can help me, Dale. You can help me by showing me that room.'

Dale still looked unsure, so Lock pressed on, his right hand on the handle of his Sig. 'Now, Dale, are you going to be a true American patriot and help me out here?'

'Absolutely, sir,' said Dale.

Visibly shaking, he reached beneath the counter for a key attached to a black fob with the room number etched on it in white, which he slid towards Lock.

Sensing that Dale was going to be on the phone to the local cops as soon as he was out of sight, Lock took the key and walked quickly towards the elevator.

★　★　★

Jalicia's room was tucked away at the back of the main motel building along with half a dozen

223

other rooms, all of which ran at a ninety-degree angle to the rest of the hotel, which faced out on to the main avenue. The room's position would have made Jalicia hard to spot as she came and went, Lock thought. Perhaps she'd chosen it for that very reason, thinking that the lower a profile she kept the safer she would be.

He opened the door and stepped inside. The room itself was basic. A double bed dominated the small space. It was still made up, although Lock noticed that the sheet stretched over the red-patterned comforter was wrinkled at the bottom right-hand corner, as if someone had sat on that part of it. Opposite the bed was a desk. Next to the desk was a wardrobe and a chest of drawers. A small portable television was perched atop the wardrobe.

Lock closed the door behind him, crossed to the desk and opened the first of three drawers. A Bible. In the second drawer were a couple of leaflets on local tourist attractions. Nothing looked like it had been moved. Lock couldn't imagine that Jalicia would even have glanced at the leaflets. Thinking about it now, he couldn't even imagine Jalicia outside work. She must have a family, he thought. Did they know she was dead? He opened and closed the final drawer, which was empty, thinking of the bitter blow it would be for them. From what little he knew, Jalicia had clawed her way up from a disadvantaged background. He could only imagine the sacrifices both she and they must have made.

Lock stood there for a moment, allowing his

anger at the injustice of it all to settle, cold and hard, at the base of his stomach, then he took a few steps and opened the wardrobe. Her clothes were still on the hangers. He'd never really registered her perfume when he met Jalicia, but he could smell it now. It was feminine, but understated. You wouldn't have been aware of it unless you were up close, which he guessed not many men had been.

He quickly rifled through her clothes, then ran his fingertips along the bottom of the wardrobe, although he wasn't sure exactly what he was hoping to find. Closing the wardrobe door, he moved to the chest of drawers. The top drawer contained Jalicia's underwear, which was mostly black and lace-edged. For the first time since he'd walked into the room he felt like he was being intrusive. He closed the drawer and went quickly through the others. Everything was folded neatly.

Finally, he moved into the small bathroom. A make-up bag lay open on the counter, and the shower curtain was pulled back. A vaguely damp towel was folded neatly over a rail. He walked back out of the bathroom and stood next to the bed. Nothing disturbed. Nothing out of place. The room told at least part of the story: Jalicia had left of her own accord.

Lock exited the room and stood outside the motel, his back to the wall. Jalicia's car was a pale blue Volkswagen Jetta. He was sure he'd seen her get into it after Reaper's testimony had come to an abrupt end.

He walked to the front of the motel but

couldn't see it. He retraced his steps back to Jalicia's room and beyond, to an area at the back of the motel. There it was, parked in a row of five lined spaces that were marked out next to two huge commercial trash containers. But her keys hadn't been in her room, and neither was her handbag. She must have left with them, Lock thought, but not used her car.

So, she would have walked out of the room some time after nine but never made it as far as her car — a distance of maybe twenty yards. Yet there were rooms all around, and people in them. If there had been a struggle, surely someone would have heard something?

Of course, maybe they had. Lock walked towards the middle of the parking lot and turned to face the building. It was a low-rent motel late at night. If Jalicia had made a noise, the other guests might have put it down to any number of things.

Even with all that, he couldn't imagine Jalicia being abducted without putting up a hell of a struggle. She was a fighter; that was her nature. He walked slowly towards her car, hunkering down, looking for something, anything; a speck of blood, something dropped from her bag. But there was nothing.

He stood back, his hands still on his knees, his head down. From close by came the trill of a cell phone. Not from a room, but outside. Just feet away. Lock looked around to see if there was anyone to whom it might belong. Maybe Dale the desk jockey had come to check on him? But no, Lock was still alone.

It kept ringing. It was coming from one of the big trash containers. Lock grabbed at the top of the first container, hauled himself up and looked down into it, spotting the flashing display almost immediately. He let go, stepped back, and this time took a running jump, almost falling into the container head first. His elbows over the lip, he swung over a leg, reached down and managed to pluck out the cell phone just as it stopped ringing.

Extricating his leg, he dropped back down to the ground and jammed the phone into the back pocket of his denims as two Medford Police Department cops rounded the corner.

'Sir, place your hands where we can see them, and do not make any sudden movements.'

43

For a full five minutes Lock argued with the cops that they didn't have probable cause to search him. But they did, they both knew it, and they took the cell phone before he had the chance to confirm that it was Jalicia's, never mind run through it properly. They also took back the borrowed key. That done, they let him go with a warning not to interfere any further in what was now a federal investigation.

Lock assured them that he wouldn't. And he might have actually meant it too, if it wasn't for the fact that the more Coburn and the cops told him to back off, that it wasn't his problem, the more determined he became to find out what the hell was really going on. Plus, Lock had a problem with authority. It was a personality trait that made for a bad soldier but a great military cop. It was also, Lock had grown to realise, a piece of his character inherited directly from his father, which inevitably had brought them into so much conflict over the years that they rarely spoke. Lock's father had, like so many parents, held to the dictum 'do as I say, not as I do'. But Lock was incapable of that. Once he got hold of something, he worried at it like a dog with a bone.

The cops stood in the parking lot and watched

him get into the car he had rented that morning from the Avis representative at the Rogue Valley airport. He waved them a friendly goodbye and headed back in the direction of Carrie's hotel.

When he got there, Carrie was perched on the bed in her room, wrapped in a white cotton robe, wet hair up in a towel, answering her cell phone. She looked exhausted, having been on air pretty much all night, reporting live from the scene almost hourly, the entire nation rising from east coast to west and tuning in to see a reporter who was still several steps ahead of the competition. Meanwhile, her newsroom back in New York had been working their law enforcement contacts hard, filling in the gaps for both her and, by extension, Lock.

She waved at Lock as he walked in, held the phone away from her ear and mouthed, 'Ty.'

'Ty?' Lock asked, taking it from her. 'How are you?'

Ty's voice came through loud and clear. 'I'm watching the news is how I am. What the hell happened?'

'Ask him how he is,' Carrie said, fighting back a yawn.

'I already did.' Lock tapped her bare knee. 'Get some sleep.'

Carrie swatted at him. 'Then ask him again.'

Lock cradled his cell between his ear and shoulder. 'Carrie wants to know how you are.'

'Stronger by the day, and just as good-looking as before.'

Lock looked at Carrie and sighed. 'Seems that

being shot has left Ty suffering from delusions of adequacy.'

'I heard that,' Ty protested. 'Any news on Reaper?'

'Thin air.'

'What about the guys who sprung him?'

'Nada.'

'That helicopter they were using was military,' Ty said.

'That's what I thought too.'

'Hard to pick one of those up on eBay.'

Carrie was scribbling something on a piece of paper which she shoved under Lock's nose. He read it, then relayed the information to Ty.

'One of Carrie's sources has had word that a Little Bird assault helicopter went missing from a base in San Diego three days ago.'

'They know who took it?'

'If they do, they're not saying. You know what the Army's like.'

'You gonna try and talk to them?' Ty asked.

'Be wasting my time, but Carrie's going to keep digging.'

'So what are you gonna do? And don't tell me nothing, Lock, because I know you must have a hard-on for Reaper a foot long by now.'

'I wish,' muttered Carrie, lying back, her eyes closed, head propped up on the pillows.

On the other end of the phone, Ty laughed.

Lock shot her a fake injured look, then lowered his voice. 'I'm heading back to the Bay. One of the AB leaders survived the attack. If he doesn't have a clue what Reaper's up to then nobody does. Listen, once I've spoken to him,

I'm coming down to San Francisco to see you.'

'Look forward to it,' said Ty, before hanging up.

'You sure you really want to go back in there, Ryan?' Carrie asked, sitting up.

'I'll be fine. I know the territory.'

Carrie gave him an even look. 'You mean like Ty did?'

44

Lock headed out of Medford on Interstate 5. He'd have to drive north first, towards a place called Grants Pass, before the highway would drop him back south and west to Pelican Bay. To his right, trees had been planted at regular intervals along the highway. The storm clouds were being sucked back out towards the Atlantic, revealing a powder-blue sky.

The smell of rental-car air freshener combined with his lack of sleep was soon making him woozy. He lowered all four windows a notch.

As he drove, the traffic fell away to a trickle of pick-up trucks and lumbering semis and the giant redwood trees closed in around his tiny car. Looking at a map he'd picked up at a gas station before he left, he'd wondered at some of the names. Rattlesnake Rapids. Wolf Creek. Starvation Heights. It was a landscape that could eat a man up whole, that was for sure.

Lock wondered if Reaper was near one of those places now. Maybe shooting the rapids with his band of fellow psychopaths, the water swallowing their trail. Or camped out on top of Starvation Heights, surveying the land below, planning a desperate last stand against the minions of what Reaper saw as an occupying government. What was the phrase he'd used? Oh yeah, the Zionist Occupation Government.

Blaming the government, Lock reflected, was

an easy out for the white inmates inside America's prisons. They had been incarcerated not because they'd peddled amphetamine to school kids, or shot some unfortunate first-generation immigrant minding the till of a convenience store, or because they'd drowned someone in their own hot tub after staging a home invasion robbery. No, it was always other people's fault, part of a wider plan to do them down, all engineered by dark forces skulking in the shadows and plotting a new world order.

With Reaper's messianic tendencies, Lock had a strong hunch that his former cellie wasn't about to go quietly. He wasn't about to do a disappearing act. No, Reaper had something else in mind. Lock was sure of it.

Aware that his eyelids were getting heavier by the minute, Lock reached down and jammed on the radio. There wasn't much choice: a couple of country music stations and something that billed itself as Rogue Valley's top-rated twenty-four-hour evangelical station. Lock would have welcomed some divine inspiration, but doubted it was going to come via this particular source. He clicked the radio back off.

Ten miles further on, Lock hit a line of traffic. It came up on him fast, and he had to slam on the brakes to avoid rear-ending a black pick-up sporting a National Rifle Association decal and a Palin for President 2012 sticker. The jolt as the car lurched to a halt convinced him that he'd have to take a nap before he got to Pelican Bay.

The local cops had set up a roadblock and were checking vehicles, and he was aware that his rental car and dragged-through-a-bush-backwards appearance would single him out for special attention.

He stayed in his car as he was approached, immediately declaring his firearm. Thankfully, one of the cops recognised him.

'Any sign of them?' Lock asked him, with a show of forced politeness.

'Not a one,' said the cop, disconsolate.

No shit, Sherlock, they left in a helicopter, Lock thought. 'Well, good luck.'

The cop waved him through, and Lock continued on his way.

Fifty miles down the road, he pulled in at a rest stop. Seconds after he'd switched off the engine, pulled on his parking brake and set the alarm on his cell phone, he was dead asleep, the doors locked and his Sig close by.

Lock rarely dreamt, and when he did he shrugged his dreams off pretty much as soon as he'd taken a leak and had his first sip of coffee. But the nightmare images that came to him now would be less easily shed, based as they were on the realities of the previous days.

At first he was tumbling down a black slide that deposited him in a heap in the middle of the yard at Pelican Bay. As he looked up and got his bearings, he saw Ty, surrounded by bare-chested white inmates, their bodies a continuous mosaic of swastikas and lightning bolts. As they closed in on Ty, knives glistening in the early-morning sun, Lock glanced up towards the gun tower. The guard's face melted into Reaper's as one of the inmates slashed at Ty and he went down.

234

There was a screech of tyres behind Lock as a black van careered across the yard, throwing up clouds of dust. Lock felt a burst of relief which faded almost immediately when he spotted the driver, her hands taped to the wheel. It was Carrie, a swastika carved, Manson-like, into her forehead. The living corpse of Ken Prager rode shotgun alongside her, helping to guide the wheel.

Lock sank to his knees, letting rip with a primal scream. Then a black tunnel was all around him, sucking him back into the sky and away from being able to help either Carrie or Ty.

Lock woke to the sound of his cell phone's alarm, the gun still by his side, the steering wheel in front of him. Disoriented by the images from his nightmare, he peered out of the windshield and both side windows, a thin sheen of sweat coating his face. He wiped the worst of it away with his sleeve, opened the door of the car and stepped out into the fresh air, shaking out the cramp from his legs. He took a walk round the rest stop area, then got back in the car, took a sip of water, wishing it were coffee, started the engine and continued his journey.

★   ★   ★

It was dusk by the time Lock drove past the unmanned security booth and into the parking lot that fronted the administration building of the prison. Coming in this way, a visitor would have little idea of the security that lay beyond.

He pushed open the main door, stepped on to the sparkling linoleum that covered the lobby floor, then took a left towards the warden's office. The two middle-aged women who served as administrators were packing up, ready to go home.

Lieutenant Williams stepped from his office next to the warden's. He didn't look particularly pleased to see Lock.

'Warden Marquez still here?' Lock asked him. 'It won't take long.'

Williams hitched up his equipment belt. 'Thought you might have had enough of this place for a lifetime,' he observed, turning into the warden's office.

Marquez emerged a few moments later. 'It's not a good time, Lock,' he said.

'The timing isn't of my choosing. I guess you heard about events in Medford?'

Marquez rubbed his prosthetic eye. 'We got the SHU and the mainline on lockdown because of it.'

'Problem?'

'Soon as word came that the AB leadership had been wiped out, the Nazi Low Riders made their move.'

'What kind of move?'

'Told all the white inmates that anyone that was AB could either switch to the NLR or die.'

'What about the AB leader who survived? I heard he was shipped back here. You still have him?'

'He was smart, he PCed up,' said Marquez.

PC, Lock knew, stood for protective custody.

There was a separate part of solitary reserved for these prisoners.

'I'd like to speak to him if I may.'

Lock waited for a speech about how his request breached protocol. Instead, Marquez glanced at Williams with his good eye while his other eye stayed on Lock.

Williams shrugged. 'He might not want to speak to you.'

'And Phileas. I'd like a moment with him too.'

Williams's moustache curled up at its tips as he smiled. 'I bet you would.'

'If anyone here knows what Reaper's next move is, he does.'

Warden Marquez crossed to a desk and lifted the phone. 'I'm not making you any promises, Lock.'

'Fine by me. I've had enough promises to last me a lifetime.'

45

The tension was plain in the faces of the guards as Williams escorted Lock across the vast expanse of No Man's Land towards the SHU. They passed through a second control point, then swung a left into the part of the SHU known as the Transitional Housing Unit. This was where the lone AB leader — William Young, Williams had told Lock, though he went by the moniker Pinky — was being held. Lock tried to conjure the man's face from the trial, but with their facial hair, the AB leaders had looked more or less broadly alike.

Pinky was waiting for Lock in a small anteroom off one of the main spurs. For someone who'd recently cheated death, he looked calm, although Lock knew better than most that appearance in this environment was essential to a person's survival. Even giving the impression of being weak or, worse, scared was a good way to get yourself killed. He was glad he had this at the front of his mind because Williams wasn't for hanging around.

'I'm going to look into your other request, if that's OK with you?' Williams said.

'I'll be fine. Would you mind if your officer here stands outside?'

Williams nodded to the guard, and they both left the room.

Lock settled into a chair opposite Pinky.

238

'Miracle we both got out of there alive.'

Pinky stared at Lock stony-faced. 'Build rapport. I like it.'

'Just making an observation.'

'You're the crazy man they brought in to keep Reaper alive, ain't you?'

'The one and only.'

'Maybe if you hadn't done as good a job my brothers would still be alive,' Pinky said, eyes narrowing.

'If you want me to pretend I have sympathy,' Lock said, holding his palms open, 'sorry, I'm all out. But I think we can agree on one thing.'

'And what's that?'

'We both got played by Reaper.'

Pinky tugged at his moustache with a cuffed hand. 'Nah, brother. *You* got played. We knew all along what Reaper was about.'

'And what was that?'

Pinky seemed to study Lock. 'Let's just say we had *i-dee-ah-logical* differences.'

'He claimed you were all about the green, and he was all about the white,' said Lock, referencing the colour of money.

Pinky smiled. 'Man, you're nothing but a tourist. You don't know our world.'

Lock put his hands up, conceding the point. 'Then explain it to me.'

Pinky seemed to mull it over. His foot tapped out a military cadence, and he stared at it as if it wasn't under his control.

'You're looking at a death sentence anyway, Pinky. The NLR are going to run things now, and they'll be looking to mop up someone like you. Maybe I can speak to someone, get you shipped somewhere safer?'

'My attorneys are already working on that.'

'So what are you going to do when the cash from selling drugs starts to dry up? The AB's a busted flush now, you know it and so do I. The people who sprang Reaper, they're the same people who killed Prager, aren't they?' Lock leaned towards him, trying to establish eye contact. 'The woman, Pinky. Who is she?'

'I've got about as much of an idea about that as you,' Pinky said. Then he too leaned in so that there were maybe three feet between his face and Lock's. 'You want to know the funny part of this whole deal?'

'Go on,' said Lock. 'I could use a chuckle or two.'

'We didn't green-light Prager.'

'So who did?'

'Reaper.'

Lock sat back. 'So why didn't you just tell that to Jalicia Jones?'

Pinky gave Lock a broad grin. 'We were about to, but Jones wouldn't deal. She had the version of events she wanted.'

Lock thought this through. Jalicia had certainly been obsessed with getting a conviction against the AB, so what Pinky was saying made sense in a weird sort of way. It still left a lot of unanswered questions though.

'Why'd you wait so long? Why let it go as far as a trial?'

Pinky glanced from one corner of the box-like room to another. 'Hell, we wasn't about to miss

240

the change of scenery.'

From there on in, Pinky clammed up. He didn't know who Reaper's people on the outside were. He didn't know who the woman was, or whether they were planning to flee the country. What's more, he was past caring. They'd all been suckered according to Pinky, and now Reaper had what he wanted. The AB was finished and he was out of Pelican Bay.

When Lock stepped out of the room, Lieutenant Williams was waiting for him in the short stretch of corridor. His arms were folded across his chest.

'I spoke to Phileas.'

'And?'

'He says you can go to hell.'

Lock sighed. He hadn't expected anything else.

'But there's more,' said Williams. 'We just decoded a kite that's been going out to all Nazi Low Rider members.'

'What did it say?'

Williams's eyes fell away from Lock's. 'You and your buddy, Ty . . . '

'What about us?' Lock asked, tensing, not liking Williams's refusal to meet his eye.

'They've green-lit you both. Any Nazi Low Rider or associate either here or on the outside is under orders to kill you on sight.'

46

Cell phone coverage was patchy this far north, whatever the main carriers claimed, so Lock used the phone in Warden Marquez's office to call Coburn and alert him to the NLR threat.

'I have someone calling San Francisco Police Department right now,' Coburn said. 'We'll make sure they get someone over to Ty's hospital room. I'm back in the city now anyway. You get anything out of the Aryan Brotherhood survivor?'

'He said Reaper ordered Prager's execution.'

'So why didn't his side tell Jalicia that?' Coburn asked.

'My first question too. He said they tried to, but Jalicia turned it down.'

'That I can believe. Once she got something in her head . . . '

There was silence, followed by a click as Coburn ended the call.

★　★　★

Warden Marquez sent Lock off to San Francisco with a cup of coffee strong enough to negate narcolepsy, and a word of caution. 'Be careful out there,' he said, punching Lock on the arm. 'The NLR don't screw about, and their tails are up right now.'

Lock shook his hand and left him to get back

to his job. It wasn't one that he envied.

'Good luck,' said Marquez.

'You too,' Lock shouted back as he jogged to his car, keen to get to Ty and see with his own eyes that he was safe. If the NLR were serious about their threat, they'd probably know that Ty was the easiest target of all right now. A stationary one.

★ ★ ★

Lock sipped at his coffee, the windows down, the Pacific roaring away on his right as he navigated the single-lane road out of Crescent City. On a sunny day it was a breathtaking drive, but night was closing in and his sole focus was getting to San Francisco.

The rental car didn't help matters, its tyres losing traction as Lock threw the vehicle into tight bends and pulled back out on to the straights. He hunched over the wheel, fatigue engrained in his bones.

Signs flashed by outside at irregular intervals. An invitation to view the world's tallest tree. To drive through a hollowed-out redwood. To view an exhibit dedicated to Sasquatch, the legendary California Bigfoot — half man, half beast.

The miles ticked down, every minute bringing him closer to the place where it had all started nearly a week ago now, when he met Ty in San Francisco. As he got within striking distance he started to relax a little. Even the place names of the small towns he passed through seemed more genteel, less threatening. Cloverdale. Windsor. Roseland.

He stopped for gas at a Chevron station on the outskirts of Santa Rosa, aware of figures in the shadows as he filled up. A couple of bikers pulled in behind him and he ducked back in the car, tucking the Sig into his jeans and covering it with his jacket. He didn't want to be ambushed, but equally he didn't want to take a bullet from an overly paranoid gas station attendant who'd spotted the gun and thought he was going to rob them. But the bikers didn't even glance in his direction as they grabbed a couple of six-packs from the fridge and made their way back out.

The traffic thickened as he neared the city, and soon he was pulling up to a toll booth on the Golden Gate Bridge. He'd made it into the city without incident.

★ ★ ★

Fifteen minutes later, as he rounded the corridor in the hospital, heading for Ty's room, Lock guessed that things weren't about to stay that way. Four cops and a couple of medical staff were clustered round what Lock guessed was the door leading into Ty's room. For a moment Lock froze, fearing the worst, then he saw Ty's head above the melee. He was fully dressed and engaged in a heated discussion with one of the cops.

'Sir, we're under orders to make sure that you stay safe,' the cop was saying.

'You think I can't take care of myself? Is that

244

what you're saying?' came Ty's belligerent reply.
Like Lock, Ty had what the Marine Corps had
designated a 'problem with authority', which had
only deepened now that he'd entered civilian life.

At least Coburn had been as good as his word,
thought Lock, as Ty spotted him.

'Hey, Ryan, can you explain to these good
people that I'd like to leave now?' Ty said,
pushing his way through the cluster of bodies.

Lock felt a rush of relief at seeing his friend,
one of the few people he was able to trust
without question.

'Are you sure you're well enough to leave?' he
asked Ty.

'Man, have you looked at your own damn self
in the mirror?'

One of the medical staff, a young resident in
his mid-twenties, touched Lock's arm. 'You
don't look great.'

He smiled. 'I've had about four hours' sleep in
the last twenty-four.'

'I can relate to that,' said the resident.

'And how do you cope?'

'Coffee and, if it's really bad, a shot of B12.'

'Then hook me up,' Lock said. He nodded at
Ty. 'Is he really well enough to leave?'

'As long as he's at home taking it easy, he
should be fine.'

Lock clasped Ty's good shoulder. 'I'll make
sure of it,' he said.

Together they had a fighting chance of finding
Reaper and his posse. But to do that, Lock knew
they had to go back to the source.

47

After a long drive and a few more snatched hours of sleep in the car, Lock and Ty pulled up next to the former Prager residence out in Lancaster. It lay in a street of foreclosed houses with yellowing, weed-infested lawns and boarded-up windows. Even amid such generalised misery and misfortune, the house gave out a vibe all of its own. Lock, however, was more concerned with the fact that Ty had insisted on them taking his car. Given that a place like Lancaster was prime territory for white supremacist skinhead gangs, and therefore, by extension, for the Nazi Low Riders, a purple classic car was not an ideal choice.

On the drive there they had debated their next move. Lock had admitted to Ty that although there were a lot of threads, nothing pulled them all together. He therefore felt it was best to go back to the beginning, back to Prager's investigation. Ty wasn't sure it was the right thing to be doing, but equally he wasn't sure what else they could do, so he'd agreed to go with Lock's hazy outline.

Next door to where the Pragers lived, a woman was packing her kids into the car. She kept on glancing over at their car.

'I'll go talk to her,' Lock said. 'You keep the pimp-mobile running in case she thinks you're a white slaver.'

Ty flipped him the bird as the woman slammed the rear passenger door on the two kids and hurried to get in herself.

'Ma'am? Excuse me?' Lock jogged the last few yards towards her. 'Ma'am?'

'Why can't you people just leave us alone?' she shouted. 'We don't have any money!'

Clearly, the much-vaunted economic recovery had not made it as far as Lancaster just yet.

Lock noticed the lack of a For Sale sign in her yard. He put up his hands. 'Ma'am, I just wanted to ask you about your former neighbours.'

'Even better,' she said, rolling her eyes. 'A reporter.'

'No, ma'am, I'm trying to understand a few things about what happened to them.'

'You're a private investigator?'

Lock stopped, deciding to tell the truth. 'Aaron was my godson. I hadn't seen his mom or dad for a few years after they moved out west.'

The woman reached in and turned on the engine so the kids could get the benefit of the air con, then she took a step towards Lock. 'I'm sorry. I thought . . . '

'It's OK. I'd be suspicious under the circumstances as well.'

'I'm not sure how I can help you though.'

'You lived next door to them.'

'Yes, but that's kind of it.'

'I heard that Aaron fell in with a bad crowd.'

'Not exactly difficult round here.' She sighed.

'Kids at school?'

'Maybe a few of them. There's a couple of those skinhead gangs round here. I think he

247

started hanging out with one of them.'

'You know which one?'

'I don't know the names. But I could tell you where they like to hang out. There's a McDonald's down on Challenger Way, I've seen 'em there.'

'What about Mrs Prager — Janet?'

'I only really got to know her before . . . They said her husband was an undercover agent?'

'That's right. For the ATF.'

The woman looked away, then spoke again. 'You know, it's so weird.'

'What is?'

The woman worried at her wedding band, twisting and turning it on her finger. 'I'm not sure I should be telling you this.'

Lock moved closer. 'Listen, it's OK. No one can hurt them now.' He clasped his hands together, mirroring the woman's body language. 'I really need some closure,' he added.

The woman studied her driveway, and nodded silently. 'The last time I saw her, she was hammered.'

'Janet? Drunk?' Lock was surprised. Ken's wife had never been a drinker.

'Yeah, as a skunk. I took her in. Tried to get some coffee into her. I didn't want her son seeing her in that state.'

'Something had upset her?'

'She told me that she thought her husband was having an affair. I didn't know he was undercover. All she said was that it was someone he'd met through work.'

Lock took in a quick breath, glancing back

over his shoulder at the Pragers' old house, the paint peeling from the eaves, the gutters choked with leaves. This changed everything.

Inside the car, the woman's kids were starting to squabble, and Lock knew his time was about up.

'She mention a name?' he asked.

The woman sighed. 'Not unless 'that blonde bitch' is a name. She said that Ken had gotten her pregnant.'

48

Chance sat in the back of a Toyota Camry rented the previous evening at San Francisco International Airport and watched as Glenn Love emerged, yawning, from his house, clambered into his work truck and backed out of his driveway. She noted the time, the make and model of the truck, the reg and the decal.

An hour later his wife, Amy, opened the blinds at the front of the house. Three-quarters of an hour after that she emerged with their two children. Chance grabbed her handheld video camera and taped them getting into their car and driving off. If they had to take the kids at the school, she didn't want any cases of mistaken identity. Killing someone was relatively straightforward. A kidnapping, however . . . well, a myriad things could go wrong.

Five minutes after Amy Love drove past them, Chance got out of the car and approached the house. She rang the bell, feigned surprise when no one answered and wandered round the back. There was no alarm system and no cameras. She noticed a plant pot near the back door. It was empty save an inch or two of mouldy compost. Lifting it up revealed a key — an unexpected bonus. It suddenly occurred to Chance that the key could cut out most of the risk if they were clever about how they approached this part of the operation.

The key fitted the rear door, and she stepped inside. Breakfast dishes lay stacked in the dishwasher; a copy of the *San Francisco Examiner* was spread out on the table. She moved quickly through the ground floor and entered the children's shared bedroom. She took several items of clothing and moved into a study-cum-office area in the hall with a desk and a filing cabinet. She jotted down Glenn and Amy's cell numbers from old bills, along with the number for the house landline. She also noted their social security numbers and a couple of other pieces of information. All this would come in handy too.

Satisfied that she'd gathered everything they'd need, she exited the house, placed the key back under the plant pot and walked casually back to the car. This time she got in the front and drove off. She'd return later when it was time to move on to the next stage of the plan.

★   ★   ★

'Fuck, man, does this guy ever leave the house?'

Cowboy drummed his fingers on the steering column. Next to him, Trooper kept his head in his copy of *Sports Illustrated*.

'He's probably not even awake yet.'

'It's nine thirty,' Cowboy said, staring across the road at the ivy-clad New England colonial which was the boyhood home and California residence of Supreme Court Justice Junius Holmes.

'So? He's old. He's probably in bed by nine.'

251

'Which means he should be up early. Old people need less sleep, don't they?'

'How the fuck should I know?'

Cowboy started to open his door. 'I'm gonna go take a peek.'

Just then a figure appeared at the gates. A man wearing tennis shorts, sneakers and a Harvard alumni T-shirt.

'See,' said Trooper. 'Patience.'

The man broke into a slow jog on spindly legs that looked barely able to support the rest of him.

'Holy shit, he might not live long enough for us to kill him.'

Trooper studied him from behind his magazine. 'You think he jogs this time every morning?'

'Guess so. Why, what are you thinking?'

'Well, we were planning on shooting him, right?'

Cowboy shrugged. 'That's usually the quickest, most efficient way of killing someone.'

'Draws a lot of attention too. Which, if you think about it, is something we don't necessarily need.'

'Where you taking this?'

Trooper grinned. 'You'll see.'

49

'Hey, I've heard about deep cover, but that's something else. You sure?' Ty asked, manoeuvring the Lincoln down another street of shattered sub-prime dreams.

'That's what she said Janet told her.'

Lock was finding it hard to reconcile the neighbour's revelation with what he remembered about Ken and Janet's marriage. They'd always seemed like such a solid couple. He guessed you never really knew what went on behind closed doors.

'Kind of explains one thing,' Ty said.

'What's that?'

'Why there's no mention of this chick in any of Prager's reports back to his bosses. I mean, you go undercover and fall into bed with a suspect, that's one thing, might even be taken that you're taking the job seriously. But then you go and get her pregnant? Damn! You imagine the kind of fun a defence attorney would have with that?'

'You'd be lucky to keep your badge,' Lock said.

'And your pension.'

Lock stared out of the window. By the looks of where Aaron's friends were living, they were surrounded by people clinging on by their fingernails.

'That's not the full explanation though, it can't be,' said Lock. Something about the whole

253

scenario was chewing away at him.

Ty pulled on to a wider street, this one with more commercial property. On their left was a gas station, on their right a couple of fast-food joints. One of them was the one mentioned by the neighbour as a favourite hang-out for one of the local skinhead gangs. They'd head back here after visiting the school.

Lock rubbed his eyes, wishing that his lack of sleep wasn't making it so hard for him to think clearly.

'You know, at Pelican Bay I got a glimpse of how seductive the whole white supremacist rap could be.'

Ty sideways-glanced at Lock as he drove. 'You got something you want to tell me?'

A pick-up truck pulled up alongside with two middle-aged white guys in it. They stared menacingly at Ty until Lock glared over at them.

'It's almost like a cult,' he continued. 'They have a way of seeing the world. They have a purpose. An ideology. And it's a powerful one. Otherwise how would a whole country have been sucked in back in the 1930s, so much so that they were prepared to slaughter millions of innocent people, women and children, pack them into gas chambers?'

'You don't think Ken went over to the dark side, do you?'

'No, otherwise why would they have killed him? An inside man with the ATF would have been a wet dream for them. But what if he was conflicted about the whole deal?'

'So he was giving his bosses some of it, but not

all of it,' Ty said slowly.

'Maybe.'

'I still don't buy it, Ryan.'

Lock looked out at the down-at-heel blue-collar neighbourhood. Even with crisp blue California skies overhead there was something depressing about it.

'Ken was a veteran agent, right?'

Ty nodded.

'Yet here he was still out in the field, while his bosses were all cosy back at base. Ken was taking all the risks and getting what in return?'

'Yeah,' said Ty slowly. 'You're reaching.'

'The Aryan Brotherhood are great at telling people that they deserve better, that somehow they're being cheated. All it needed was for a couple of seeds to be planted. Then Ken falls for this woman. Hard.' Lock rubbed at his face again, closing his eyes for a second. 'I'd say that's all any man would need to start questioning where his loyalties lay.'

They pulled into the entrance of the local high school. Kids were streaming out, the older ones heading to their cars. A few were checking out the Lincoln 66. A fat white kid sporting a dorag and a soul patch stopped in his tracks as Ty lowered the window.

'Sweet ride,' he said.

Ty beamed. 'Kid's got taste.'

'See what I mean about people getting confused?' Lock said. 'He's white, but he thinks he's Snoop Dog.'

'We have the more interesting culture, that's all.' Ty leaned out of the window towards the teenager. 'Yo! Where's the principal's office?'

The kid pointed to a side entrance.

Over in a corner of the parking lot, Lock spotted a bunch of other youths. Hair cut short and wearing English Doc Marten boots, they were scowling at the car and, in particular, Ty.

50

They stood outside the principal's office, unable to escape that sense of being back at high school themselves.

'Bet this takes you back,' Lock said to Ty.

'Déjà vu all over again, baby.'

'Me too. I spent more time here than in class.'

The door opened and a severe-looking African-American woman in female school principal uniform of long heavy skirt and ruffled blouse stepped out. A brief thought crossed Lock's mind, that he'd rather go back to the SHU at Pelican Bay than spend too much time in her office.

Her opening line didn't exactly fill him with joy either: 'I have three and a half thousand young people to look after, so would you gentlemen kindly explain what you want?'

'May we step into your office, ma'am?' Lock asked.

Ty shot him one of his trademarked 'Are you out of your freakin' mind?' looks.

The principal stood aside.

'Nice move,' Ty whispered as they stepped inside. 'Who knows if we'll ever get out alive again?'

She gestured for them to sit. They did. She didn't say anything, just stared at them — a tactic beloved of salesmen, interrogators and school principals. When neither Lock nor Ty said anything, she looked at her watch.

Lock swallowed. Yup, definitely worse than the SHU at Pelican Bay.

'Aaron Prager was a student at your school,' he said at last.

She didn't give any of the standard responses, or at least any of the responses Lock had anticipated. She didn't say, 'I can't discuss current or former students.' She didn't say, 'What's your interest in Aaron Prager?' She didn't even say, 'Yes, it was a terrible tragedy, he was a fine young man.' What she did first was stare at Lock's right hip, where his 226 bulged under his jacket. Then she picked up her phone.

'Yes, Jessica, could you call 911 and ask them to respond to the school?'

Then she calmly put the receiver down.

'Now, unless you gentlemen can show me some bona fide credentials, which doesn't mean some private investigator's certificate you scammed off the internet, I'd like you to not only leave my office, but to leave school property immediately, and never return. Nor should you contact either me or anyone else at this school by any other means. Do you understand me?'

Lock nodded. Ty nodded. They both rose, and almost in a daze walked swiftly out of her office, down several corridors and out of the school gates.

Back in her office, the principal lifted her phone once more.

'Jessica, you may call the police back and assure them that it was a false alarm.'

258

* * *

Out in the parking lot, Ty turned to Lock. 'What was that?'

'I don't know, but if I ever land a job which requires the ability to garner total cooperation, I'm kicking you to the kerb and hiring her.'

Ty opened the driver's door, then stopped. 'Goddamnit.'

'What is it?'

Ty hunkered down and rubbed at the paintwork. Someone had taken something sharp, keys probably, down the side of the Continental, leaving a thin grey scar.

Lock looked up to see the white Snoop-wannabe staring at them.

'It was some of those Hammer Skin kids,' he told them. 'They give everyone a hard time.'

'You saw them?' Lock asked.

The boy shrugged. 'Wasn't like they were trying to hide doing it.'

'The cops are on their way,' Lock said. 'Will you tell them what you told us?'

The boy smiled. 'Are you out of your mind? I like having my teeth in my head. Listen, bro, I got three more years in this dump, then I'm outta here. Anyways, what are the cops gonna do when the Hammer Skins are their own kids?' The boy looked beyond Lock to the school. 'What did the principal say?'

'Nada.'

'That figures. She's scared of them too. She tried to make a stand a few years back and they put a pipe-bomb under her car.'

259

Lock saw Ty perk up to the extent that he lost interest in the damage to his car. He stepped towards the boy. 'The cops investigate?'

'What did I just say? No one wants any trouble.' The boy airquoted the last three words.

'So the skinheads do what they want?'

'If you don't mess with 'em, they leave you alone. For the most part.'

'What grade you in?'

'Ninth.'

Same as Aaron. Even in a school with such a large number of students, Lock knew that they'd just caught a break. Rather than go the direct route, he took a different approach.

'I guess some of the kids hang out with these skinhead gangs to stop themselves getting picked on.'

'Some, yeah.'

'You friends with any of those kids?'

'Not once they join up,' the boy said, spitting on the ground and jamming his hands into his pockets. 'Man, why don't you just ask me what you want to ask me?'

'We're trying to find out what happened to Aaron Prager.'

The boy choked back a grin. 'I can help you with that. He got motherfucking shot.'

Ty moved in on the boy. 'Have a little bit of respect. You wanna be ghetto, you'd better understand, you step to us wrong and you know what's gonna happen.'

The kid's eyes fell back to the sidewalk. 'I'm sorry. I didn't mean anything by it.'

Lock could see that what the boy aspired to,

Ty simply was, with all that entailed. He decided to let Ty handle him.

'Did you ever speak to Aaron after he hooked up with this gang?' Ty asked.

The boy's smirk was back, but there was a touch of something else there too. Lock guessed at a creeping understanding of how people could change, and not always for the better.

'The only time he spoke to me was to call me a wigger.' The boy kicked at the ground. 'He used to be a nice guy.'

'Do they have a leader?'

'Roach, I guess.'

'What's he look like?'

'Big sucker. Shaves twice a day. You'll know him when you see him.'

'He a student here too?'

'No, he got kicked out last year.'

'Where can we find him?'

The boy gave Ty the name of the same fast-food restaurant as the one provided by the Pragers' neighbour.

'Thanks for your help, bro,' Ty said, bumping fists with the boy.

'Just don't mention my name, OK?'

Lock and Ty got back into the Lincoln, leaving the kid on the sidewalk. Lock waved a thanks but the kid was too busy jamming his headphones into his ears. Lock didn't blame him. If he'd grown up here, he'd have wanted to shut out the world too.

As they pulled away from the school, Ty sideways-glanced at Lock. 'This Roach kid sounds like a real charmer.'

Lock puffed out his cheeks. 'Big fish in a small pond. Maybe if we drain the water a little we can get him flapping.'

'You think he's caught up in this?' Ty asked.

'I can definitely see him giving up Aaron. I'm not so sure about anything else. Although, if he wanted to make a name for himself, then who knows.'

Lock fell silent for a moment, his jaw clenched tight.

'I'll promise you one thing though, Tyrone.'

'What's that, brother?'

'He's gonna tell us everything he knows about what went down.'

51

The boy they'd spoken to at the school was right, Roach was hard to miss. Six foot plus and maybe a hundred and eighty pounds. He wasn't up there with Reaper or the other members of the AB, but he would hold his own in most prisons, which in Lock's view was exactly where he was heading.

He greeted Tyrone with a faux-menacing 'What you looking at, nigger?'

Tyrone's expression read mock-offended but he kept his hands by his side as Roach's compatriots snickered. He and Lock hadn't exactly expected a ticker-tape parade, and they weren't going to be disappointed.

'I get it,' said Ty. 'This is the part where I say, 'Who you callin' a nigger?' And then you say, 'I'm callin' you a nigger, nigger.' And then I throw a punch at you. And that gives you and your cronies here the perfect excuse to triple-team me and beat me to a pulp.'

Ty's speech seemed to throw Roach. He looked to his fellow skinheads for a reaction, but they seemed equally perplexed.

'Except,' Ty went on, 'there's a couple of problems. One, I've been called all kinds of names. And you know that saying about sticks and stones . . . ' He pulled down his T-shirt to expose the fresh wound on his shoulder. 'And I been shot too. Recently. You ever been shot?'

263

Roach looked at his cheerleaders. 'Nigger's crazy.'

Lock eyeballed Roach. 'Answer the man's question.' He parted his jacket just enough that the butt of his 226 was on view. 'You ever been shot?'

Roach backed up a step. 'Fuck you, nigger-lover.'

Before anyone had a chance to react, Lock's gun was in Roach's face. Roach's mouth shaped to say something, then he changed his mind.

'Get in the car,' Lock whispered to him.

Roach's bravado was very slowly ebbing away. Easy to be top dog in a town like this, thought Lock, especially when you were big and stupid.

'You're playing in the big leagues now, Roach.'

Roach reacted to hearing his name. 'Who are you?'

The longer the delay, the more chance someone would call the cops, Lock knew, smashing his gun into the side of Roach's face. His buddies did some sidewalk dancing and shouting, but none of them made a move to help their fallen leader.

Ty grabbed Roach, dug both thumbs under his jaw and propelled him towards the Lincoln. Together, he and Lock bundled him into the back. Lock climbed in with him, giving Roach a few digs of his elbow for good measure.

'You guys are dead!' Roach shouted.

Ty caught Lock's eye. This was going to be fun.

★ ★ ★

They drove for more than an hour in total, heading due east towards the desert. The longer they drove, the more Roach's self-confidence peeled away in layers. He quickly moved from threats to a sullen silence, finally settling on a couple of half-hearted pleas for leniency, all of which were met with studied silence by Lock and Ty.

As the traffic on the highway thinned out, Lock finally spoke.

'You bring the shovel?'

Ty glanced in the rear-view for the briefest of seconds.

'In the trunk with the quicklime.'

Five minutes later, Ty pulled the Lincoln off the road and they hauled an unwilling Roach out. They walked him for ten minutes, hitting a rise and putting them all out of sight of the highway. Every time Roach tried to look over his shoulder, Lock prodded him with the gun.

'This looks as good a spot as any,' Ty said.

'Get down on your knees,' Lock ordered.

Roach was crying now. Big mucus-filled sobs. Just like Aaron Prager. Lock contemplated starting out by cutting off one of Roach's many Nazi-themed tattoos. He jammed his gun into the back of Roach's neck.

'This is bullshit, man. You're going to kill me because I called someone a name?'

'Oh, I'm sure you've done a lot worse. Sure there's been more than a few blacks, or Hispanics, or gay folk, or people who just looked different, who've run into you and your little jerk-off crew. Haven't there?' The Sig was ready to fire. He withdrew it from Roach's neck. 'I'm going to use this, but I don't want any contact burns. It makes the gun easier to trace if they find you.'

Taking a step back, Lock aimed the Sig six feet to Roach's right, then pulled the trigger. Roach let out a choked scream and, judging by the smell, emptied his bladder and bowels simultaneously.

'Damn, that's rank. You want to get a bit more variety into your diet there, son,' Ty said.

Roach turned to them, tears streaming down his face. 'You motherfuckers! If you're going to do this, just do it, OK?'

'Why shouldn't we torture you a little bit first, like your friends did with Aaron?' Ty said. 'Eyes front, cockroach.'

Roach complied.

Lock raised the Sig again. 'Now, you have one chance and one chance only to tell us who you ratted Aaron out to.'

Roach sucked some snot back up his nose. He shuddered a sob. 'He never told us his real name.'

'He must have called himself something.'

'Cowboy.'

'What did he look like?'

'Like six two. Bigger than average. Real fit. He was in the military.'

Another look between Lock and Ty.

'Ex-military?'

'No, still serving. He was trying to get us to sign up too. He said that was the best shot the movement had. For as many of us as possible to join up, get the training and then use it when the time came.'

'What unit was he in?'

'He never said.'

'Infantry? Air Force? Navy? What?' Lock pressed the Sig into Roach's back.

'He just said something about Special Forces.'

Lock noticed Ty's wry grin. Every wannabe Walter Mitty character — and the white supremacists had plenty of those — claimed some kind of connection to Special Forces.

'Did he say where he was based?'

'He said they came from all over, but he was down in Coronado.'

'You got the Seals down there, far as I remember anyway,' said Ty.

Lock jabbed the gun into Roach's flesh. 'That ring a bell?'

'No. I swear.'

'So this Cowboy guy came down and hung out round here?'

'Yeah.'

'After you told him about Aaron and who his father was?'

'No, I met him before that.'

So much for Aaron dicking about on the wrong internet forums. The Feds had called that one wrong. Lock could see Ty thinking the same thing.

'He come on his own?'

'Apart from one time. There was a woman with him.'

'Catch her name?' Lock asked, his attention sharpening.

'Chance,' said Roach.

Lock sighed. Another street name.

'What was she like?'

'Like maybe twenty-five, twenty-six. Blonde. Super-hot. Nice rack.'

'She military as well?'

'No, but her father had been. She talked about him some. He was a martyr to the cause. You know, like David Lane and those guys in the Order.'

'He was in the Order?'

'No, he came after those guys. She said he was up in Pelican Bay.'

Lock breathed in sharply. 'She have a name for him?'

'No.'

'Think hard, Roach,' Lock said, pushing so hard into Roach's neck with his gun that he could see a welt starting to form.

'Cowboy called him something. It was kinda cool.'

'Reaper?'

'Yeah,' said Roach. 'That was it.'

52

Cowboy woke with a start. The engine was idling, and he was in the passenger seat. He started to sit up. 'What the hell's going on?'

Before he could get an answer, Trooper floored it and Cowboy was flung backwards.

'He's up ahead.'

'Jogging?'

'Taking a walk. You know that little rise we came over when we got here?'

'Yeah,' said Cowboy, hauling himself up so he could see through the front of the windshield.

'Well, right now, he should be just about over that.'

The speedometer of their SUV crept past fifty, then sixty. Either side of the road was grass and trees. They had to make sure they stayed on the road. And so did the man up ahead of them.

'Keep the speed up but the revs down,' Cowboy said. 'He hears the engine, he'll jump out of the way.'

'OK, but he's probably going to think it's kids, not someone who's aiming for him.'

★ ★ ★

Junius Holmes heard the car behind him as he crested the hill. There was the road and then three feet of asphalt beyond the white line where it was safe to walk. Anyone passing him, and

269

recognising him, might have guessed he was thinking about weighty matters. A case the Supreme Court had before it, or what he was going to say at a seminar he was to give shortly at Harvard about law and philosophy. In fact, he was thinking about what he was going to have for dinner. Even a justice of the highest court in the land had to eat, he told himself. He was thinking chicken, with mashed potato and broccoli.

Ahead of him there was a low roar — a big rig struggling to get up the sharp gradient. It wasn't a road ideally suited to such a wide vehicle, but there was rarely much traffic here and it would be on the opposite side to where he was walking, so he didn't deviate from his path.

★ ★ ★

The SUV was up to seventy now. They couldn't see Holmes, so unless he had ducked into the woods to take a leak, he was just ahead of them over the hill.

'OK,' Cowboy said to Trooper, 'keep that speed.'

'Dude, you're worse than my ex-wife. Shut the fuck up and let me do this.'

★ ★ ★

Junius glanced round and saw an SUV behind him. Life didn't go into slow motion. Instead, he froze like a rabbit for a second as the big rig which had climbed the hill shifted up a gear.

* * *

Cowboy could see Junius Holmes, but he could also see the driver of the big rig, who was shifting the path of his vehicle to avoid the pedestrian.

'Do it then, man!' he shouted at Trooper. 'Do it now!'

53

They left Roach in the desert, naked and bleeding. A less than fitting punishment for him, thought Lock, but it would have to suffice. Ty had argued the merits of throwing him into a cactus bush, but Lock had countered by pointing out that most of the cacti out here were endangered species which didn't deserve having a low-life such as Roach thrown at them.

They had thought about taking Roach up to San Francisco themselves (where Lock wanted to talk to Coburn) and handing him over to the Feds there, but they wanted away from this part of the state as fast as they could. No, Lock decided, once they had some distance they would put a call in to the authorities. If they got lucky with the timing, by the time Roach found his way back home he would have someone from federal law enforcement there to take him in for questioning about his role in the death of the Pragers. But at least Roach had been useful, Lock thought: he'd established the identity and parentage of the woman who was almost certainly Ken's killer.

They pulled in to an off-site lot next to LAX, parked the Lincoln at the back and caught a shuttle bus to the terminal, where Lock used his credit card to get them two seats on the next flight up to San Francisco. Because they would have to check their firearms at the check-in desk,

Lock made sure to wipe off any residue of the Sig's contact with Roach's head before he stowed it in its lockable carry case.

Inside the terminal, they headed to the Virgin America counter, filled in the appropriate paperwork and checked their bags. Then, boarding passes in hand, they made for security, both, thankfully, passing through the detector without incident. A swipe might well have showed positive for cordite, and that wasn't a conversation they wanted to have with a member of the Transport Security Administration, whom Lock regarded with an informed contempt.

Instead, they watched as a ninety-year-old woman in a wheelchair was led into the Perspex search box and asked repeatedly to stand so that they could wand her. Lock, who was gathering his wallet and belt from the end of the conveyor, quickly lost his patience. The door leading out of the Perspex box was ajar, so he turned in the direction of the female TSA officer as she said for a third time, 'Ma'am, do you think you could stand up, just for a few seconds?' and said, 'Miss?', taking a leaf from the TSA officer's book and being an asshole, politely, with a smile on his face.

Ty nudged Lock. 'What about the grey man?' he said, referring to Lock's belief that a good close protection operative had a duty not to call attention to himself.

Lock ignored him.

The TSA officer looked over. 'Can I help you, sir?'

'Does she look like she can stand?' Lock asked, still polite.

'Are you travelling with her?'

The elderly woman opened her mouth.

'She's my aunt,' he said firmly. 'Now, we have several hours until our plane actually departs, so I'd like to see your supervisor and register a formal complaint regarding your behaviour towards an elderly, not to mention disabled, passenger.'

The TSA officer flushed under the two inches of make-up she'd plastered over her face. 'There's really no need — '

'I'd say asking someone in a wheelchair to stand three times means there's every need. Now, will you call your supervisor, or shall I?'

Lock kept his tone even and low, like a parent explaining to a toddler why they shouldn't run with scissors.

'I'll just run the wand and then you can both be on your way,' the officer said, hurriedly.

Lock sighed. The TSA had caught a lot of flak since their formation. They had some good people — ex-law enforcement and military — but they also had more than their fair share of people who couldn't read a leaflet without moving their lips and who confused brusqueness with thoroughness.

The officer waved her wand vaguely in the elderly woman's direction. 'Thank you, ma'am.'

Lock stepped forward, took the woman's wheelchair by its handles and pushed it out of the box as the female officer went to look for someone else to give a hard time to. Maybe a nun, he thought, or a boy scout. Someone who fitted the profile of crazed terrorist bent on bringing the western world to its knees.

Once they were well clear of the security area, the elderly woman craned her neck back to get a view of her rescuer. 'Thank you, young man,' she said, sweetly. 'Those people are such assholes.'

★ ★ ★

At their gate, a knot of passengers and ground crew were standing in front of a plasma screen tuned to a twenty-four-hour news station. Lock and Ty shuffled to a halt, hoping that they weren't the main feature, but no one gave them a second glance. Instead everyone stared intently at the screen as a news update rolled along the bottom: 'Supreme Court Justice Junius Holmes Killed In Multiple Vehicle Auto Smash'.

Lock edged closer to a middle-aged cleaning woman holding a mop.

'When'd this happen?' he asked her.

She shrugged, grabbed her mop and bucket and shuffled away.

Lock was reaching for his cell as it rang. Carrie.

'You see the news?' she asked him.

'Just now.'

'Well, we're getting early word that it wasn't an accident.'

This didn't make sense to Lock. These kind of incidents usually took days of piecing together. For law enforcement to be hinting at foul play so early in an auto smash was almost unheard of.

Even if it did involve someone like Junius Holmes, who despite his WASPy name had made his reputation getting down and dirty in the trenches as a prosecutor in the Department of Justice before being appointed by the new President to serve on the Supreme Court.

'Why do they think that?' he asked.

'Because of reports from the scene. A truck driver who got tangled up in it said there was an SUV containing two white males who'd aimed straight for Holmes.'

'Maybe the driver lost control of the car?'

'Oh, he lost control OK.'

'So why do the authorities think it was deliberate?' Lock asked, taking a few more steps away from the throng staring up at the screen.

Ty edged away with him. 'Carrie says they don't think it was an accident,' Lock said to him.

'Ryan, you still there?'

'Yeah, I'm here.'

'The two white guys in the SUV. One died at the scene. The other fled. The one who died was sporting a swastika tattoo.'

'Neither of them female?'

'No. Why?'

'Well, it turns out that the woman who pulled the trigger on Prager was almost certainly Reaper's daughter.'

Carrie made a low whistling noise down the phone. 'That would explain a few things. But how did she persuade everyone else to get involved in taking that kind of risk to spring him?'

'I'd guess, judging from something else I've

found out about Ken, that she had her methods.'

'What?'

'Well, there's no way of knowing for sure, but we think she was sleeping with Ken even though we think she knew who he was right from the get go.'

Carrie was quiet for a moment as she digested this. 'Poor Janet,' she said at last.

'Yeah,' Lock agreed. 'Can you see what you can get on Reaper's daughter for us?'

'I'm on it. Anything else?'

'Do we know if Junius Holmes ever went after any of the white supremacist groups?'

'Better than that. He helped put away Reaper in the first place.'

Lock could hear someone speaking to Carrie.

'Ryan, hang on.'

Lock's eyes tracked back to the TV screen and the carnage at the scene of the accident, then Carrie came back on the line.

'Got one more thing for you. When Jalicia was coming up through the ranks at the DOJ, guess who her mentor was.'

Onscreen, a body was being loaded into the back of an ambulance.

'Junius Holmes,' said Lock.

54

Glenn Love waved the truck into the rear of the Bureau of Street and Sewer Repair depot on Cesar Chavez Street. The driver climbed down along with two other members of the crew and Glenn slapped them each on the back.

He went into the tiny office and started filling out the paperwork. People called up to report a pothole or some other piece of sidewalk or road that needed to be fixed, it went into the system, someone was sent out to take a look, and within forty-eight hours it had to be repaired. Like the mail, cracks in the asphalt and holes in the road kept appearing. It was an unending task, like painting the Golden Gate Bridge.

Same shit, different day.

All that said, there were parts of the job Glenn enjoyed. Getting to work outside rather than in an office, at least when the weather was halfway decent. The camaraderie he had with the rest of the guys. The feeling that, even though no one really ever came up and thanked him for holding up the traffic while they did their work, he did actually do something that improved life for people in the city. Not like some of the assholes in BMWs or Mercedes or Lexi who gave his crew the finger as they drove past, annoyed that they'd lost a full sixty seconds waiting in traffic. No, Glenn felt like he made a difference.

Paperwork done, he left the depot and

clambered into his five-year-old car for the thirty-minute commute back home. He drove past the Presidio, then took the Golden Gate Bridge. The bay was clear of fog and the air felt warm. Having grown up in this area, Glenn still got a jolt of excitement from the city, especially on a day like today.

As he cleared the bridge, a couple of Hell's Angels cut round his car, both riding fat-boy Harleys with ape hanger handlebars. A regular enough sight, they sped off, diving in and out of traffic, then they were gone from sight.

Glenn didn't notice the vehicle that had followed him all the way from the depot. Nor did he see the occupants. After all, who would possibly want to follow Glenn Love?

But the car kept trailing him, all the way home. As he turned into his driveway, it kept on going. He didn't notice it then either. He was too busy gathering up his stuff from the front passenger seat.

He took off his boots and put them in the trunk. Then he walked up the driveway and through into his house by the back door. His wife, Amy, had her back to him, washing her hands in the sink. He crept up on her and slid his hands around her waist.

She jumped. 'Glenn! You frightened the life out of me.'

'Got your heart racing a little faster, did I?'

'You are such an ass,' she said, but with a smile on her face.

His hands slipped down her waist a little. 'I was thinking maybe we could get away this weekend. Leave the kids with your mother.'

She turned, kissed him on the lips. 'We have that thing at the Spicers'. Then Patrick has soccer on Saturday. And Rebecca has a play date over at the Myers' on Sunday. Maybe another weekend?'

'Sure.'

'Oh, come here,' she said, pulling him towards her for another kiss.

Patrick, their eight-year-old, came in, bouncing his soccer ball.

'Hey, tiger,' Glenn said, breaking away from his wife and tousling his son's hair. 'Now what did Mom say about having the ball in the house?'

Patrick sighed. Eight going on eighteen. 'I'll take it outside.'

Glenn made his way to the refrigerator and pulled out a beer.

'Where's Becky?'

'Up in her room.'

Glenn popped open his beer. 'Now Patrick's out in the back yard . . . '

Amy turned round and dried off her hands. 'What *is* up with you?'

'Must be the weather.'

★   ★   ★

Outside, the car circled the block and parked a few houses down from the Loves' house.

A cell phone rang.

'I have a date for you,' said a voice.

'When?' Chance asked.

'The fifth.'

Today was the evening of the first. The fifth was about as fast as they could have hoped for.

'What's the venue?'

'The one you'd expect.'

This was good news. It also meant that they would have to act fast.

Chance ended the call, then dialled another number.

'We got three days,' she said, leaning forward and eyeing the house.

The family inside was blissfully unaware of the storm gathering less than a hundred yards away. Unaware of how life could be changed for ever by one single event. Like Chance had been when Reaper went to prison for his beliefs.

'Tonight?' Reaper asked her.

'Yes. Tonight.'

'Means we're gonna have to keep 'em for three days and four nights. That's a long time.'

Chance kept her eyes on the house as a soccer ball rolled down the drive and a little boy chased after it, followed by Glenn Love, who scooped up his son and then the ball.

'Maybe we won't keep 'em,' she said.

55

A sea of blue uniforms greeted Lock and Ty outside San Francisco International Airport. The last time Lock had seen such a show of strength by law enforcement was in the weeks following 9/11. Cars, limos and taxis lingering for more than a few moments at the kerbside were being swiftly dealt with.

Amid the crush of stressed-out passengers, Lock spotted Carrie piloting the mini-van towards them. He and Ty forced their way through the crowd. They clambered inside and Carrie edged out into the traffic. She leaned over and touched Lock's hand.

'You want me to drive?' he offered.

'Relax, Ryan,' Carrie said, picking her way past a cab with its trunk open, the driver loading luggage as a burly cop screamed at him to pick up the pace, 'I got it. How did you get on?'

'Nothing we can use to find Reaper. But you know how you wanted me not to keep things from you?'

'Yeah,' said Carrie.

'Well, the Nazi Low Riders have a contract out on me and Ty.'

Carrie hit the brakes and honked her horn as a pick-up truck cut her off. Lock put his hands on the windscreen and braced. Carrie behind the wheel was only marginally less stressful than babysitting Reaper.

'Then maybe we should go back to New York,' she said. 'The network can get someone else to cover the funeral.'

Lock closed his eyes, trying to let go of some of the tension of the last forty-eight hours. 'It's gone too far for that now. Reaper's my responsibility.'

★   ★   ★

Soon they were out of the worst of the airport tangle of traffic and on the Bayshore Freeway, which would take them into San Francisco. There was a low fog rising from the water but, up above, the sky was clear. Lock sat back, allowing himself to relax a little.

'So, you want to know what I dug up on Reaper's daughter?' Carrie asked as they rolled along. 'Chance is a street name. Her real name is Freya Vaden.'

Lock opened his eyes. 'Not Hays?'

'Mom didn't want anything to do with Frank Hays after he went to jail. She moved herself and little Freya to the Inland Empire.'

'Where's that exactly?'

'Los Angeles, right where we just were,' Ty said.

'So how'd she hook back up with Dad?' Lock asked.

Carrie shook her head. 'No idea. But clearly she got curious. It wouldn't take much digging to find out he was in jail.'

'So Chance grew up in California?'

'Until she was about twelve, when Mom died

of a drugs overdose. No grandparents around, so she went into foster care. Ended up with a family called the Grisaldis.'

'You're shitting me, right?' Ty said.

'What?' asked Lock.

'You never heard about the Grisaldi case? They fostered dozens of kids. Molested them too. Papa Grisaldi was convicted about four years ago and sent to Corcoran.'

Lock knew that Corcoran was one of California's heavy-duty prisons. Not as hardcore as Pelican Bay, but still pretty tough. 'How long did he last there?' he asked Carrie.

'Less than a week,' she said. 'He was murdered by a two-man Aryan Brotherhood hit squad.'

Ty leaned forward from the back seat. 'And here's the kicker, Ryan. Papa Grisaldi was a black man.'

'And her long-lost father's a race warrior. Perfect,' said Lock, pinching at the bridge of his nose. 'So we got her psychology. But how do we find her?'

'I'm not so sure that we will. All the regular checks seem to indicate that she dropped off the grid some time last year.' Her eyes still on the road, Carrie dug in her bag and tossed over a wad of printouts. 'This is everything I have.'

Lock quickly riffled through the papers. He stopped at one particular page and held it up to Carrie. It was a crumpled colour printout of a young woman in her mid-twenties. 'This her?'

'Only picture I could find. Of course it was taken a few years back so she might have

284

changed her appearance since.'

Ty leaned forward and studied the picture of Chance. 'You can see how Prager got drawn in.'

Carrie laughed. 'Don't get your hopes up, Ty. Somehow I don't think you'd be her type.'

'No shit,' Ty said.

'You pass this on to the FBI?' Lock asked her.

'Via Coburn,' Carrie said.

'He's speaking to you?' Lock asked. 'He seems kind of pissed at me.'

Carrie's cell phone trilled. 'Speak of the devil,' she said, plucking it from her bag on the dash. She flipped it open and listened for a moment. 'OK, where?' she asked. There was another pause. 'What else?' she said, before killing the call and turning to Lock. 'They've had a sighting of Reaper. Travelling north on PCH about fifty south of us. California Highway Patrol stopped a vehicle he was travelling in. At least they think that's who it was.'

'North?' Ty said.

Carrie nodded.

'So why don't they have him in custody?' Lock demanded.

'He came out shooting, Coburn says. Destroyed the patrol car, and shot the two officers inside.'

Lock slammed the palm of his hand against the dash in frustration. 'He kill them?'

Carrie nodded. 'One of them. The other's pretty badly injured.'

Lock sighed. This sounded more like the Reaper he knew. Whatever he was planning, he clearly had no intention of going back to prison, even if it meant killing anyone who got in his way.

And there was something that worried Lock even more. Any fugitive looking to flee justice should have been heading south. But Reaper was heading north, straight towards them.

56

Carrie had a suite for her and Lock, and a room for Ty, booked at the Argonaut Hotel on Fisherman's Wharf. Pulling up on the street outside, she handed the keys to the valet, then headed up to the suite. The hotel itself was beautiful, with a hell of a view out across the bay to Alcatraz. These days, reflected Lock, he couldn't seem to avoid prisons.

As Carrie ordered some coffee and sandwiches to be sent up, Lock laid out the pictures Carrie had amassed of the key players on the nautically themed kingsize bed that dominated the room. There was one of Reaper. One of his daughter, Freya, aka Chance. One of Ken Prager. One of Jalicia Jones. And, finally, one of Junius Holmes. Three of them dead. Two on the run.

Ty put his cup of coffee down on the nightstand next to the bed. 'You getting anything?' he asked Lock, rubbing his injured shoulder.

'Not apart from the obvious.'

'Which is?'

'Junius Holmes had a track record of going after these guys. That's one score settled right there for Reaper. Ken — that's a slam-dunk too. And, Jalicia — revenge works as a motive for her as well, just like Coburn said.' Lock picked up the picture of Reaper, tapped the edge of the paper against the desk. 'So why the hell is he heading north when anyone in their right mind would either be staying put or moving south or east?' He shuffled the pictures around like he was playing three-card Monte, then looked up to see Carrie filtering back into the room from the bathroom.

She tapped him on the shoulder. 'Come on, Ryan, you need to get some rest.'

'I think we all do,' Ty said, with a grimace. Lock knew that his injured shoulder was playing him up.

He glanced back at the pictures. The clue to what was going on lay in front of him. But why couldn't he see it?

'You can play detective tomorrow,' said Carrie.

Lock stood up, gathered the faces into a pile and put them on the desk. Carrie was right. He was exhausted. Maybe some rest would clear his mind a little.

Carrie's cell rang again, Coburn's name flashing up.

'He wants to speak to you,' she said.

Lock took the phone from her. 'Reaper?' he asked.

'Maybe,' Coburn said. 'We got a tip-off a few minutes ago that someone saw an individual matching his description entering a building in the Tenderloin.'

'Credible witness?'

'Little old Vietnamese lady.'

'The Tenderloin would make sense,' Lock said slowly.

The Tenderloin had originally gained its name because cops patrolling its streets were paid more for the privilege, thus being able to afford a better cut of meat than their colleagues who patrolled more salubrious parts of the city. It was the kind of place where the mice wiped their feet on the way out of the apartment buildings. Now a haven for the destitute, deranged and the desperate, as well as a burgeoning influx of Vietnamese, most San Franciscans gave the relatively small area a wide berth, unless they had people visiting who wanted to pack in some gritty reality as well as the tour of Alcatraz and a snap of the Golden Gate. Given how paranoid the majority of residents were, not to mention the dim view they took of law enforcement, it was a place where a raid had the potential to go badly wrong.

Lock frowned as he worked through the implications. If they went in heavy, especially with racial tensions running high in the city and beyond, it could be the spark that provoked a riot. Even if they didn't go in heavy, these things had a habit of getting out of hand rapidly. Anyone in their right mind wouldn't want anything to do with such an operation unless they were being paid to do it.

'So, you want to tag along?' Coburn asked him.

'I didn't think you wanted me involved in this any more.'

There was a chuckle on the other end of the line. 'Like that's going to happen. At least this way I know where you are and what you're doing. Plus, you're good at sneaking around.

That's the kind of expertise we could use right now.'

There was a moment of silence on the other end of the line.

'Hey, it's up to you,' Coburn said.

'Don't worry, I'll be there,' Lock said, reaching for his gun.

57

Glenn Love woke to a dog barking next door. He rolled over and threw an arm over his wife, pulling her towards him, enjoying the warmth of her body. She cuddled into him and he closed his eyes.

A few seconds later he heard a noise downstairs like someone tapping against one of the windows. He disentangled himself from his wife.

'What is it?' she asked sleepily.

'Nothing, honey,' he said, getting out of bed.

She rolled over, grabbed a pillow from his side and snuggled into it as the sound came again, more distinct this time.

Glenn grabbed his pants from the laundry basket and put them on as his wife sat up.

'Glenn?'

'It's probably a bird or something. Go back to sleep, Amy.'

Downstairs there was another sound. Different from the tapping. Like wood splintering.

'Should I call 911?' Amy asked.

Glenn sighed. His heart rate was elevated a little, but he was more curious than scared. He was a big guy. And he was in his house. The last thing he needed was the cops turning out because something had worked its way inside the house and was trying to get back out. 'Let me see what it is first.'

Amy was wide awake now. The phone was next to her on the night stand. Waiting there, should they need it.

Glenn got down on his knees next to the bed. 'Just in case,' he said, retrieving the baseball bat from underneath the bed. Glenn had bought it from one of the guys on his crew. It was lead-weighted. The heft of it in his hands felt reassuring. He held it now with his right hand and tapped it on to the palm of his left like some old-school Irish cop with a night stick.

'Relax,' he said to Amy, slipping into a bad impersonation of a Boston accent. 'If it's a raccoon he's gonna regret he was ever born.'

Amy's smile faded as another sound came from somewhere downstairs. The creak of a floorboard? A footstep?

Glenn's heart rate was picking up pace now. He was hyper-alert.

But when you're hyper-alert, don't noises you might otherwise not register take on more sinister connotations?

Amy seemed to have fewer doubts. She reached over for the phone.

'Listen,' Glenn said, 'I holler, then you call 911. OK?'

He walked slowly out of the bedroom, carrying the bat. Out in the hallway he wondered why he was trying to be so quiet.

If there is someone in the house I should be making some noise to let them know that they've been rumbled, maybe even spook them.

Then he passed the doors leading into the kids' bedrooms.

*No point me screaming like a madman,
swinging a bat around and terrifying the life out
of them if it is indeed nothing.*

He listened again. Nothing. He thought about
reaching over and flipping on the light in the
upstairs hallway, then noticed that his son's
bedroom door was ajar. The light might wake
him, so he started down the stairs in the dark.

The hand rail was on his right so he switched
the bat to his left hand and took the steps one at
a time. He didn't stomp down them but he
didn't tiptoe either. If there was someone in the
house, he'd let them have a chance to do the
right thing and get the hell out. He'd seen a talk
show once where this guy who'd been a serial
burglar had said that the last thing these guys
wanted, the professionals anyway, was to
confront a householder.

Glenn took the last step and turned right into
the long narrow hallway. Ahead of him was the
front door. Closed. Locked. That was good.

Glenn turned the other way, towards the back
of the house and the kitchen, where he'd thought
the noise was coming from. With each step he
felt himself relax a tiny amount. Even the deafest
intruder would have heard him by now. In case
they hadn't, he switched the bat back to his right
hand.

He walked into the kitchen. Nothing out of
place. Nothing at all. The clicker for Amy's car
was hung up in its place. So was the clicker for
his truck. Her handbag was still on the counter
where he'd seen it as he turned out the lights
and went up to bed.

He crossed to the sink and filled a glass with water. He glugged it down, then checked the back door. Locked, with the chain on.

Then he heard them. Two sets of heavy boots hammering up the stairs. Sheer panic coursed through him. He raced out of the room.

They were at the top of the stairs now. Two figures. Then the thing that he most dreaded: Amy racing out of the bedroom straight into one of them.

A door opened and Patrick stumbled out in his PJs, rubbing his eyes. 'Hey, leave my mom alone!' he shouted.

Glenn froze five steps from the top. The intruder had a knife to Amy's throat. Not a switchblade. A big hunting knife, like the kind you'd use to gut a deer.

'OK, take it easy,' Glenn said. He tore his eyes away from the knife to his son. 'Patrick, it's OK.' His daughter was out of her room now. 'Honey, it's fine,' he told her.

One of the intruders stepped forward. He was a huge guy with a shaved head, big walrus moustache and lots of tattoos. He put his hand out and said, 'Give me the bat, Glenn.'

How does he know my name? Who are these people? What do they want?

The man appeared to be reading Glenn's mind. 'Glenn, we're here because we need your help.'

The way he said it, it sounded like the most reasonable request in the world. But it wasn't. For the first time since he'd woken up it occurred to Glenn that maybe he was having a nightmare. No way could someone who looked like this man be so calm, so rational.

There was nothing else he could do — his wife and his children's lives were at stake here — so he flipped the bat round and reached out with it.

The intruder took it. 'Thank you, Glenn. Now, Amy, why don't you try and settle the children somewhere? Don't put any lights on.' He nodded to his accomplice to release her.

Amy seemed to Glenn as though she was in complete shock. Only when the knife was moved from her throat and sheathed did she nod that she understood.

The man, who still seemed like a giant, turned his attention back to Glenn. 'I'll need all your cell phones. Then I want you to get dressed for work. We have a job for you. A very important job. Do it well and everything will be fine.'

58

In any other area of the city they would have arrived to a sleepy neighbourhood of empty streets. But the Tenderloin existed in an inverse state to the rest of San Francisco, like the negative image of an old photograph. At three in the morning every sidewalk was crowded. It was like walking on to the set of a B-rated horror movie with junkies filling the role of the living dead.

On the way there, Lock and Ty had driven past the bombed-out Federal Courthouse, a reminder of not only where this whole crazy journey had started, but also of how far Reaper and his daughter were prepared to go to achieve their aims.

The cab driver had dropped them, at Lock's request, next to a weed-infested lot two blocks away from the address Coburn had given them. A crack-ridden prostitute sporting a battered blonde wig and an Adam's apple the size of a grapefruit tottered over towards them on clear-plastic stiletto heels.

'How you boys doin' tonight?' he asked Ty.

'Beat it,' Ty said gruffly, as Lock did his best not to laugh.

The prostitute put a hand on his hip and waved a finger at Ty with his other hand. 'Beating it's ten bucks.'

'Thanks, ma'am,' Lock said, 'but we'll take a rain check.'

'Your loss, baby,' the prostitute said, tottering back again towards a small knot of co-workers, all of them sporting short skirts, ample cleavage and biceps like longshoremen.

As they exited the lot, Lock glanced over at Ty. 'Don't know why you didn't get her number.'

'Dude, that was a chick with a dick. You know what one of those is?'

'Do I know? Sounds like my dad's second wife.'

'How's your old man doing anyway? Still in God's waiting room?' Ty asked.

'Down in the Florida Keys, making out like he's Humphrey Bogart.'

Ty jerked his head up the street towards the address Coburn had given them. Lock followed Ty's gaze. There was no sign of the promised US Marshals arrest response team, which they'd been informed would be handling this.

'Could use him now,' Ty said.

Damn straight, thought Lock. Lock's father, even though he was now in his sixties and had lived in America for most of his adult life, had lost none of his Scottish toughness. He was a good man to have in your corner — especially when, like now, your corner was next to empty.

Lock took another look around for signs of support but there was none in sight. He got on his cell phone to Coburn.

'Where the hell are you?'

'There's been a delay in getting the search warrant,' Coburn told him.

Lock kicked out at the edge of the sidewalk in frustration.

'Are you there?' Coburn asked him.

'Yeah,' Lock answered.

'OK, then sit tight. Whatever you do, do not go into that building until we get there.'

Lock didn't say anything.

'You hear me, Lock?' Coburn said.

'I hear you,' Lock said, hanging up and looking at Ty. 'No harm in at least taking a look.'

'Nothing illegal about it either,' Ty agreed. 'Just two private citizens checking on someone.'

'Right,' Lock nodded, jamming a fresh clip into his 226.

★ ★ ★

The apartment block where Reaper had been sighted was next door to a homeless shelter and directly opposite a brightly painted Vietnamese restaurant. A group of three men were stretched out on the sidewalk, their backs against the building. The youngest of them looked up at Lock and Ty, his eyes yellow and vacant, a line of drool running from the corner of his mouth down his jaw and on to the collar of his jacket. He put out his hand. 'Help me out, man?'

Lock made eye contact with him. Peel away the beard and the crank-pocked skin and the man was early twenties, no more than a kid really. Lock wondered what had happened to him to bring him here. He dug into his back pocket and pulled out a ten-dollar bill, bending down so that he was at eye level with the young man.

'I'm looking for someone who we think lives here,' Lock said with a nod towards the apartment block.

The young man's eyes flitted from the ten spot to Lock and back again.

'He's white. Real big. Shaved head. Lots of ink. Nazi shit.'

Lock spotted a flicker of recognition, and then fear.

'Relax,' he said to the young man. 'If we find him, he's not coming back here.'

'2G,' the young man said, his hand shooting out towards the ten spot.

Lock kept the money pinched between his thumb and fore-finger. 'You're sure?'

The young man nodded.

'You'd better be,' Lock said, relinquishing the ten-dollar bill. 'Because if you're jerking me around, I'll be back to put you out of your misery.'

Lock got back up and, with Ty, stepped towards the building entrance.

There was an entry system. Ty pushed a button for an apartment on the top floor. A few seconds later a woman's voice, sleepy and disconnected, answered, 'Who is it?'

'Got something for you,' said Ty, slurring his words slightly.

It worked. There was another silence, then the lock clicked open with a buzz, and Lock and Ty stepped into the grubby, dimly lit foyer.

The building reeked of urine, sweat and stale food. The smell took Lock back to Pelican Bay. He sucked it in through his nostrils, more convinced than ever that Reaper had to be here for a reason. Why else would he have traded one fetid hell hole for another when there was a whole country full of fresh air and wide open spaces out there?

Lock and Ty split up, Ty taking the elevator while Lock took the stairs. As Lock pushed through into the stairwell, he took out his Sig, holding it down by his hip. He didn't want to be caught cold if he met Reaper on the way down. If Reaper was here, he'd be armed, of that there was no doubt.

Up on the second floor, Lock pushed open the door and stepped out into a corridor. He didn't have to do any more searching for apartment 2G. It was right in front of him.

The door was closed. Set into it was a peephole. Lock skirted it, hugging the wall to one side of the door as he waited for Ty.

There was a loud clank as the elevator shuddered to a halt and Ty stepped out. They both moved slowly towards the door.

★ ★ ★

A shadow fell over the young man slumped outside the apartment building that Lock had entered a few moments before. He looked up from the ten-dollar bill Lock had given him to see a woman standing beside him.

'What you tell him?' she asked.

'What you told me to tell him,' the young man replied. 'Apartment 2G.'

'Good,' the woman said, peeling off a fifty

from a roll of bills and handing it over. 'Now get out of here.'

The young man scrambled to his feet as Chance crossed the street and climbed into a white San Francisco works truck which pulled away from the kerb and disappeared from view along Leavenworth Street.

★ ★ ★

Lock waved Ty back towards the stairwell, all the while keeping one eye on the door.

'I don't like it,' he said.

'How come?' Ty asked.

'It's too easy.'

Lock frowned, rubbing at the scar that still ran round his scalp, a memento of walking through a door rigged with a shotgun. Fool me once, he thought, shame on you. Fool me twice, shame on me.

'So what you want to do?' Ty said.

'Let's wait. You go downstairs, see if there's a fire escape he can climb down. I'll stay here.'

Ty nodded, then he was gone, his movements awkward as he jogged down the stairs, his shoulder clearly still troubling him.

Lock set his phone to silent and texted Coburn, letting him know he was there. Coburn texted back within a minute saying that they finally had the warrant and to stay where he was.

The minutes passed slowly. There were no sirens, but then a low roar of commotion rose from the street outside, alerting Lock to the arrival of the arrest response team, which was deployed for high-risk fugitive raids.

Lock tensed, waiting for the door of the apartment to burst open, but it remained resolutely shut. Soon, the sounds of toilets being flushed and water running into sinks could be heard from behind the other apartment doors as the building's occupants flushed away anything they shouldn't have. But all that emanated from behind the door of 2G was a heavy silence.

Footsteps echoed in the stairwell below Lock. Then three storm-trooperesque US Marshals came into view, one of them wielding a mini battering ram, one a shotgun, all of them clad in black body armour and sporting Kevlar helmets with visors. Lock pointed them towards the door, then moved away.

The Marshal with the battering ram hefted it against the handle of the apartment door. It flew open. From where Lock was hunkered down, in the door of the stairwell, weapon drawn, he could see a short length of corridor on the other side of the apartment door. Directly facing it was the apartment's bathroom. The door was ajar. It opened inwards, although it didn't look like there was enough room to conceal a man as big as Reaper.

Then Lock saw it. A thin coil of wire stretched across the bathroom door. The Marshal holding the battering ram stepped towards it as his two colleagues side-stepped the bathroom, moving towards the tiny living area beyond.

'Bomb!' Lock screamed, diving towards the stairs.

The Marshal with the battering ram half-turned, taking another step at the same time and stumbling across the wire, which broke, coiling on the floor.

There was no explosion. Nothing. He flipped up his visor and turned to remonstrate with Lock, who had his head below the top tread of the stairwell.

'Relax. It's clear.'

Then there was a dull boom from the bathroom and the Marshal was lifted off his feet by the waves of the blast, his face splitting against the edge of the door, the flesh at the back of both his thighs parting to reveal splintered femur. Pieces of wood from the apartment door sailed over Lock's head, one shard embedding itself in the plaster of the wall behind him.

Lock called out to the other two Marshals to get the hell out of there. When he got no reply, he got slowly to his feet. His heart was pounding out of his chest. As the dust settled, he saw the two Marshals emerge from the apartment, one of them supporting his buddy. Lock rushed over to help the injured man. Between them, they got him down the stairs and on to the first floor, where they helped him off with his helmet. Blood was seeping from his ears and nose.

Lock looked behind him to see Ty heading up the stairs with a couple of paramedics.

'You OK?' Ty asked.

Lock nodded.

As the paramedics set to work, Lock headed back out on to Leavenworth Street. He looked around for the young man who'd given him the apartment number but, like Reaper, he was nowhere to be seen.

59

Four San Francisco Fire Department engines screamed past them as they headed up California Street. They had heard the explosion, and Glenn had noted the utter lack of surprise on the face of the man sitting next to him.

Back at the house, it had taken Glenn a few minutes to calm down enough to realise that he knew who the man sitting next to him was. He'd seen his picture on the front page of the newspaper and on the TV news. It was the guy who'd escaped from that trial up north in a helicopter. He was some kind of Nazi or something. He hadn't caught the guy's name, only that he was armed and considered highly dangerous, and that members of the public were not to approach him under any circumstances. OK, so you weren't supposed to approach the guy. But what if the guy broke into your house and threatened to kill your wife and kids? What were you supposed to do then?

Glenn had decided that the best thing, the only thing, he could do was exactly what they told him to do. Right now, with his wife and kids back at the house with the other intruder, if they asked him to jump off the Golden Gate Bridge and into the freezing cold waters of San Francisco Bay, he'd do it.

'OK, pull up here,' the guy said, directing him to a spot opposite the front entrance of Grace Cathedral. He'd put on a John Deere tractor ball cap, pulling the brim down low so it was almost touching his eyes. He told Glenn to get out, and as he joined him on the sidewalk said, 'Now remember, if we don't call in every ten minutes, you know what happens.'

Glenn did. Unless the woman back at the house heard from him at regular intervals his family would be killed.

'But what if your cell phone runs out of power, or there's a network problem?' Glenn asked, trying to keep the gut-churning fear out of his voice.

'Over here, I'm gonna show you something,' the man said, ignoring his question and leading Glenn across the wide street.

They stopped short of the sidewalk by a few feet.

'Right here,' he said, looking down.

Glenn was more confused now than ever.

'You don't see that?' the man asked.

All Glenn could see was asphalt on the street. 'What am I looking for here?'

'You mean, you don't see that huge goddamn pothole right there?'

There was no pothole. The road surface was cracked, but nothing out of the ordinary.

Glenn caught on. 'Oh, yeah, that.'

The man tilted his head slightly so that Glenn could see the light from a nearby store glinting in his dark grey eyes. 'Needs repairing, don't you think?'

Glenn fought the urge to laugh. *Is this what this is about? They broke into my house, scared me and my family half to death because they want a goddamn pothole that doesn't even exist repaired?* He tried to keep his voice even. 'You know, you can just call this in. We have a phone number. The city promises to make a repair within forty-eight hours.'

'Yeah,' the man said, 'we did that already. Someone came out, said they couldn't see anything.'

Maybe that's because there is no pothole, you psychopath. That was what Glenn felt like saying, but instead he said, 'Well, I can see that it needs fixing. I can get my crew on it first thing.'

'Good,' said the man. He paused and looked at Glenn, and once again Glenn felt a stab of pure terror. 'So what are you going to say to them?'

'What do you mean?'

'Well,' said the man, 'there ain't no pothole here. Even a blind man can see that. So what you going to say to them?'

Glenn thought fast. 'I'll just say that we've had a burst water pipe underneath. That's what has caused these cracks.' He kicked the toe of his right boot at where the top layer of asphalt had puckered into two ridges. 'Better to fix it now than let it get worse.'

It was a bunch of baloney but it sounded plausible. Plus, his guys wouldn't really care too much anyway. They fixed roads. It didn't really

307

matter to them where or why.

'Good,' said the man, patting Glenn on the shoulder. 'Now, I don't want a patch job. I'm going to need you to go down a ways. And remember, you breathe a word of this and you'll never see your family again.'

60

'What's the matter, man?'

Glenn stared at his supervisor, jolted by the question. 'What?'

'You're an hour early.'

His supervisor seemed to study him for a moment.

'I had some paperwork to catch up on.'

'Uh-huh,' said his supervisor, clearly not buying it. Which was bad news because the kidnappers had been as good as their word, ensuring he would do what he was told by wiring him with a tiny microphone.

Glenn searched for a more plausible excuse for showing up early. 'Listen, don't say anything to anyone, but I needed to get out of the house. Me and the wife have been going through a rough patch recently.'

The supervisor, who'd only been in the job a few months, having transferred from a different city department, wiped at a dried mustard stain on his tie. 'Been there.' Then he wandered back to his office, leaving Glenn on his own.

Glenn quickly grabbed his list of jobs and set to work. He'd have to fill in the repair request form himself, so he pulled one out and set to work. He inserted the address, the nature of the repair. In the section where the name of the person who'd requested the repair went, Glenn wrote what they'd told him to write — with one slight adjustment.

Once the form was completed, he lowered his head so that his chin was on his chest and his mouth was close to the microphone. 'OK, the paperwork's all done.'

He tore off his copy and took the original back to his supervisor. The supervisor took it without a word, then looked at it.

Glenn's heart jumped. 'Problem?' he asked.

'Nah. It's just with it being outside Grace Cathedral.'

'What about it?' Glenn's heart was racing.

'Well, they got that big funeral there on Tuesday.'

'They've always got funerals, ain't they?' Glenn said, knowing this wasn't true. Funerals at the cathedral were a rare event, reserved only for the great and the good.

'It's the one for that judge — you know, Junius Holmes?' said the supervisor. 'So just make sure you get to this today.'

Glenn exhaled with relief. 'Don't worry. I will.'

★ ★ ★

An hour later, Glenn and his crew had signs set up, traffic diverted, and were busy at work excavating the road outside Grace Cathedral. He took comfort in the familiar routine although his mind kept slipping back to his home and his wife and children, and what might happen to them if something went wrong.

There had been a couple of questions from one of the guys in the crew when they set to work but Glenn passed it off easily enough. Yes, the cracks didn't look too bad, but their job was to repair what they were asked to repair. The guys on the crew had shrugged and got on with it, using a mini excavator to tear up the existing road surface and deposit the contents into the back of a dumper truck.

Glenn's heart leapt when a couple of cops on mountain bikes cruised to a stop next to him. He knew them both — not well, but in his job it was impossible not to get to know at least some of the cops. The older of them, a guy in his late fifties with greying hair, propped his bike against the truck and sauntered over.

'Didn't know you guys were working here today,' he said.

Glenn could feel his face flush. 'Kind of a last-minute thing.'

'No surprise,' said the cop, hands on hips. 'Lot of bigwigs'll be here for the funeral. Guess they'll want everything looking good.'

'That must be it,' said Glenn.

'OK, man, see you later.'

The cop took his leave and Glenn got back to work.

About two hours later, all the prep work having been completed, Glenn looked up to see a man striding towards him wearing jeans, a sweatshirt and a hi-visibility vest. A construction worker's hard hat rested on the man's head and a red bandana shielded his mouth and nose from the dust. When the man pulled the bandana down, Glenn saw that it was Reaper.

He headed him off, worried that one of the

311

guys on his crew might see him, but none of them even looked up. Nor did any of the hundred or so passers-by in the immediate area around the cathedral. But then, he reflected, guys doing their kind of jobs were pretty much invisible to the rest of the population.

'Tell your guys to move on to the job you were supposed to be doing today,' Reaper told him.

'What?'

'Just do it.'

Reaper stood in close to Glenn, who suddenly remembered the knife at Amy's throat and her look of horror. 'We'll start work again at midnight.'

'But the guys go home at six.'

'You and me are going to finish up this job together,' Reaper said. 'You don't mind doing some overtime, do you?'

61

Ty held the piece of paper up to his mouth and kissed it. Then he lowered it and studied the amount. They were waiting in line at the bank to deposit the cheques that had come through for services rendered to Uncle Sam.

'That's one hell of a lot of zeros,' Ty said.

'Yeah,' said Lock.

Before she was killed, Jalicia must have pushed hard to make sure they got paid. Standing here now, with Reaper still on the loose, it felt like blood money.

Ty must have caught him staring sombrely at the piece of paper. 'Man, shouldn't you be happy?'

'Why? Because I have a lot of money?'

'Well, yeah.'

Lock shifted his body so he was facing Ty. 'Sometimes there are more important things in life than dollar bills.'

'I'll pretend I never heard you say that,' Ty huffed, reaching over and grabbing a pen to endorse the cheque. 'Look, I was shot and almost died for this, so, way I see it, I reckon I deserve every penny. I'm going to take that vacation I've been talking about. You should see if Carrie can get some more time off work, extend the romantic weekend you guys've been having.'

'She's busy covering the Junius Holmes

funeral,' Lock said, his eyes flicking to a TV in the corner of the bank where the ticker was announcing that the President would be in attendance.

'When is it?'

'Tomorrow.'

'Then we could fly on Friday. Listen, Ryan, you need to chill the fuck out.'

Lock squared his shoulders. 'Not until I find Reaper.'

Back on the TV there was footage of the President at a press conference, the rolling banner reporting that he was making a statement about events in Asia and a new terrorist outrage in Pakistan.

Ty stepped up to the teller, a huge smile plastered over his face as he slid the deposit slip and cheque over the counter towards her. 'Wanna come to Cancun this weekend?' he asked her.

'You are such an asshole,' said Lock, as the teller smiled.

'Hey, but at least I'm not a miserable asshole,' Ty said, throwing the comment over his shoulder, then fixing his attention back on the teller. 'My business partner thinks that somehow being unhappy all the time makes him deep.'

Sighing, Lock stepped up to the next teller and slid over the money he'd received. Something was nagging at him, though, as he glanced back at the TV screen to see the President departing the podium.

'OK, I'll speak to Carrie and see if she can take some time off — after the funeral.'

314

'That's more like it,' said Ty. 'What about you, baby?'

'Thanks, but I'm engaged,' the teller said sternly.

'So you got one last chance to have some real fun,' Ty protested, before Lock dragged him away.

They stood on the sidewalk outside the bank. It was a perfect day. Mid-seventies. No fog, just clear blue skies. On either side of them, office blocks sparkled in the late-fall sunshine.

'Ty?'

'Yeah?'

'Reaper might not have been in that apartment, but he's still here in the city.'

Ty put his hand over his eyes and made a show of looking around. 'Where?'

Lock raised his hand to silence Ty. 'What do you think it would take to really start a race war in this country?'

'Right now? You refusing to shut the hell up.'

'You kill a member of the Supreme Court, who cares, right?' Lock said. 'But you kill the President, our first black President . . . well, that's like JFK and Martin Luther King all rolled into one.'

Ty turned to Lock, shock etched on his face. 'Holy shit, man, are you crazy?' He stepped back and spread his hands. 'Say Reaper really does want to kill the President. There's a world of difference between wanting to do something and being able to do it.'

'That's true,' Lock conceded. 'But say you want to assassinate someone specific. What's the first thing you have to know?'

Ty shrugged an 'I dunno'.

'First you have to know where they're going to be. And tomorrow, the President's going to be right here, at Grace Cathedral, with his family.'

Ty was silent as he thought it through. 'OK,' he said reluctantly. 'But how are they gonna do it? You know what security's like around the President. He carries the biggest, most advanced security detail in the world. Killing a Federal Prosecutor, that's one thing. Running over some little old judge who's already a bazillion years old, that's something else. But taking out the President?' He clapped Lock on the shoulder. 'Maybe you don't need a vacation. You're already tripping.'

62

'Do you know how many threats against his life a President of the United States receives on a weekly basis?' Coburn asked, kneeling down to tie an errant shoelace as Lock took in the ongoing work to the Federal Building where he had first met Jalicia.

'A couple hundred?' said Lock.

'Times that by ten and you're getting close. Now, you want to take a stab at how many threats *this* President gets on a weekly basis? Times that by ten. You want me to go on?'

'Sure,' said Lock. 'This is an education.'

Coburn sighed. 'Ever since we got our first black President, gun ownership has gone through the roof. So have sales of ammunition. The Secret Service and other federal agencies have identified over three hundred domestic groups who would love to take a shot at him. Plots have been uncovered and thwarted to kill not only him but the First Lady and their daughters. There have also been threats to kidnap the kids and execute them. The Secret Service deal with this shit every day. What makes tomorrow so different?'

'You gonna allow me the right of reply?'

'Sure. But as soon as I hear the word 'hunch' or 'feeling' or any other guesswork bullshit, this conversation is done.'

Lock took a breath. 'There are threats and

317

then there are credible threats from individuals and groups who can action them. You with me so far?'

'You going to keep stating the obvious?' Coburn asked.

'Maybe someone should. Now, Reaper and the people who sprang him — '

'At least one of whom is dead,' Coburn interrupted.

Lock gave him a 'yeah, I kinda know that' look before continuing. 'This group is not only highly motivated and determined, as proved by not one but two attempts to free their de facto leader, they are also highly trained. Not to mention ingenious. They appear to have the resources required. And here's the kicker: their leader is still at large and active.'

'Agreed,' said Coburn, not exactly softening but finally seeming to listen to what Lock was trying to say.

'We know Reaper is in town. And it's a fair guess that he — '

'Guess? You're getting close to saying you have a hunch here, Lock.'

Lock changed tack, a trick he'd picked up from Jalicia. He wished she was here with them now. 'Why would Reaper and his buddies go to the trouble of killing Junius Holmes?'

'Isn't it obvious?'

'Not to me.'

'Then go back and read the files. He went up against them. This was payback.'

'Not good enough, Coburn. If I'm guessing here, then so are you.'

'OK. So let's say for the sake of argument that you're right, that Reaper is here in San Francisco lying in wait to kill the President. How's he going to do it?'

Lock scuffed a shoe against the sidewalk. 'That I don't know. But I think you should have some people there as well.'

'Oh, you mean in addition to the two hundred or so Secret Service men and half of the San Francisco Police Department?'

'What about the route? Where's he coming in from?'

'Listen, Lock, I'm going to be nice about this, because although you're a major pain in the ass, you're either crazier than a crack-head or you've just got way bigger balls than anyone I've ever met. Take your money and go take that long vacation. We'll catch up with Reaper, and the President will be just fine. We don't need you.'

'At least pass on my concerns to the Secret Service,' Lock said, walking away.

Coburn cupped his hands in a cone to his mouth. 'Take that vacation, Lock. You hear me?'

★   ★   ★

Still feeling uneasy, Lock walked back to his car, pulled out on to Golden Gate Avenue and headed east towards Grace Cathedral. Traffic was already being diverted ahead of the funeral, so he had to park five blocks away.

Heading back towards the cathedral, he tried to approach it as Reaper would. The first thing he noticed was that all the mail boxes and trash

319

cans had been removed. Manhole covers had been sealed. All standard practice for a presidential visit. As was the case protecting any other VIP, there were certain points where they were more vulnerable than others. Lock looked around him. The cathedral would have undergone a detailed search. Once this was completed, those who could gain access would be strictly controlled. The same went for the guest list.

The route from the airport or the helipad that was being used might normally be a worry, but Lock reckoned that the presidential limousine removed much of that risk. Nicknamed 'The Beast' by the Secret Service, it was an up-armoured Cadillac with run-flat tyres and, if rumours were to be believed, its own air supply. A new one was usually rolled out for every inauguration, and the latest incarnation was said to weigh in at close to eight tonnes.

All this meant that the main threat would lie between The Beast and entry to the cathedral. Given that the authorities would have taken every sniper position for themselves, that left a rush from the crowd. Or, if Reaper and his accomplices stayed true to form, a full-on armed assault.

Lock looked around again, then crossed the street, trying to get a sense of the place from Reaper's perspective. Where would he make his move from? What would be his best entry point?

Standing there, he noticed a freshly laid patch of asphalt. A truck with crash barriers loaded on to the back rolled over it. Once it had passed, Lock recrossed the street to take a better look.

Absence of the normal. Presence of the abnormal.

In and of itself there was nothing abnormal about a patch of road having been repaired. Lock didn't know much about road repair either. But a couple of things did stand out to him. The first was that the road surface around the newly laid area was immaculate. No cracks. No damage. Lock guessed that it could have been a pothole, but why would the city go to all the trouble of resurfacing the whole area?

He looked back at the cathedral. The repaired area was directly parallel to the entrance. Exactly where the disembarkation point would be for the President.

Lock kicked away at where the new surface met the kerb with his boot. He kept kicking until he had chipped away the top layer of asphalt. Underneath that layer the filler looked fresh as well. He knelt down, pulled out his Gerber knife and dug into it, as far as the blade of the knife would go.

Nothing. He bit down on his lip. Ty, Coburn — hell, even Carrie — would tell him he was being paranoid. Of course the disembarkation point would have been freshly repaired. Just like the steps would be freshly swept. It was said that the Queen of England must think the world smells of fresh paint because everywhere she goes there's some poor bastard twelve feet in front of her with a pot of paint. The same probably went for the President.

Lock resheathed his knife and stood up,

feeling the warmth of the sun on his back. Across the street, people strolled through Huntington Park, enjoying the weather.

He'd get Carrie to swing them an invite. Just in case.

63

Tuesday morning, eleven a.m. Snipers dotted the rooftops. A San Francisco Police Department helicopter buzzed low over Grace Cathedral. On the ground there were plenty of uniforms. The streets immediately surrounding the cathedral were closed to all but official traffic.

At a perimeter barrier formed by half a dozen sawhorses, Lock showed his invitation along with identification, and was checked off a list. He stepped through and waited for Ty to go through the same rigmarole. Carrie had come through, as Lock knew she would, securing them seats inside the cathedral.

'Where do you think we'll be sitting, huh?' Ty asked, excited at the prospect of seeing the first African-American President in the flesh.

Lock shrugged, his mind on Reaper and the threat he posed. 'How should I know?'

Ty stopped walking, forcing Lock to look back. 'Will you just chill the hell out? Look around. No one's going to be making any moves against the President with all this security. And even if they do, they got America's Top Bodyguard in attendance.' Ty smirked. 'So where do you think we're sitting?'

'I'm sure you'll be front and centre, right in between the President and the First Lady.'

'Sweet. So, when's this thing supposed to start?'

'You make it sound like a concert.'

Ty craned his neck to check out the queue of guests in front of them. Here and there, Lock recognised a senator or some other major political figure. There were even a couple of high-profile actors and media types, presumably drawn in by the presence of the President. As people chatted excitedly, Lock wondered how many of them had ever even met Junius Holmes. The vibe was definitely not that of a funeral. Instead, the whole thing came off like the funeral was the hottest ticket in town. Lock reflected that it made for one huge upside: a rampaging gang of white supremacists making for the President was definitely going to stand out.

Leaving the crowds already gathering behind the barriers on the streets outside, Lock and Ty slowly headed up the steps of the cathedral. At the entrance, the funeral-goers were being searched. There was an airport-style metal detector and a separate X-ray machine for bags. By the way they were fumbling with belts and shoes, Lock guessed that most of this crowd flew private jets.

A sinewy brunette who was accompanying a Republican senator was in hushed conversation with a female Secret Service agent as Lock stepped up to take his turn. The machine had gone off and she was being asked to remove anything metal that she had on her person. 'I have a piercing which can't be removed,' she was saying, her New York accent loud and pronounced. 'Not here anyway.'

Ty was already through the detector and standing on the other side. 'Come on, man,' he said to Lock while peering towards the altar. 'I can see a couple of good seats down the front.'

Yup, like we're going to be allowed to sit there, thought Lock, knowing that most of the pews in that part of the cathedral would be reserved for the President and his entourage.

The detector beeped as Lock stepped through.

'Sir, could you remove your belt?' asked one of the agents.

Lock stepped back and, hitching up his lightweight jacket, saw that he still had his Gerber hanging from it. Stupid. He'd remembered to leave his 226 back at the hotel, but the Gerber he'd forgotten about. It was a new knife too. A gift from Carrie. An LMF II Infantry Knife with a 4.8-inch blade. Not easily missed.

Ty was still hopping up and down on the other side, watching as the New Yorker with the secret piercing and her septuagenarian date walked past him in the direction of the two seats he'd scoped out.

Lock made no attempt to hide the knife. One of the security people by the scanner had already seen it. 'Sorry, forgot I had it on me. Can I leave it with you?'

Two agents were heading towards him now at speed. No big deal, thought Lock.

'Sir, can you step over here?' said one of them, ushering Lock off to one side.

The other agent picked up the knife, still in its sheath, from the plastic tray. Lock could see in his eyes that this was going to take a lot of explaining. Rather than dive in and offer up a *mea culpa*, he waited to take a cue from the two agents. He glanced around, hoping to spot Coburn or one of the other local guys, but there was no one he recognised apart from Ty, and he had given up waiting and was hustling to take a seat.

'You usually bring a knife to a funeral?' one of the agents asked as he palmed the Gerber off to his colleague.

Lock suppressed the urge to fire back with a wisecrack. Or to tell them that he had in fact, at one funeral, snapped the wrist of a suspect in a child abduction. 'I had it on my belt, forgot it was there. Confiscate it if you like. Or give it back to me later?'

The agent who had been handed the knife had disappeared with it behind the scanner. He was running a swab over the blade.

The agent who was with Lock said nothing. Lock joined him in staying silent.

'Could I see some identification, sir?' the agent said at last.

Slowly, Lock dug his wallet from his pants pocket and flipped it open.

If the agent recognised the name, he showed no hint. Instead, he took the wallet and headed over to join his colleague by the scanner.

'Stay right there,' he said.

Lock checked his watch, feeling self-conscious as guests streamed past and the place began to fill up.

Then the two agents were back, their demeanour different. There was a tightness to their features, even more pronounced than before, and they'd been joined by a couple of San Francisco Police Department uniforms, one of whom had his hand on his gun. His partner was unclipping her cuffs.

Lock turned towards her, squaring his shoulders as she approached.

'Sir,' she said, 'can you explain why the knife you're carrying just tested positive for explosives?'

64

They called it living in the bubble. You couldn't really understand it until you had experienced it. Even something as simple as going for a walk had to be cleared with the Secret Service.

Together, he and the First Lady had tried to keep things as normal as possible, especially for the kids. But no matter how hard you tried, the fact remained, when you were President, life was no longer normal.

The motorcade was whipping through the outskirts of San Francisco on the way from the airport to Grace Cathedral. He leaned towards the window, caught sight of the Golden Gate Bridge.

'Hey, girls,' he said to his two daughters, pointing it out.

They unbuckled their seat belts. His wife rolled her eyes.

'Let them take a look, honey,' he said with a smile.

Then he turned to the agent sitting next to him. 'Can I put the window down so they can take a look?'

'I'd really prefer if you didn't, sir,' the agent said.

The President let it go. He could overrule the guy, but he tried his best not to. The Secret Service people were there to protect him and his family, to lay down their own lives if they had to.

Under those circumstances it didn't seem fair to make their job any more difficult.

'Sorry, girls.'

They sank back into their seats, and his youngest daughter stuck out her tongue at the agent.

'Ashley!' his wife scolded.

'I'm sorry,' Ashley singsonged.

The agent managed a smile. 'That's OK. We're a big bunch of spoilsports, right?'

'Worse than Dad,' said Ashley.

'And that's saying something, right?' the President joked.

It was tough on the kids, though. He tried to keep to a minimum the number of official engagements they went to, but sometimes it was the only opportunity he had to see them.

He turned to the agent. 'How long until we get there?'

'About twelve minutes, sir.'

'You know,' said the President, addressing his two daughters, 'if you're real good, maybe there'll be a surprise later.'

'Ghirardelli?' they both asked, wide-eyed.

The Ghirardelli soda fountain on North Point Street near Fisherman's Wharf was a San Francisco institution, famous for its chocolate and ice-cream sundaes. You could gain twenty pounds just looking at one of them.

'Depends if you're good.' He nudged the agent. 'I might even get you one too, Mike.'

'Not sure my wife would thank you, sir,' said the agent.

The President winked. 'Then don't tell her.'

The First Lady rolled her eyes again but kept a smile on her face. It was part of their married shtick. He'd misbehave, she'd scold him.

'So, what d'you say, kids? Sundaes?'

The two little girls bounced up and down on their seats with anticipation as The Beast rolled inexorably ahead, freeway rolling under its run-flats, two motorcycle outriders sweeping the First Family towards the cathedral.

65

The Secret Service had hustled Lock and Ty out on to the back steps of the cathedral, away from the assembled dignitaries. Over the crush, Lock spotted Coburn walking towards the cathedral. His head was down. He looked troubled.

Lock shouted out to him, but Coburn didn't react.

'Ask that guy,' said Lock, pointing towards Coburn, as a burly Secret Service agent stepped in front of him. 'He's ATF. He can vouch for me.'

The Secret Service agents gathered round them didn't move.

'OK, I'll ask him,' said Lock, stepping around them.

'The hell you will,' said the burly agent. 'You still haven't explained how you came to have explosives residue on a deadly weapon you were carrying in here.'

Coburn was heading up the steps towards them. 'Coburn!' Lock shouted. 'Coburn!' He turned to one of the agents. 'Just ask him, would you?'

Coburn pulled out his ATF badge and showed it to someone standing halfway down the stairs. The agent checked it and let him pass.

He was just feet away from Lock and Ty now.

'Hey,' said the burly agent, 'you know these guys?'

Coburn stopped, looked straight at Lock and Ty, and smiled. 'Never seen them before in my life,' he said, then ducked past the group and into the body of the cathedral.

Lock and Ty exchanged a look of disbelief.

'Hey, Coburn!' Lock shouted. He went to push past the agent, which only signalled to the cops to move in to cuff him.

'Get this guy the hell out of here before POTUS gets here.'

'OK, OK,' Lock said, giving up.

'Him too,' said the Secret Service agent, nodding at Ty.

'What the hell did I do?' Ty protested.

The second Secret Service agent hitched his thumbs into his belt. 'We need you both out of here. If everything checks out, you'll be released later in the day.'

'Place your hands behind your back,' said one of the cops to Lock.

'Fine,' Lock said, doing exactly as he was told.

'You have any needles, any other sharp objects in your pocket?' a female cop asked.

'No.'

She came up with a comb in the right front pocket of his jeans and his wallet, which she left where they were. Once they were satisfied that they posed no threat, Lock and Ty were perp-walked down the steps of the cathedral.

Ty twisted his head round. 'Hey, take it easy, I got a bad shoulder.'

His plea was met with a growled 'And if you don't keep moving it's gonna get a lot worse.'

The crowd gathered at the crash barriers

jeered as Lock walked down the stairs and across the sidewalk, propelled towards a patrol car parked directly across the street next to the park. He watched as Ty was given the same treatment, the only difference being that Ty wasn't going quietly. He couldn't make out the words but he guessed they weren't pretty.

Lock's head was forced down and he was placed into the back seat of the cruiser. He checked out the crowd once more: hard faces peering in his direction. The locks on the rear doors thunked shut, and then they were inching forward, away from the cathedral.

From his position on the back seat, he scanned the faces of those gathered at the front entrance but didn't see Carrie. In a way, he was relieved. He'd go to the station, follow procedure like he'd been asked, and be out again in a couple of hours.

As they inched away from the kerb, he thought frantically about the explosive residue on the tip of his knife. Had it been near his Sig? That way it might have picked up a few specks of cordite. No, the closest the Gerber had been to either live rounds or his Sig was being in the same room. No way would that have been enough to leave a trace.

He glanced back at the cathedral through the cruiser window, across the freshly repaired patch of asphalt and up the steps.

Shit. The road. It had to be! He'd bent down and used the knife to dig a hole into the newly laid road surface.

'Stop the car!' he shouted, leaning forward.

The female cop riding up front bumped the brakes, the momentum propelling him forward so that he smacked his head against the hard Perspex divider which separated him from her, then accelerated again.

Unless he acted fast, his next stop was the station house, and the President's next stop would be the morgue.

66

Chance sat astride a purloined Ducati and watched the San Francisco Police Department motorcycle outriders whip past her, along the Embarcadero, followed by half a dozen other vehicles in the presidential motorcade.

She clicked on her intercom headset, which was Bluetoothed to her cell phone. 'They just went past.'

'How fast they moving?' Reaper asked.

'They're booking it. I'd say we've got under three minutes until we can RV.'

'Freya?'

'Yeah?'

'Just don't move in too fast, 'kay? We need the dust settled before we hit.'

'Got you.'

Chance hitched up the straps of her backpack full of goodies, toed up the kick-stand on the bike and slipped back down the street, away from the route the presidential convoy was taking. The plan was to run parallel, then after initial detonation move in to mop up. The objective was straightforward in terms of those inside The Beast, and she was looking forward to it.

Leave no survivors.

★ ★ ★

Lock slumped back on the bench seat of the cruiser. No amount of pleading was getting the driver to stop. 'At least patch me through to someone who can check it out.'

The female cop eyed him in the rear-view mirror with a jaundiced look that spoke of having had to endure too many crazies. 'Listen, buddy, the Secret Service know what they're doing. If there was a bomb they'd have found it already. There was sniffer dogs there just this morning. I saw them.'

But the dogs, no matter how refined their sense of smell, might not have been able to detect anything apart from the overpowering whiff of fresh tar. He had to get out of the car. And fast.

As the driver turned her attention back to the road, Lock slipped his right hand into the front pocket of his jeans and pulled out the comb with his fingertips. Without looking, he felt for the final, thickest tooth of the comb, and again by feel used the tooth to press down on the pawl of the right-hand cuff, in an attempt to disengage the swing arm from the ratchet. The cuff on his right hand clicked open. He waited a second to see if the cop had noticed anything, but her eyes were fixed on the road ahead.

'Listen,' he said, leaning forward again, 'I gotta pee.'

'Hold it.'

'I can't. Can you at least pull over so I don't make a mess of your back seat here?'

'Forget it.'

336

It was the answer he'd been expecting. Keeping his hands low, he opened the zip of his jeans. 'I'm sorry about this, officer, but I ain't wetting my jeans.'

She squinted in the rear-view mirror. 'Aw, Jesus. OK, OK, wait.'

She pulled sharply over to the kerb, and got out. As she opened the rear passenger door, Lock kept his hands low, figuring that her eyes would be everywhere but waist level or below. He guessed right.

He had a second, maybe two.

As she began to usher him to a patch of barren ground which doubled as a street-side parking lot, he hit her hard in the face just below her nose, sending her tumbling to the ground. As she fell, he was on her, freeing her service weapon from its holster. Next, he ripped her radio from her belt.

Picking her up under one shoulder, he tossed her into the still-open rear door and slammed it, then climbed in the front, jammed the cruiser back into drive and spun it round in a thick one-eighty turn that drew honks from oncoming cars as he cut directly across their paths.

He glanced back at the female cop in the back seat. She was sitting up now, trying to staunch the blood from her nose.

'Lady, I'm sorry, but we're short on time, so buckle up.'

She glared at him and mouthed the word 'motherfucker'. He could hardly blame her.

Finding the switch that engaged the lights

and sirens, he flicked the toggle and jammed his foot down on the accelerator, weaving through the traffic, scattering pedestrians and other vehicles behind him as he raced to the cathedral, praying he wasn't already too late.

67

The motorcycle outriders slowed as they edged within a block of the cathedral. People crowded every sidewalk, children hoisted on to aching parental shoulders, while others craned their necks over police sawhorses, everyone eager for a glimpse of the President and his family.

Then, from a side street, came screams, the roar of a car engine at full throttle and the whip-crack of gunshots.

★ ★ ★

The needle of the cruiser's speedometer hit seventy miles an hour as Lock's mantra played out in real time.

Fast.

A patrol officer, set in a Weaver stance, his gun pointed straight at Lock, dived for the sidewalk as the patrol car Lock was piloting bore down on him.

Aggressive.

In front of him, three blue San Francisco Police Department sawhorses disintegrated, splintering under the wheels as the road opened out in front of him, shots pouring in, the presidential limousine in plain sight. Lock spun the wheel so that the limousine's trajectory matched his own.

Action.

As the heavily up-armoured SUV to the rear of The Beast spun out, the tailgate dropped to reveal two Secret Service agents sporting M-4s. As they opened fire on him, Lock's hands slipped down to grip the bottom of the steering wheel, his foot lifted from the accelerator, and he wedged himself as tight as he could into the footwell.

With determination.

Seconds before The Beast moved on to the fresh asphalt in front of the cathedral, the front of Lock's patrol car concertinaed into it at the driver's-side front wheel arch. Lock's shoulder rammed into the base of the steering column, sending a screaming pain through his body. A few more shots poured in, shattering what was left of the windshield. There was a fresh whimper from the officer in the back.

Lock closed his eyes and didn't move. The engine block was directly in front of him, which was about all he had in his favour.

Voices, panicked and urgent, emanated from outside the vehicle.

'Officer inside! Officer inside!'

'Cease fire!'

'Stop firing, you assholes! We got a cop in back!'

Lock stayed still. Any movement could get him killed. The preferred method of dealing with a suicide bomber, which is what they might safely assume he was, was to fill him full of lots of holes, quickly and without mercy.

The rear door was flung open first. Then his door.

'Do not move, you fucking asshole!'

Big hands rushed in and scooped him out, dumping him face down on the street. A gun was pressed into the back of his neck. Not a good sign.

More gunshots, then the rip of a single motorbike engine. The cold metal tickle of the gun lifted from his neck and he could hear the man holding it say, 'Holy Mother of God.'

Lock opened his eyes, lifted his head from his prone position and caught sight of a man mounted on a fat-boy Harley with a teenage boy, presumably plucked from the crowd to serve as a human shield, in front of him. He was dropping flares behind and to either side of him, creating a thick, acid-trip-surreal soup of multicoloured fog around him. It took a second for Lock to shift from looking to seeing, a second before he recognised the lone gunman as Reaper.

Lock grabbed for the sill of the driver's door, pulling himself back inside the patrol car. The female officer's service weapon had fallen into the passenger-side footwell. He reached in and grabbed it, aware of the screams of panic and confusion from the crowd.

Just in time, Lock emerged to see Reaper toss the M-4 he'd been spraying in all directions to the ground and reach back into the saddle-bags of the Harley. Lock took a quick breath in. He knew what was coming next.

There it was: an RPG launcher.

Reaper pushed his temporary hostage off the bike and took aim. And there was Chance, her blonde hair marking her out in the crowd, hunkered down at ground level among the terrified onlookers. Lock could see her hands working the zip of a large designer-leather backpack that lay on the sidewalk in front of her. Her knees and elbows were pumping as she slithered forward, unnoticed by those around her.

Could any of the police snipers positioned on the rooftops around the cathedral see Reaper? Lock assumed not: the smoke from the flares was still far too thick. He crawled back out, belly on the ground, aimed his Sig towards Reaper and fired a quick shot. It was enough to distract him. Lock fired again, this time finding his target. Reaper was blown backwards from the bike, the leather jacket he was wearing shredding into pieces to reveal Kevlar body armour. As Reaper scrambled back to his feet, Lock took his chance, punching out another round which caught Reaper at the very top of his nose. Reaper's forehead opened up. Blood and chunks of his brain spattered across the sidewalk. He fell with a thump backwards on to the sidewalk, his arms splayed out at his sides.

Lock's focus snapped back to Chance as she opened her backpack and pulled out a matching compact RPG launcher. Most women carried Mace, or at most a taser, but Chance wasn't most women. Moving on to one knee, the RPG launcher slung over her shoulder, she took aim.

So did Lock. Aiming for her chest, he began to squeeze down on the trigger. Then he froze.

The hard swell of her belly, made visible by her T-shirt riding up as she hefted the RPG launcher, stopped him cold. Something primal, or maybe something hard-wired from years of protecting life, kicked in. He shook his head. She was every bit as dangerous as her father, he told himself, resighting and moving his hands up less than half a foot so that now it would be a head shot.

But the two-second hesitation was enough. There was a zip, then a bang, and finally the roar of an impact as the grenade tore into the hood of The Beast. The front of The Beast arched up, then a hundred yards in front of it the newly repaired patch of road erupted, sending earth and debris high into the air and twisting The Beast in the other direction.

When Lock looked up, his mouth, nose and eyes clogged with dust, The Beast had come to rest on its side. The windows and the inner core looked intact, but what about the people inside?

There was a moment of stunned silence, then the screams began again, but where exactly they were coming from was anyone's guess.

Through the smoke, what was left of the Secret Service detail poured towards The Beast, fanning out to surround it, while others worked to prise open the doors that lay air side up.

Lock got to his feet, the muscles in his legs shaking as he tucked the Glock into the waistband of his trousers.

Ty suddenly appeared through the murk.

Lock was as surprised as he guessed Ty was to see him out of custody, but there was no time to dwell on that now. Already the limp body of a child was being lifted carefully from the wreckage of The Beast.

68

As Lock stared at the scene before him, through the fog emerged the President and the First Lady, their arms around each other and their eldest daughter. Lock put a hand on the cruiser to steady himself, wiped the dust from his mouth and took a big gulp of fresh air. They were safe.

Ty clamped a hand on his shoulder. 'Good shooting, brother.'

Lock glanced round. 'Thanks.'

They stayed there for a few more minutes, until they heard the first Emergency Medical Service ambulances approaching.

Lock straightened up. 'Let's go see if we can find her.'

★ ★ ★

Together, they roamed the streets for close to an hour. There was no sign of Chance, and the shocked state of most people didn't help matters.

Rounding the corner on to California Street, Lock caught sight of Carrie reporting live to camera. He waited for her to finish, admiring her quiet composure in the middle of all the chaos.

She threw her arms round his neck when she saw him. 'You OK?'

'Yeah, but one of 'em got away.'

'Jesus, Ryan, will you switch off for two seconds? That's not what I asked you.'

'I'll switch off when she's found. I had her right in my sights too. I just couldn't pull the trigger.'

'Because she was a woman?'

Lock looked straight into Carrie's eyes. 'Because she was pregnant. I was aiming dead centre.'

Carrie smoothed her hands across his face, and kissed him softly on the lips. 'You did the right thing.'

'But if I'd taken the shot everyone inside the car would have been OK. Have you had any word on how they are yet?'

'Shaken up real bad, but OK. No word yet on the daughter.' She hesitated. 'We've also had a report of a multiple homicide over in Oakland. Mom, Dad, two kids. All with their throats cut. Think that had anything to do with Reaper and his daughter?'

'Sounds like their work.' Lock took a deep breath and turned towards Ty. 'Let's keep looking.'

As he leaned in to kiss Carrie, he swayed, his legs almost folding beneath him. Carrie and Ty caught him between them.

'I'm fine,' he said, brushing off their help.

Carrie pointed behind them where an EMS ambulance was parked, the two-man crew taking a brief water break.

'I got it,' said Ty, jogging towards them.

'You need to take care of yourself, Ryan,'

Carrie said. 'Please, for my sake?'

'OK,' Lock said, sighing. 'But if they give me the all-clear we keep looking for Chance. We're not safe yet.'

One of the paramedics headed back over with Ty. 'Sit down on the kerb for me, sir.'

Lock sat, his head in his hands. He was dog-tired.

The paramedic began to run through the usual checks.

'We're looking for someone who got lost in the crowd,' Lock said.

'Open your eyes for me,' said the paramedic, checking out Lock's pupil dilation.

'White woman. Mid twenties. Blonde hair. She was wearing jeans and a white T-shirt, sneakers. They were white as well.'

'Could you look up for me?' the paramedic said.

'And she was pregnant. Maybe, I dunno, about four months. Not huge, but enough of a bump to be noticeable.'

'Couple of tattoos? Kind of fucked-up ones?'

Lock made eye contact. 'Yeah. Where'd you see her?'

'See her? We just dropped her off at St Francis. She said she was having a miscarriage. I tried to take a look at her, but she freaked out. I think she might have just been in shock. But better safe than sorry with someone in that condition, right?'

Elbowing the paramedic aside, Lock jumped to his feet. Carrie was standing by the mini-van, Ty at her side. Exhaustion forgotten, he ran over to them. 'Quick, where'd they take the President and his family?'

Carrie thought for a moment. 'St Francis. Why?'

'Because we have to get over there — now!'

69

The hospital was chaotic. Cops, doctors, nurses and the walking wounded from the blast filled the waiting area. Chance had been handed a stack of forms then left to her own devices. No one gave her a second look.

She flagged down a passing nurse. 'Is there a ladies' room?'

'Down there, honey,' the nurse said, gesturing further down a corridor that led towards the treatment rooms.

Chance had dumped her backpack back at the scene. All she had now was the clothes she was standing in, and her knife. But that was hidden. Which was why she'd freaked out when the paramedic had tried to examine her.

She slipped into the relative cool of the ladies' room and locked herself in one of the stalls. With the knife retrieved, she walked back out, using the pretext of getting cleaned up to wait at the sinks without arousing suspicion.

She didn't have long to wait for what she needed. A harassed-looking resident ran towards a stall, firing a 'Can't even get the time to have a pee in this place' before stepping inside.

With three quick steps, Chance was at the stall door before the woman could lock it.

'What the — '

Chance pushed her back and held the knife to her throat. 'One more word and you die. Nod if

349

you understand me. Now, get undressed.'

The resident stripped out of her scrubs. Chance took off her own jeans and T-shirt and donned the scrubs. Then she slashed a strip from the jeans, and did the same with the T-shirt. She jammed a piece of T-shirt into the resident's mouth and tied the young woman's hands behind her back with the denim strip.

'OK, turn round.'

The resident banged her shins against the toilet bowl as she did so, her cry of pain and then her screams muffled as Chance reached round and slashed her throat, making sure to slice the carotid artery.

One good thing about what she was wearing, Chance thought as she left the ladies' room; no one was going to notice a little blood.

70

St Francis Hospital was four blocks away and the roads were crammed with bumper-to-bumper traffic. Lock and Ty ran, as best they could, towards it, as Carrie tried to get word to the hospital — a task complicated by the fact that the cell phone network was seriously overloaded, as was the hospital's switchboard.

There was no sign of the civil unrest or the race war Reaper had been aiming for. From what Carrie had gleaned, the country was still in shock. But, so far at least, people were being drawn together by their collective fear rather than divided by it. Lock, however, knew that this might not hold if Chance got to finish her mission.

He was forced to stop to catch his breath, hands on knees. He could see the entrance to the hospital up ahead.

'We're gonna have to clear people out of the way,' he told Ty. 'If she's in there and about to make a move, she's going to be relying on hiding in the crowd.'

'OK, I'll see you up there,' said Ty, moving off, his long legs carrying him faster than Lock could manage.

Lock straightened up and broke into a semi-run, pushing himself through the pain. He turned left on to Pine Street, the doors of the emergency room in plain view.

It was chaos, far beyond a normal big-city emergency room. Triage had spilled out on to the sidewalk. Lock managed to walk straight in, past Ty, who was engaged in a heated argument with a couple of security guards. In the main foyer he spotted a couple of Secret Service agents having a vehement discussion of their own with a guy in a suit and a St Francis Hospital badge that identified him as some sort of manager.

'We need this whole front area clear,' they were yelling. 'The President's going to make a statement.'

'Then book a goddamn hotel,' the manager yelled back. 'This is a hospital.'

Lock left them to it, walking on, up a long corridor with rooms off it. Ten doors ahead he saw a phalanx of Secret Service personnel, some in suits, some in T-shirts or windbreakers. He jogged towards them.

★   ★   ★

Chance stood in a private room, her back pressed against the door. The patient occupying the room was too far gone to offer any resistance. Rather than stab him, she had cut his oxygen line and let nature take its course.

Further down the corridor was where she guessed the President was holding vigil with his family. There were too many people there, so she'd waited. There was chatter about a press conference out front — she had heard a couple of yuppie types talking about it just before she

352

elected to duck in here. All she had to do now was bide her time.

★ ★ ★

The President held his youngest daughter's hand, watched her heart monitor and prayed. Right here, right now, the weight of parenthood was making him feel like the most impotent man in the world rather than the most powerful.

The door opened. A staffer tiptoed in and bent down next to him. 'Sir, they're ready for you out front.'

He nodded and got to his feet. 'Give me a second here, Rob. Then I'll be right out.'

'Yes, Mr President.'

He bent down and softly kissed his daughter's forehead. 'I'll be right back, sweetheart. OK? And I still haven't forgotten about that sundae I owe you and your sister.'

He straightened up, sliding on his game-face at the same time as the door opened again and the head of his personal escort section walked in.

'Sir, we've had a change of plan. The woman involved in the attack — we have credible evidence that she's inside the hospital.'

The President blanched. 'Ashley can't be moved.'

'I understand that. We want you and the family to stay exactly where you are.'

'And where is the woman who tried to kill us?'

'We're trying to locate her right now.'

★ ★ ★

Lock nudged Ty's elbow. 'Come on, you have to get dressed.'

Ty broke off from his argument with the hospital security guards. 'What you talking about?'

Lock was joined by one of the Secret Service agents. 'Come with us.'

The agent led Lock and Ty back out of the front entrance and around the side of the building. A fire exit door opened and a suited Secret Service agent ushered them inside. They were led down another short stretch of corridor and into a side room.

A woman handed Ty a suit carrier, brushing off some dust from the vinyl covering. 'Here, put this on. The quicker we get this done, the quicker the President can address the nation.'

Someone else flung Ty a lightweight vest. 'You'll want this on under the shirt.'

'Someone mind telling me what the hell's going on?' Ty protested.

'Remember how everyone thought we were nuts trying to stop someone killing Reaper?' Lock asked him, stripping off himself.

'Uh-huh.'

'We're about to prove to them that they were right. We really are nuts.'

71

The door at the far end of the corridor opened and the President strode out, four Secret Service agents immediately falling into a diamond formation around him. His head was bowed in thought as he studied his speech. Six steps further along, where the corridor widened another foot, four more suited agents fell into step, filling the gaps in the diamond so that the President was almost completely obscured.

Lock, who was now sporting a suit similar to the other members of the personal escort section, took the rear point of the diamond, which gave him the best eyes-on in the narrow corridor.

He'd never had much time for the Secret Service before, disliking their whole frat-boy, shade-wearing, talking-into-their-sleeve shtick. But he had to hand it to them, when it came to walking drills they had their shit down cold.

Up ahead, a man on a gurney was being propelled towards them by a three-person medical team. The man had an oxygen mask over his mouth and his chest was shredded with shrapnel wounds. They shifted as far as they could to try and let him pass before the President raised his hand, signalling for them to stop.

'Wait. I want to see how this guy's doing.'

'I think you can see how he's doing, sir,' Lock

355

snapped from the back. 'What we really need to do is keep moving.'

Yeah, he definitely wasn't cut out for the Secret Service, Lock thought.

The President did as he was told and the medical team squeezed the wounded man past them on their right as a door on the left-hand side of the corridor opened and a woman in bloodstained medical scrubs stepped out parallel to the front member of the President's personal escort. She had a mask pulled over her face but seemed startled because she flattened herself against the closed door to allow them past with a deferential 'Excuse me.'

As she straightened out against the door, Lock saw the hard swell of her belly. This time there was no hesitation.

'Threat left!' he screamed.

As the personal escort pivoted round and the President was propelled out of the way, Chance made her move. The knife, which had been down by her side, came up in a slashing arc, cutting the throat of the agent closest to her.

From the corner of his eye, Lock saw a flash of hand as the next closest agent reached for his weapon. A gun might be handy in a knife fight, but only if you had some distance, and not when you were dealing in fractions of a second.

Lock threw himself forward at Chance as she lunged past the stricken agent and sprang towards the President, her knife held in a hammer grip. Rather than move, though, the President shrugged off his designated bodyguard and, stepping back, bent low, so that the arc of the knife caught air rather than flesh.

As Chance fell, the President punched back his elbow, catching her in the throat — hard. The knife tumbled from her hand and there was a scramble to retrieve it. Lock caught her feet, his arms wrapping her ankles as she kicked back, catching him in the face.

The President followed Chance and Lock to the floor. She landed on her face, the President on her back. The President grabbed for her wrist, levering it up, bringing her arm with it, twisting the joint and breaking it with an audible snap.

Chance gasped with pain. Her eyes closed. When she opened them, she found herself staring up at Tyrone.

'What's the matter?' Ty asked her, his teeth bared, his eyes narrow with fury. 'We all look alike to you people?'

72

'Wait, I want to see how this guy's doing,' Lock said, parodying Ty's only line as President.

'Hey, I got into the role a little too much. Sue me.'

Treble-cuffed, Chance was being loaded into the back of a patrol car at the rear of the hospital, having been checked over by the medical staff to make sure that both she and her unborn baby were fine. The knife was already gone for forensic examination, but it looked eerily like the one that had been used on Ken Prager.

Lock hadn't stopped to count the total dead, but with the family over in Oakland and bombings added in, it was well into double figures. Even if Reaper hadn't achieved what he'd set out to, a lot of people had been sacrificed to his unholy war.

A voice from behind them: 'Mr Johnson, Mr Lock.'

They turned to see the President. He had a cigarette in one hand. He took a puff, waved it in the air at them. 'I think I'm allowed, just this once,' he said. He switched the cigarette to his left hand and extended his right hand to each of them in turn. 'Thank you. Both.'

Lock shook his hand first. In his line of work he was used to encountering celebrities, but this was a little different. This President had a movie-star halo with none of the accompanying ego.

'How's your family?'

The President closed his eyes for the briefest of moments, and Lock got a rare glimpse of a man who already had the weight of the world's problems on his shoulders. 'My wife and our eldest are both fine, and the doctor's just told me that Ashley's off the critical list and she's going to be fine.'

'That's great news, sir,' Lock said.

'Gentlemen, thanks again.'

And then he was gone, his regular security detail falling in behind as he walked back into the hospital to resume his private vigil over his daughter.

★ ★ ★

A small phalanx of FBI agents was making its way across the parking lot towards Lock and Ty. This is going to be one hell of a debrief, thought Lock as they closed in.

The agent in front put out his hand. 'FBI Agent Breedlove. We'd like to talk to you.'

'And I'd like to talk to you,' Lock said. 'But I haven't slept in a hundred years, so it's going to have to wait.'

'This can't wait,' said Breedlove, lifting his sunglasses, as if somehow this gesture conveyed the gravity of the situation.

Lock looked at him. 'You can either arrest me or you can wait. If you arrest me, I won't be cooperating. If you let me get some sleep, you can have everything my scrambled brain contains.'

Breedlove hesitated. His cell phone sounded — a James Bond ring tone.

'Hey, 007, you want to get that?' Lock said.

Breedlove killed the call, then turned to his colleagues. 'We'll speak to him in the morning,' he said, trying to make it sound like it was his idea.

In truth, Lock was bone-tired, but he needed time to himself to order what had happened in his own mind. Even with Reaper dead, Chance in custody and the President safe, something was still bothering him. He understood Chance's desire to see her father free. He got that Reaper would have used giving testimony as a way of allowing himself an opportunity to escape. He even got how Reaper saw liberty as a way of fulfilling his sick fantasy of sparking a race war. But there was something else, a piece of the jigsaw that hadn't yet slotted into place.

Carrie stayed behind to call in reports from the scene while Lock and Ty walked back to the hotel. News of what had happened, and the fact that the President was fine, had spread through the city. People were out on the sidewalks, drawn together by a need to share their relief at a crisis averted.

But, Lock noticed, beyond the shock imprinted on people's faces, a sense of togetherness seemed to pervade the air. Outside a grocery store, a wizened acid casualty in his seventies embraced an equally elderly Asian man. A group of female college students sat together in a small park a few blocks shy of the hotel, lighting candles next to a picture of the President's injured daughter. A little further towards the piers that faced the bay, a good-looking young couple, the guy black, the woman white, hugged each other as they watched a couple of fighter aircraft sweep low over the Golden Gate Bridge.

Rather than the death, mayhem and hatred Reaper had so confidently predicted, events had served to bring the country together. When Martin Luther King was gunned down, it had plunged the country into spasms of violence. Maybe this time they had truly moved on.

Lock and Ty wandered into the lobby of the Argonaut and took the elevator to their respective rooms. They clasped hands for a moment, then headed off in opposite directions.

Lock opened the door into his suite and stepped into the bathroom. He stared at his reflection in the mirror. There were dark patches under his eyes and a nasty bruise on one side of his face where Chance had kicked him.

He washed his hands and face and dried off with a towel. Then he walked into the bedroom area and lay back on the bed fully clothed. There would be time to sleep later. He had a strong feeling the game wasn't over yet.

73

Coburn's name flashed up on Carrie's cell phone. She clicked the answer button. Behind her, activity at the hospital had slowed to a crawl as the media mopped up the last shreds of information about the failed assassination attempt on the President.

'You've got some nerve,' she said. Lock had told her about Coburn leaving him hanging back at the cathedral.

'Where is he? I need to speak to him.'

'Emergency's over, so he's getting some rest,' she told him.

'You're staying at the Argonaut, right?'

Carrie couldn't remember either her or Lock telling anyone where they were staying. 'What is it with you people?' she snapped. 'I told you, he's resting. You can talk to him tomorrow.'

'It won't wait until then. What room's he in?'

Carrie hesitated. 'Room 426,' she said at last.

'Thanks,' he said, and hung up.

★   ★   ★

Coburn put his cell phone back into his pocket and glanced at the crowd of people packed into Capurro's Restaurant and Bar, which sat on the opposite side of Jefferson Street from the Argonaut. With some difficulty he muscled his way over to the man nursing his beer at the bar.

362

He ordered himself a beer and leaned in towards the man.

'Room 426,' Coburn told him.

'I got it,' said Cowboy, raising his beer bottle in salute to Coburn and tilting the dregs into his throat.

Coburn slapped Cowboy a high five and watched as he elbowed his way towards the front door of the bar. The bartender slid Coburn his beer, and he took a big gulp. In a few minutes, Lock would be dead, and he could relax.

74

Cowboy tipped his hat to a well-dressed Asian couple pushing a stroller as he exited the elevator on the fourth floor and they got in. He waited for the doors to close on them, glancing across to his right at the room number guide. Then he turned right and followed the corridor for around twenty yards, counting off the numbers as he walked, before hanging another right.

A long corridor stretched ahead of him. His boots sank deep into the blue- and gold-patterned carpet. Aside from a maid's cleaning cart parked at the far end of the hallway, the place was deserted. Still, the cart meant that he would have to force Lock back inside before he killed him. Once he had him inside, Cowboy would crank up the volume on the TV and take care of business. Coburn had warned him to be careful, that Lock was dangerous, but Cowboy had dealt with guys like Lock before.

★ ★ ★

Coburn finished his beer, left the bar and waited across the street from the hotel, sticking close to a group of tourists checking out T-shirts in the next-door gift shop. Once Cowboy had killed Lock and taken care of Ty, he would head upstairs and take care of Cowboy. That only left Chance, and with her in custody, he would have ample opportunity to deal with that problem.

Coburn picked up a hat from the rack in front of him. Emblazoned across its front were the words 'Alcatraz — Mental Ward — Outpatient'. He turned it over in his hands, then put it back on the rack, and waited.

★　★　★

Standing in the corridor outside Lock's room, Cowboy finally caught a break. The velvet bag holding that day's newspaper was wedged in between the door and the frame of room 426. Lock must have opened the door, left the bag still swinging on the handle, and gone back into the room. As the door had closed, the bag had jammed in there, preventing the door from clicking shut.

Cowboy pushed the door open and snuck in, making sure to close it behind him, as quietly as he could. Directly ahead of him was a bedroom. There was also a living area with a couch and a coffee table. Off to one side was a dark wooden door. It was open a few inches and Cowboy could hear the blast of a shower running. Perfect.

He crept towards the bathroom, then stopped. He'd need more than the sound of running water to cover the noise of a gunshot. He walked slowly into the bedroom and picked up the remote control for the TV. He clicked it on, and kept the remote in his left hand. As soon as he had Lock in front of him, he'd max the volume.

He crossed back to the bathroom door and pushed it open, his gun raised in his hand. The

365

shower curtain was pulled over the bath. He stepped back to the doorway and snuck his left hand back round the door frame, aiming it towards the TV, clicking on the volume up button. He was all set.

'Hey, Lock,' he called out.

There was no response other than the white noise of water blasting into the bath.

'Game's up, Lock,' he announced, a little louder this time.

The curtain didn't even move. Cautiously, Cowboy dropped his right foot back and reached out with his left hand towards the shower curtain. He yanked it to one side.

The shower was running but the bath was empty. He whipped round, expecting to see Lock standing behind him, but he was alone in the bathroom. He took a deep breath, tipped his hat back on his head and swiped the moisture that had gathered on his face from the hot blast of the shower away from his eyes.

Then he stepped out of the bathroom.

He was sideways on to the door leading into the room when the bullet slammed into his neck with a wet thud.

★ ★ ★

Lock walked over and toe-poked Cowboy's limp corpse. Behind him, Ty looked on.

'Wrong room, asshole,' Lock said. 'I'm staying in 427.'

'One down,' said Ty.

Lock nodded. 'Coburn can't be far behind.'

366

He stared down at Cowboy's body, noting the tiny shamrock tattoo on his right hand. 'Let's get him moved.'

Together, they dragged Cowboy into the bathroom, leaving a smear of blood on the carpet, which didn't matter, Lock concluded. Coburn would be expecting blood, and, contrary to the white supremacists' beliefs, one man's blood looked the same as any other's.

With Cowboy's body hidden from plain view, Lock handed Ty his room key card. Ty crossed the five yards to the other side of the hall to wait while Lock reset the door of room 426 with the newspaper bag. Coburn, who was surely less gullible than the dead man in the bathroom, would assume his buddy had done it.

Lock stepped back into the room and took a seat on the couch, facing the door. If Coburn bolted, Ty would be watching from across the corridor, ready to take him down.

★ ★ ★

Lock didn't have long to wait. Less than five minutes later, the door was pushed open.

'Lock, you OK?' Coburn called out, stepping inside.

The concerned ATF agent, thought Lock bitterly.

Coburn froze when he saw Lock, then, looking down at the carpet, he caught sight of the bloody trail leading into the bathroom. 'Jesus H. What the hell happened here?'

'I could ask you the same,' Lock said, taking

his time. 'Don't you knock first?'

Coburn looked behind him. 'Sorry. I . . . I thought you might be in trouble when I saw the door open.'

Lock smiled. 'Close it.'

This was the moment of truth. Coburn could either close the door, step back into the room and try to front it out, or he could make an escape. Either way, Lock thought grimly, he was going to take him down.

Carrie had called him about five minutes after he'd arrived in his room to tell him that Coburn was looking for him. Going on gut feeling, and after what had happened back at the Cathedral, she had decided to give Coburn the wrong room number.

Coburn leaving him to hang like that had also been preying on Lock's mind. His disquiet prompted him to make a call he'd been avoiding. He called the police department in Medford and tracked down one of the cops who'd taken the cell phone that he'd found outside Jalicia's motel from him. With a lot of persuasion the cop confirmed that it was Jalicia's cell phone. He told Lock something else as well.

On the night she was abducted outside her motel the last phone call she'd received was from an agent with the ATFE. It was the same agent who was standing in front of Lock now. Through all the bad decisions, bloodshed and mayhem, he was the one constant.

Coburn was turning towards the door. Lock felt his whole body tense.

'Your buddy with the cowboy hat's in the bathroom.'

Coburn stopped. 'What are you talking about?'

He was one hell of an actor, Lock conceded that much. More of an actor than Ken Prager. Although Ken wouldn't have stood a chance anyway, not if Coburn had let slip to Reaper and his daughter that he was an undercover ATF agent.

'Go ahead,' Lock said. 'Close it.'

Coburn looked puzzled. 'Whatever you say.'

Lock watched as Coburn grasped the handle. Then, with a sudden jerk, he made his move, throwing the door open and launching himself through it.

75

Lock squeezed the trigger, but rather than run, Coburn had gone to ground, and Lock's shot went high.

The room door began to swing shut. Lock got to his feet and ran towards it. He could hear the door on the other side of the corridor being thrown open and Ty shouting at Coburn to stop. Then there was the sound of a struggle.

Lock stepped out into the corridor. It was a long stretch to where it turned at a right angle back towards the bank of two elevators. Coburn was running towards them.

Ty was on the floor just outside the door, clutching his shoulder, his face contorted in pain. For a heart-stopping second Lock thought he'd been shot again, but there was no blood.

'Son of a bitch hit me,' Ty spat at Coburn's retreating figure.

Lock took to his heels in pursuit of Coburn, who now had a good thirty-yard start. At least, thought Lock, there was no longer any doubt as to what Coburn was, or which side he was on.

As Coburn closed in on the end of the corridor, Lock was gaining on him. With doors either side, Lock hadn't wanted to risk taking a shot which might take out a curious hotel guest who had opened his door to see what all the commotion was. Coburn, however, had no such qualms.

He spun round on his heel and took aim.

Lock flattened himself against a door. Coburn took the shot anyway, missing by a mile but buying himself a few more valuable seconds.

When Lock looked up, Coburn was already rounding the turn at the end of the corridor. Lock followed him, pulling up short of the turn, aware that he could fly round the corner only to find Coburn waiting for him. Reaching the end of the corridor, he took a quick look, catching sight of Coburn's back as he ran past the elevators, heading for the stairs.

Driven on by adrenalin, Lock ran for the exit to the stairs. He burst through the door and, leaning over the railing, saw Coburn already on the way down. Lock stood there, tracking Coburn's progress, waiting for the right moment, praying that Coburn wouldn't duck back out into a corridor before he made it to the ground floor.

Steadying his grip on his 226, Lock took aim and squeezed the trigger. The tight confines of the stairwell amplified the sound of the gunshot, leaving an echo ringing in Lock's ears. The single blast of gunfire was accompanied by a sharp, guttural scream of pain from below as Coburn tumbled down on to the second-floor landing.

Lock started down the stairs, taking them two at a time. He could see Coburn lying prostrate on the ground, his gun ten steps below him, safely out of reach. Blood oozed from Coburn's right boot where Lock's bullet had found its target.

Coburn was rocking back and forth with the

pain. Finally, he twisted his head round, staring up at Lock. 'Prison ain't so bad,' he said.

Lock took a moment to catch his breath. He looked around the stairwell. He was alone with Coburn. No CCTV or witnesses of any description. All anyone would have seen was two men, both armed and firing at each other, disappearing into the stairwell.

'You think I'm going to take you in?' Lock asked him.

Coburn half-shrugged a 'yes' and clutched at his bloodied foot with both hands. 'You're a boy scout, Lock,' he said. 'Why else would you have taken that suicide mission Jalicia gave you?'

Lock took one more step towards him. Then another. Coburn's foot looked bad, but not bad enough to kill him. Not even close. He turned over the situation in his mind, then took a breath, the stairwell seeming to tunnel in round them. A cold breeze had picked up from somewhere. It took him back to the redwood clearing where Ken Prager had been butchered before being forced to watch the execution of his wife and child.

The question facing Lock now wasn't whether Coburn deserved to die. He did. The question was, could he kill a man in cold blood? Even a man such as Coburn.

If he did, Lock would be crossing a line into a different country. And once he had crossed, there would be no return.

He stared down at Coburn's twisted features as he writhed in pain in front of him. He thought of Ty lying helpless on the yard back at Pelican

Bay, and how Reaper and Phileas had seen Ty as less than human because of the colour of his skin.

'See,' Coburn said, pushing down his sock to get a better look at his wound and revealing a tiny bloodied shamrock on his ankle, 'I knew you were a boy scout.'

Lock wasn't sure whether it was seeing the symbol of the Aryan Brotherhood hidden away on Coburn's ankle or the smirk on his face, but he felt something in him shift at that moment. Slowly, he raised his gun so that it was aimed right between Coburn's eyes.

'I'm going to tell you what I told Reaper on that plane down from Pelican Bay,' he said softly. 'I'm not a cop, or a Marshal, or the FBI. I'm a private contractor, and right now I'm off the clock, working on my own time, so the only person I have to answer to is myself.'

Coburn blinked, and his expression morphed from a look of pained amusement to genuine fear. 'You wouldn't,' he said.

Lock's index finger closed round the trigger and he squeezed off a single round, the bullet catching Coburn square in the face. His left arm twitched in spasm, his neck snapped violently back, and then he was perfectly still.

The sound of the gunshot reverberated around the empty stairwell, fading slowly away until all Lock could hear was a distant hum, overlaid by the sharp keen of sirens and his heart pounding in his chest.

'I just did,' he said, turning his back on the twisted corpse and starting back up the stairs.

Epilogue

Hand in hand, Lock and Carrie climbed the steps of Grace Cathedral and walked through the Gothic façade into the cool of the nave. The visit had been Carrie's idea, a way of both of them finding some closure before they headed home, although Lock had been grateful that she hadn't used those words.

The last few days had involved endless variations on the same set of questions. Lock's answers had not changed. Gradually, and with no appetite to wash the ATF's dirty laundry in public, the questions had fallen away to a distant echo until Lock was alone with only his own thoughts for company.

In the body of the cathedral was a limestone labyrinth. Unlike a maze, Carrie had explained, a labyrinth had no dead ends. You followed the path to the centre, stayed there for as long as you wanted, then followed the same route back out.

She dropped Lock's hand from hers and stepped back.

'You don't want to walk it with me?' he asked her.

Carrie shook her head. 'I'll be over there if you need me,' she said, nodding towards a candle-lit area off to one side.

He watched her walk away. Calm. Composed. More precious to him than any woman he had ever known. In the days since those final

374

moments alone with Coburn in the stairwell, she had allowed him his silences, letting him know with a look, or a hand at the small of his back, that if he needed to talk she was happy to listen, but not pressing him on it.

She seemed to understand that for him there was no release to be found in taking another man's life, no surge of excitement from the metallic tang of blood that filled your nostrils, no joy in pulling a trigger.

Feeling more than a little self conscious, Lock stepped onto the labyrinth and slowly began to follow it round. The past week had given him the time to think about the path he had chosen in life, the places it had taken him, and the things it had taught him about the best and the worst of human nature.

Even with all that baggage, nothing had prepared him for seeing Ken Prager and his family being slaughtered. Nothing would ever erase in his mind the first sight he had had of Ty lying on the yard at Pelican Bay. Nor would he ever forget the shiver in Coburn's eyes as he'd watched him squeeze the trigger. All of these things Lock would carry with him — perhaps for the rest of his life.

Reaching the centre of the labyrinth, he stopped and closed his eyes, letting it all settle inside him. Then he followed the path all the way back to where he had started.

He found Carrie by a small shrine commemorating a visit to the cathedral, or church as it then was, by Martin Luther King. King had spoken of many things. Of hatred. Of fear. Of the power of

375

love. A little over three years later, his own life had been snatched away by an assassin's bullet.

The labyrinth had held no answers for Lock. But maybe, he thought as he watched the yellow candlelight flicker over the resigned expression on King's face, this tiny shrine did.

There was the world as most people wanted it to exist, and then there was the world as it was, and standing in the middle, trying to make sure that people like King or the President could do their job were men like Lock.

Lock gave Carrie's hand a squeeze.

'Let's go home.'

Acknowledgements

My thanks to: Selina Walker for her friendship and guidance; my agent Luigi Bonomi and the rest of the team at LBA for their continued hard work on my behalf; Lieutenant Ken Thomas and the rest of the staff at Pelican Bay; Jimell Griffin of the United States Marshals Service; Andy Carmichael for his ongoing advice and support; Pete Mitchell, and Stitz, for their steadfast work in facilitating my borderline-suicidal research tendencies; Larry, Martin, AK47, Jo, Rich, Polly and the entire Transworld family for all their hard work and enthusiasm; Daniel Balado-Lopez for his stalwart efforts in making me appear more detail-orientated than I actually am; Madeira James for running my website; our family and friends on both sides of the Atlantic for their encouragement and belief, especially Jim, Lorna, Ali, Pat, Gordon, Lee, Patsy, Lisa, Ron, Kathy, Gregg and Delinah.

We do hope that you have enjoyed reading this large print book.

Did you know that all of our titles are available for purchase?

We publish a wide range of high quality large print books including:
**Romances, Mysteries, Classics
General Fiction
Non Fiction and Westerns**

Special interest titles available in large print are:
**The Little Oxford Dictionary
Music Book
Song Book
Hymn Book
Service Book**

Also available from us courtesy of Oxford University Press:
**Young Readers' Dictionary
(large print edition)
Young Readers' Thesaurus
(large print edition)**

For further information or a free brochure, please contact us at:
**Ulverscroft Large Print Books Ltd.,
The Green, Bradgate Road, Anstey,
Leicester, LE7 7FU, England.
Tel:** (00 44) 0116 236 4325
Fax: (00 44) 0116 234 0205

LOCKDOWN

Sean Black

It's Christmas in New York, but for ex-military bodyguard Ryan Lock it's business as usual. His mission is to protect the head of America's most ruthless corporation. When gunshots suddenly ring out, people run for cover and innocent bystanders are mown down. Amid the chaos, Lock's hunt for the killers turns into a game of cat and mouse. Lock's search for the truth takes him from the rooftops of a New York skyscraper to a heavily fortified warehouse on the Hudson, where he confronts one of the world's most dangerous women. As the clock ticks towards midnight on New Year's Eve, all routes into and out of Manhattan are sealed. Lock's life is in terrible danger — but so are the lives of millions of others . . .

NEVER LOOK AWAY

Linwood Barclay

David Harwood is hoping that a carefree day taking a trip to Five Mountains amusement park with their four-year-old son Ethan, will help dispel his wife Jan's depression and frightening thoughts of suicide. But the day turns into a nightmare. When Jan and David become separated he goes to the police to report her missing — terrified that she's planning to take her own life — the nightmare reaches a new level. The police suspect that she might already be dead, murdered by her husband. To prove his innocence and keep his son from being taken away from him, David must face a terrifying possibility. That he's become the victim of a cold, calculating schemer prepared to destroy him and his family to keep a dreadful secret.

THE BURNING WIRE

Jeffery Deaver

A killer is crippling New York City with fear. His weapon — the electrical grid. The killer harnesses huge arc flashes with voltage so high that steel melts and his victims are set afire, or he reconnects the wires in buildings, so that sinks, lamps, or computer keyboards, can kill. The first attack reduces a city bus to a pile of molten metal, and officials fear terrorism. Rhyme, a world-class forensic criminologist, is tapped for the investigation. Long a quadriplegic, he assembles NYPD detective Amelia Sachs and officer Ron Pulaski as his eyes, ears and legs on crime sites, along with FBI agent Fred Dellray. The attacks continue — the team work desperately against time. And whilst Rhyme's health falters — his determination could drive away his closest allies . . .

CONTROL

John Macken

Two deaths, days apart but clearly linked. Each victim has had the tips of their fingers removed with a hacksaw. Reuben Maitland, freshly returned to GeneCrime, is heading up the case. The forensics come in, DNA is sampled, the clues begin to mount up. Then the killer strikes again, but not to kill. Reuben's young son is snatched. The murderer sends Reuben a message: 'Stop hunting me. Come after me and your son will die.' Reuben now faces the choice every cop dreads: the price of stopping a psychopath from killing again could be the life of his own child.

9TH JUDGEMENT

James Patterson with Maxine Paetro

A young mother and her infant child are ruthlessly gunned down while returning to their car in the garage of a shopping mall. There are no witnesses, and the only evidence for Detective Lindsay Boxer is a cryptic message scrawled across the windshield in blood-red lipstick. The same night, the wife of A-list actor Marcus Dowling walks in on a cat burglar who is about to steal millions of dollars' worth of precious jewels. In seconds there is an empty safe, a lifeless body, and another mystery that throws San Francisco into hysteria. Before Lindsay and her friends can piece together either case, one of the killers forces Lindsay to put her own life on the line — but is it enough to save the city?

THE THINGS THAT KEEP US HERE

Carla Buckley

It's been a tough year for Ann Brooks, bringing up her two young daughters alone, but it's about to get worse, and she's about to discover just how strong she can be. Panic has gripped America. A virus, so deadly it kills every other person it infects, is moving across countries and oceans. Society grinds to a halt and ordinary families quarantine themselves in their own homes, desperate to avoid its spread. Ann must face her worst fears and try to protect her family from an invisible threat. Sealed inside their home, Ann, Maddie and Kate will have to battle the cold, the dark, food and water shortages, and the greed and violence of their former neighbours if they're to survive.